BEYOND REGRET/PYTHON

Serpents MC/Las Vegas

BARBARA NOLAN

Gabby
Happy Reading!
B. Nolan

D1264473

ACKNOWLEDGMENTS:

Published by: Barbara Nolan

Edited by: Lisa Cullinan

Proofed by: Read by Rose

Photographer: Jean Maureen Woodfin

Model: Theodore Brown

Cover Design: Cosmic Letterz

Promotions: CJG Consulting

❀ Created with Vellum

Dear Readers,

My hero, Python, is all alpha, tough and hard-edged, but with a fierce loyalty, and a deep sensitivity he tries to hide— until Virginia. My heroine, Virginia, is a bit shy and a little klutzy, but when it comes to fighting for what she wants she finds an inner strength that Python can't resist.

My cover model, Theodore Brown, owns a black German Shepherd who I incorporated into Beyond Regret. I appreciate Theodore sharing his love for this beautiful animal as it inspired some touching scenes.

I hope you enjoy reading about Python and Virginia as much as I enjoyed writing them.

Love,

Barbara

FREE Bonus: **Joker's Story**

There was still so much that needed to be uncovered about Joker's past, that I felt compelled to write his back-story. Now, all you have to do is hit the link in the back of the book, and you can uncover Joker's very complicated past.

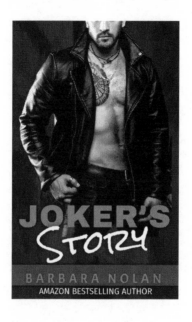

SERPENTS MC

LAS VEGAS

CHAPTER ONE

Python hadn't given his birthday much thought. After all, what was the big deal about turning thirty-five? It wasn't a decade birthday like thirty or forty. Shit, forty. He was five years away from forty. There were times when Python didn't think he'd make it to twenty-five no less thirty-five. Back then he'd been muscle for hire—waking up at three in the afternoon, busting some heads, partying, fucking random snatch, then blissfully passing out, only to start all over again. Those were the bad old days after he'd done some time in Ely State Pen and before he'd hooked up with Cobra to form the Serpents.

Okay, no more deep thoughts about that—at least not now—not when he had an outstanding brunette named Crystal and a stunning blonde named Tina or Tara or something like that ... in his bed.

"Outstanding" and "stunning" weren't his words. The new ad agency he'd hired used them on the billboard along I-15, advertising Ecstasy Gentlemen's Club, the strip joint he ran for the Serpents. If someone would've asked him, he'd have said that they were both hot as fuck and, right about now, had his dick hard as steel.

"Baby, I don't like the way he keeps looking at us." Crystal shifted closer as she eyed Kobi, Python's black German shepherd, who was staring at them from his dog bed in the corner of the bedroom.

"He's just jealous." Python patted the sheets. "This is usually his spot."

Yup, the ninety-pound German shepherd acted like a big baby anytime Python entertained.

"He's making me nervous," she squeaked. Crystal had a beautiful face, killer body, but a voice like an ice chipper. Sharp and screechy.

"He's harmless." Python slung his arm around her. "It's me you gotta worry about." He waggled his eyebrows and when she laughed, he kissed her. She couldn't squeak while they kissed.

Python could overlook her voice. He'd never been too picky and loved all types of women, sometimes too much. His biker buddies were always up his ass for lending women money. As sergeant-at-arms for the Serpents MC, he took care of the muscle, which meant he busted heads when needed. Nobody would've suspected the six-foot-five, hard-ass biker to be a light touch, but give him a sob story and he fell for it—every time. Can't make rent or your ex is late with the check? Call Python. Your kid wants the latest high-tech toy? Call Python.

Crystal sat up in bed and the sheet fell away from her bangin' body. Python smiled at who he was sure would be Ecstasy's next headliner.

"I was thinking about what my costume should be. Maybe a harem girl or a female construction worker or maybe even a cop," she babbled on. "Like ... maybe every night I could do a different profession, you know, like the Village People."

He grabbed up her hand and shoved it under the sheet, but she kept talking. *Definitely, ice chipper meets squeaky door.* He hadn't noticed that earlier. Probably since they hit the bed, her tongue had been halfway down his throat.

He glanced at the blonde still passed out on the other side of him. At least she was quiet.

"So, like I was saying, do you have any ideas?" she asked. "Is there some costume you'd like to see? Maybe I could—"

Python leaned in getting directly in her line of vision. "Babe, with your body, you could wear a burlap bag and the guys would be coming in their pants." He adjusted her hand over his painfully hard cock. "I'm really not interested in conversation right now. I just wanna fuck."

"Sure." She cuddled into him, pushed back the sheet, and crawled down his body. As soon as her wet mouth clamped down on his dick, he was a goner.

"That's what I'm talking about."

She was good, real good, but once they were employees, it would be hands off. Although he'd hired them last week, technically they wouldn't start working at the club until tomorrow night; but they knew the rules up front. The club protected the girls and had their back, and the girls showed up sober and on time. He ran a clean place: no hard drugs, no prostitution, just a little money laundering from their less legit businesses. Python took his job seriously, but overseeing a strip club with half-dressed, knock-out women every night?— wasn't too much of a real hardship.

Life was good. He had his Harley, his club, his brothers, and two hot women in his bed—one who was currently tonguing his dick.

Happy fuckin' birthday to him.

———

"Don't worry, I'll be fine," Virginia said through her phone as she maneuvered the late model Toyota into the parking lot of Ecstasy. A strip club where, according to the sign, All Your Dreams Come True.

"You should've taken someone with you. You should've taken me with you."

Virginia rolled her eyes. The last thing she needed was her co-worker, Nicole, with her. She loved the girl dearly, but the frenetic energy that woman exuded could put anyone on edge.

"I know what I'm doing." She hoped. "Anyway, I have an appointment."

"Who has appointments at strip clubs?"

"It's where he works. Apparently, Python manages the place, and Cobra said I should interview him there."

"And that's another thing. Who has names like Python and Cobra? Yikes."

"They're the Las Vegas Serpents."

Truth, Virginia did think it was odd, although she'd never admit that to Nicole.

"I still think you're making a mistake going out there alone."

"Don't worry." Virginia circled the parking lot, avoiding the valet just in case she had to make a quick getaway. Another detail she'd keep from Nicole's prying ears. "I'm here, so I'm going to hang up."

"But just—"

She turned off her car and the phone disconnected, filling the air with blessed silence. Nicole had been her first friend at KLAS-TV News, serving greater Las Vegas. Six months later, she'd become her best friend, and Nicole's vivacious, super confident, outgoing attitude was everything Virginia wasn't.

Psychology 101 told her their friendship worked because

they were such extreme opposites, but it was more than that. Virginia liked Nicole's easy, laidback ideas about life. Even though she might talk a mile a minute, Nicole didn't stress the small stuff. That was something Virginia admired, especially coming from a family that competed and stressed over every subject, large or small.

Virginia flipped down the vanity mirror, then stared into her light brown eyes and said out loud, "You can do this." Those four words were used as a mantra whenever her confidence threatened to do a disappearing act. She took a deep breath and then pushed the car door handle with more force than necessary.

Her apprehension had more to do with her career and less to do with entering a strip club at eleven at night. An odd time to do an interview, yes, but then again this was a strip club, or as they like to be called now, "a gentlemen's club," owned and operated by bikers. As a reporter, Virginia knew a good story was all in the word choice.

She'd like to say she volunteered for this assignment, but in truth, no one else wanted it, so her editor, Mr. Larson, threw it to her. And that right there was the problem. As the low woman on the totem pole, she covered car dealership openings, restaurant openings, and the latest jackpot winners at the Flamingo. Virginia was now the proud owner of an Audi brochure for a car she'd never be able to afford unless she won the next Flamingo jackpot.

Her three-inch heels clacked along the blacktop of the large parking lot. The shoes pinched a bit, but at only five foot three, the heels added to her confidence as well as her height. Walking into a strip club threatened to push every one of her low self-esteem buttons, even though she made a promise to force herself out of her comfort zone as soon as she'd hit Vegas. And what could be less comforting than stepping into a place where women with perfect figures strutted around half naked? She glimpsed down at her petite frame and modest breasts—*no, don't go there.*

Virginia could do this, and she would do this, because excelling would hopefully mean achieving a career she'd wanted since she was a teen, a career she would get on her own without the help of her father, her family name, or their money. It was the main reason she used her mother's maiden name when she applied at KLAS.

Nicole insisted she needed to break out of her shell and be more adventurous, therefore she stormed forward like *Wonder Woman.* So, how come she felt more like Dorothy about to step into the Land of Oz?

As she approached the door, she pulled out her wallet. Still getting carded at twenty-six years old annoyed her. Some women might be flattered by that, but to Virginia it was just another way that the world wasn't taking her seriously—more like her father not taking her seriously—but that was another subject entirely.

The human block of cement standing by the door was easily a foot taller than her, even with her wearing the heels from hell. His narrowed eyes blatantly ran over her body without shame, probably trying to figure out if she was from the same species as the women who danced inside the club. Before she got close enough to show him her ID, he flicked his thick fingers at her and said, "Dancers enter around back."

"Excuse me?" She stepped back as the double doors swung open and four guys barreled out, followed by the pounding bass from within the club.

The bouncer pointed to the double doors. "This entrance is for customers; dancers go around back."

She laughed and he furrowed his brow. "I'm not a dancer. I'm meeting Python here."

His brow knitted further together as if processing what she said equated with the theory of evolution. Either that or he'd been in one too many fights defending the honor of said dancers.

"Hmmm," he grunted, as his eyes roamed over Virginia and lingered on her chest ... or lack thereof. He dragged his gaze back to hers and she offered her ID, which he waved away. Assuming there'd be a cover charge, she dug in her wallet and pulled out some money, but he dismissed that too.

"Sunday is ladies night."

Great. If, for some reason this night went as disastrously wrong as Nicole suspected, at least it didn't cost her anything.

He jerked his head toward the entrance, and his lips twitched into what she thought might be a smirky grin?

After clearing the entrance, she walked about six feet further inside and stopped. Her writer's mind wanted to take it all in and examine every nuance. Expecting the flashing neon lights and the loud driving music, Virginia was surprised by the upscale furniture. Leather banquets were spaced around the room with smaller tables by the three stages, and high-gloss wood flooring led to a raised granite bar along the entire length of one wall. The clean, fragrant air dispelled all her assumptions of a typical smoke-and-cheap-perfume-filled, sleazy strip club. Even the dancers had an elegant upmarket tone. She'd be sure to include all this in her article. So much for stereotypes.

The Serpents needed a bit of good press after some recent bad publicity. They wanted the story to cover their charitable donations, thus shedding a favorable light on their motorcycle club. Choosing Ecstasy as a meeting place seemed counterproductive, but where else would an outlaw biker conduct business, right?

Virginia walked along the perimeter of the room, then climbed the few stairs to the raised bar. Because most of the men and a scattering of women were by the stages, the bar area was manageable. She found an opening, wedged herself against the black granite, and motioned to the waitress. The female bartender assessed her with her dark almond-shaped eyes.

"Can you tell me where I might find Python?" Virginia asked.

The girl craned her neck around the bar, causing her straight, waist-length ebony hair to fan out across her back, then pointed to the far side of the room. "He's probably at the back table with Cobra."

Virginia glanced where she pointed and saw quite a few men at the tables. "I don't know what either of them looks like."

She chuckled. "They're not hard to miss. They'll be wearing a Serpents cut." Someone called the dark-haired beauty, and she moved down the bar.

In preparation for this interview, she'd done extensive research on outlaw biker clubs. It proved to be very interesting reading, and because of it, she knew a cut was the leather vest all bikers wore. Knowledge had always been her friend.

She pointed herself toward the back of the room, hoping some divine intervention would make Python or Cobra magically appear.

Her eyes had adjusted to the dim lighting, but straining to see made them water, which wasn't helpful when trying to pick out a stranger in a place one has never been to before.

Virginia stopped just short of the end of the bar to get her bearings, blinking and swiveling her head. Thankfully, most of the attention was on the stage and she could stand in the shadows and observe.

"Can I help you?" A deep rasp of masculinity said behind her.

She spun around so fast, momentarily losing her balance,

that the raspy-voiced stranger gripped her arm to steady her. Damn high heels.

She craned her neck back like a child looking at a skyscraper. The man's muscled forearms and biceps swirled with colorful tattoos under a black leather cut over a black t-shirt and jeans. She squinted to focus and did some speed reading. A rectangle patch on the right side of his massive chest said Serpents MC, and under that was a diamond patch with a number one and a percentage sign, which meant they were outlaws. On his left side, another rectangular patch said Cobra - President.

"You're Cobra?"

"Sure am." His lips twisted into a smirk not unlike the bouncer at the door. It was as though each of them was trying to figure out what she was doing at a strip club. Similar to seeing a baby bird in the middle of the highway, you just know it's not going to end well.

"I'm Virginia, from KLAS." She stuck out her hand but retracted it, remembering from her research that many bikers didn't do traditional handshakes. Most had some secret hand gestures. Oh god, where was her mind going?

Cobra cocked his head like she was an exhibit at the circus.

"My editor said we had your approval to do a story on Ecstasy, and that I'm to meet with Python, and that he would—"

"Forgot you were coming tonight."

With all the plundering and pillaging, outlaw bikers probably didn't have time to check their iCalendar.

"Sit." Cobra extended his arm to the small round table off to the side of the bar. Virginia followed him and took a seat, happy to be off her torturous shoes. She drew in a deep breath and regrouped, but this intense man staring at her did nothing for her nerves.

He flicked his wrist at a waitress and a bottle of tequila appeared. "Drink?" He motioned to the bottle.

"No, no. No, I'm good." One too many no's there.

"You sure?" Cobra held up the bottle like he was offering her some much-needed medicinal elixir.

"I'm sure." Tequila and Virginia had a love-hate relationship. The few times she drank it, she loved it—but hated herself the next day.

Cobra poured himself a shot and downed it like it was water, then slammed the glass on the table and stared at her with the lightest blue eyes she'd ever seen.

Virginia looked over her shoulder. "Is Python here?"

"Upstairs."

Cobra certainly wasn't into long run-on sentences. His communication skills were short and to the point. He'd be every editor's dream back at the station, but for a woman who currently felt like a fish out of water, he was a bit nerve-wracking. Cobra's phone vibrated on the table, and a second after he answered it, he put the call on hold and flagged over another guy wearing the same leather cut. "This is Rattler."

Then he turned to Rattler. "Show her around and answer her questions."

Rattler flicked a look at Cobra that Virginia couldn't decipher.

"C'mon," Rattler said, his voice deep and somewhat bored.

Rattler, yes, another snake name, was younger than Cobra, maybe in his mid-twenties like herself, she guessed, and while he stood at least six feet, he had a leaner, rangy build and longish black hair. Rattler turned away from her so abruptly that she hadn't gotten a good look at his face. She scurried behind him down a wide hallway to the back of the club as fast as her stilettos allowed, barely keeping up with his long-legged swagger.

He stopped at the first door and pushed it open. "This is the kitchen. The dancers get one meal a shift."

Cooks hustled around the remarkably clean, stainless steel kitchen preparing simple bar food. She suspected most men weren't there for the food and that the fare was mainly to help soak up the alcohol.

Then they moved further down the hall to another door. Rattler knocked and announced his entrance, then opened the door to another room bustling with sequins, skimpy lingerie, and women in all stages of undress.

Virginia instinctively stepped back until she realized that her presence as well as Rattler's wasn't even noticed.

"This is the dressing room." Rattler stated the obvious as women of every shape and size applied makeup at the long, mirrored tables, adjusted skimpy costumes, or practiced their routines. "You're responsible for your own costumes." He patted his pockets and came up with a pack of cigarettes. "You show up on time. No booze or drugs while you're on stage." He knocked one out of the pack and stuck it between his teeth.

Virginia started to correct him, but the sheer energy of the room captivated her, and the writer in her longed to sit down with them right now and ask what life was like as an exotic dancer.

Maybe along with praise for the club, she'd add a touch of human interest to give it "people appeal." Her mind started outlining and inventing questions because she was sure that each of those girls had her own personal story. Probably some were very different than what the public perceived. It could be a breakout report that abolished stereotypes and got to the truth.

Rattler's gaze raked over her. "Use the back entrance the next time you come in."

Same thing the bouncer said. "No, I'm with—" No sense in explaining it all to him, she'd just wait for Python.

A stunning brunette in four-inch stilettos sidled up to him, flicked a lighter, and lit his cigarette. She wore a fringed g-string and a western-themed bra that barely covered her enormous breasts. "Hey, Rattler."

"Hey, darlin', how're you doin' tonight?" Rattler inhaled deep on the cigarette, seemingly unimpressed and unaffected by the statuesque beauty that stood almost as tall as him.

"Good, now that you're here." She ran her hand over his tattooed bicep, but he remained uninterested. Maybe it was like working in a bakery surrounded by sweets everyday: after a while you became immune.

The girl flicked her manicured fingers at Virginia. "Is this one of the new dancers?"

Rattler gave Virginia the once-over, then laughed, and yes, she was insulted because an outlaw biker didn't think she was an exotic dancer. There was definitely something wrong with her thinking.

The tall, gorgeous entertainer glanced at the clock on the wall. "Almost time to go on." As she strutted out of the dressing room, Virginia admired and envied her confidence.

"That's about it," Rattler said. He eyed her from head to toe. "I gotta say ... That's a great fuckin' costume."

"Costume?"

"The whole buttoned-up librarian look. Some guys get off on that."

"You don't understand, I came to see Python because—"

"You should've said that before."

"I'm from—."

"Yeah, yeah, I get it." From the expression on Rattler's face, she and this subject bored him about ten minutes ago. "Python's upstairs in his apartment."

"Oh, I thought he'd want to do it down here."

He suddenly cracked a broad smile. "Nah, I don't think so." Rattler was rather handsome when he smiled. It softened the multiple piercings in his nose, ears, and lip.

He led her to the end of the hall and pointed to a staircase. "He's probably waiting for you."

"Oh, all right." It actually made more sense. They could talk away from the loud music and maybe set up a future date to interview the dancers.

He mumbled something that sounded like "lucky fucker," then held up his phone. "I'll text him that you're on your way up. Top of the stairs. It's the only apartment up there."

"Thanks."

Virginia hoped that Python was more chatty than Cobra and Rattler, or this interview would be very tedious. She climbed the one flight as Rattler instructed, then squared her shoulders at the top of the small hallway with the one door. If she wanted to be a successful investigative reporter, she had to be bolder, pushier, more assertive.

CHAPTER TWO

Python reached for the joint in the ashtray on his bedside table. He fired it up and sucked deep. The Serpents grew the best weed in Clark County. The thick smoke filled his lungs just as Crystal gripped his thighs and sucked him in deeper. Maybe outstanding did describe her 'cause right now his whole body was tingling. Talk about deep throat.

"Fuck yeah!" His guttural shout rumbled through the bedroom, waking the blonde sprawled out on the other side of him. She rolled over and leaned up on her elbow, then proceeded to suck on his nipple ring. Pain and pleasure at its finest.

Kobi raised his head for a better look, then slowly crossed the room. Python loved the animal more than most people, but if the beast jumped up and interrupted this show, Python would definitely hold back his doggie treats later.

His phone buzzed on the nightstand beside him, and he glanced down at it, barely able to concentrate.

Rattler: I'm sending you up another present. Happy birthday, fucker.

Python glanced down at the two girls draped around him.

He'd done plenty of threesomes, but never a foursome. And if the one on her way up was half as good as these two ... oh, shit yeah.

He nodded to the blonde. "Go unlock the door. We got somebody else joining the party."

She scurried off the bed, and a few seconds later she was back. Python stuck the joint between his lips and let his head sink into the pillows. Thirty-five was looking like a goddamn good year.

A few minutes later, the sound of knocking seeped through his smoke-filled brain. He couldn't wait to see what stood on the other side. A redhead would round out the trio nicely, but he wasn't picky.

"C'mon in, darlin'," Python called out from the bedroom. He heard the main door open and close, then footsteps down the hall.

"Hello?"

"I'm in the bedroom." He panted out. Crystal picked that moment to look up at him, so he angled her head back where it belonged.

The door creaked open slowly and a short, thin blonde dressed in black pants and a white button-down shirt froze in the doorway. Her outfit resembled what someone would wear while waiting tables. Not exactly sexy, yet something about the way this girl looked, all innocent and insecure, could definitely work in her favor.

Cobra hadn't told him he'd hired another dancer, but this one could definitely rock that costume of the chick that lost her sheep. Little Peep something. She had that innocent look going on for sure, maybe a little too innocent.

He flashed his shittiest grin, held up the joint, then waved her toward the bed. "Don't just stand there, babe. Strip down and join the party.

———

Virginia's feet were rooted to the floor like someone had nailed her shoes to the carpeting. Had there been another door in the hall? Had she stumbled into the wrong apartment? Her brain flashed with ridiculous questions as she gawked at her own personal HD porn show.

The seductive scent of weed and sex seeped from the room while her mind tried to make sense of the situation. Clothes were scattered over the plush carpet. An end table was crammed with an overflowing ashtray and a bottle of Jack Daniels.

The massive bed took up most of the room. Virginia didn't know they even made beds that big. Must've been custom. The man sprawled out over the sheets was massive, too, and when the two naked women were added, an over-sized bed made perfect sense.

She tried to stop her analytical mind, but stress had put it in overdrive, and in this situation, she feared there would be no reining it in. Assuming this was Python, she examined every minuscule detail.

His broad chest and rippling muscles rose and fell under a myriad of tattoos that extended to his biceps—biceps that were the size of Virginia's waist. Her gaze fell dangerously lower to the brunette firmly planted between his thick, muscular thighs, whose head bobbed with the rhythm set by his palm buried in her hair while his other hand nipped the joint from his lips after a long drag.

A steady stream of smoke flowed from his mouth as he mumbled, "Suck it harder, baby."

The other woman in their trio plucked the joint from between his fingers and sucked in the smoke, expanding the largest breasts Virginia had ever seen. She stared, transfixed, as the blonde leaned within inches of Python's full, sexy lips and blew the smoke into his mouth. He inhaled and cupped her neck as their tongues teased and tangled around the exhaled smoke. The act aroused Virginia in a sensual, primitive way that scared her and caught her by surprise.

Apparently, the brunette didn't need any organic stimulation. She had her own nature show going in full force. And thank god for that because it made it impossible to peek at his other body part. She could only imagine what a man of his physical size would look like and—*Stop!*

Then the blonde made eye contact and stared. "Don't just stand there, hun, join the party."

The brunette remained silent. Apparently, she'd been taught not to speak with her mouth full.

Python patted the mattress. "C'mon, babe, there's plenty of room for one more."

When Virginia gasped, Python squinted through the smoke, then shifted enough for the brunette to slip free with an unsettling smacking noise.

The women stared at her and she marveled at the four huge breasts pointed in her direction. Erotic bookends that flanked Python on either side.

The words *sleazy* and *seedy* came to mind, but the tingling between her legs told her something different, something that made her mind scream—*Run.*

"No, no." She held up one hand. "I'm the reporter from KLAS. I'm here to— Sorry, for interrupting." She pivoted, but her damn heels caught in the plushness of the carpeting. She did a quick shuffling spin and managed to grab the doorjamb seconds before slamming the side of her head into the molding.

"Ouch." Her hand flew to her head.

"Shit, babe, are you all right?" Python asked.

Virginia heard the rustle of sheets and then bodies behind her as she rubbed her temple. Her cheeks flamed and she wasn't sure if it was from witnessing the porn show or her act of clumsiness.

"Hey." The low gravelly voice surrounded her, then a warm, firm hand covered her own. "You really banged yourself."

Python gently turned her and she squeezed her eyes shut knowing that they'd only be inches from each other. If he was still naked she didn't think she could—

"Open your eyes, babe." His finger lifted her chin. "I'm not gonna bite."

She peeked through her lashes and, thankful to the almighty powers, he had clothes on. Well, sweatpants. Faded gray sweatpants hanging precariously on his hips. Her gaze traveled up his broad ... no, make that ... his *expansive* chest and settled on the multi-colored python tattoo that wound its way over his pecs and ended at the base of his neck. Snakes freaked her out, but she had to admit this piece of body art impressed her.

"Python," she mumbled, as the heat in her cheeks increased.

"That's me." His soft, whispered rasp belied his size.

"Three guesses how he got that name." A screechy voice came from behind him on the bed. She couldn't tell which of the women spoke because Python's bulk made it impossible for her to see past him. The man was a human mountain.

"It's because his dick is—"

Python shot a look over his shoulder that put the buzzsaw voice on pause. "Let's call it a night, ladies."

The sounds of rustling and mumbled protests were within earshot, but just minutes later, the brunette and the blonde were dressed, which wasn't a surprise considering how they made their living. No, she wouldn't judge. After all, she didn't even know if the girls were exotic dancers.

The blonde leaned up and brushed a kiss to his cheek,

whereas the brunette wedged herself between them and threw her arms around his neck, then full-out kissed him and stepped away. "Oh, and thanks for taking care of my mother."

Virginia speculated what that comment had meant as both women strutted out of the bedroom, leaving her alone with him.

Python smiled down at her wary expression. "The landlord where her mother lives was trying to raise the rent. I told him I didn't think it would be a good idea."

"I see." Oh, dear God, she really didn't want to think about how that must've gone down.

"Let me grab a t-shirt and we can sit in the living room." He plucked a shirt from the pile of clothes on a nearby chair, and as soon as he dragged it over his head, her brain disapproved his covering of that glorious torso.

Her gaze traveled around the room and landed on a large dog sitting atop his own bed in the corner of the room. "Wow, he's beautiful." As if the animal understood the compliment, he trotted over and nuzzled her leg. She scratched the top of his head, noticing that he almost came up to her waist. Her hand wandered down to the soft fur under his ears, and she smiled at the red bandana jauntily tied around his neck.

"What's his name?"

"Kobi."

"Hi Kobi." She bent over and rubbed at his chest and swore the dog smiled.

"You got a friend for life now. That's his sweet spot."

Virginia smiled, then she speculated if Python had a sweet spot.

"What kind of dog is he?"

"German shepherd. Probably weighs more than you."

"You like that, don't you?" she said to Kobi. She loved dogs and always wanted one growing up, but her mother would've never allowed a dog of any size to traipse through her Beverly Hills monstrosity.

He patted the dog's head, then rested his hand on her back and nudged her down the hall with Kobi trotting behind them. When they got to the living room, Python motioned to the black leather couch, and he sat in the matching leather chair while Kobi lay down on the floor beside him.

The tables shone with chrome and glass, giving the living room an ultra-modern, almost sterile mood—very different from the smoldering vibe surrounding this man.

Python stared at her, and for the first time she noticed his startling blue eyes. She'd been so focused on his other body parts that she'd missed his eyes. They were bright blue like the color of a cornflower crayon, and definitely as impressive as the rest of him.

"I feel like something got screwed up here," he said.

Her mind spun off a thousand flip remarks before she said, "Yes."

"When Rattler texted me before he said ... well, he made it sound like you were ... I guess there's not a good way to say this."

"It's fine." She'd just caught him having sex with not one woman but two, and yet this huge man with a day-old scruff, scrolling tattoos, and numerous piercings had a teddy bear quality about him. Crazy and ridiculous as it sounded, but yeah, Python was a big, scary biker teddy bear.

"Why don't we start over," he suggested.

"Good idea. I'm Virginia Swanson from KLAS."

"The TV station?"

"Yes. I came to do the interview about Ecstasy. Your other friend, Cobra, had set it up. It's a documentary of sorts following the evolution of gentlemen's clubs from the early days when they were a bit underground to current day as big business and quite sophisticated."

"I'm gonna fuckin' kill Rattler," Python mumbled, then his face twisted and the teddy bear image vanished.

She experienced the need to save Rattler from whatever horror was floating around in Python's head. "To be fair, I don't think he knew who I was."

"Doesn't matter." He swept his broad hand in her direction. "Anybody with eyes can see you're not the kinda bitc—*girl* who would ... you know what I mean."

She drew her lips inward to keep from smiling at his unease. "It was just a mix-up."

He leaned in with his muscled forearms on full display. Virginia dug her fingers into her palms just to keep from reaching out and tracing each intricate tattoo.

"You look like you could use a drink." He blew out a breath. "I know I could."

Close up, she noticed his eyes had flecks of silver—like little ice chips. Interesting and sexy. The kind of eyes you could get lost in; the kind of eyes—

Before Virginia did something she'd regret, or maybe *not regret,* in any case still unprofessional, she pushed herself off the couch so suddenly that Python reared back. Even Kobi's head popped up from the floor.

"I should go."

He unfolded himself from the chair, easy and almost graceful. "You sure?"

She focused on the floor and noticed his bare feet. He had nice feet too.

"Yes. Why don't we set up another appointment for a time when you're not busy? I mean, not ... well, you know what I mean." She stepped around him, then said over her shoulder. "I'll call you."

"You don't have my number." He sauntered toward her.

"Right, I'll get it from Cobra, or I'll call Cobra and then

he can give it to me … or I can set up another time with Cobra." Now she was rambling like a crazy person.

He closed the distance between them, held out his hand, and again his body eclipsed her. "Give me your phone."

She rummaged through her huge purse, digging through year-old receipts and gum wrappers, thinking for the hundredth time that she needed to clean it out, until finally coming up with her phone. She unlocked it and then handed it to him. After he swiped at it, he punched in his number and handed it back to her.

"Call me." His lips twisted, and she couldn't figure out if he was going to smile or laugh at her.

She nodded because there was nothing else to say. She'd already babbled her way into idiocy. She didn't think there was any other way to possibly embarrass herself, so she headed for the door and opened it. When she looked back, he winked. Normally a jerk move, but coupled with his soft smile, it was almost like he could read her mind. A terrifying thought.

She left the apartment, then quickly walked to the stairs with one thought on her mind: get out of there and into the safety of her car. As she clomped down the stairs, she dug into her purse for her keys. At the bottom of the steps she spied a back door at the end of the hall. Perfect. She passed another bouncer but luckily no one else.

What a colossal screw up. In one night she'd hit all the bases: mistaken identity, a live porn show, tripping over her own feet, then topping it off with a devastatingly handsome, no … edgy, rugged … ahh, she couldn't nail his looks down. Usually the adjectives flowed through her with ease, but Python stumped her. In a short time, she'd seen him morph into so many different personas. He was a paradox, a man who had threesomes yet helped an elderly woman with her rent and obviously loved his dog. Then he sensed her unease, and correctly assessed that she would not be the type of woman to have group sex. Although witnessing that ménage à trois before did set off a fantasy of her own.

She'd reached her car by the time that thought hit and she paused. A niggling unease crept through her. He'd sensed her dull, boring sexual experiences and didn't even know her. What tipped him off? Of course, she'd looked shocked, but it was more than that. Rattler threw off a similar vibe, like he couldn't believe that she could be an exotic dancer. A more unsettling thought—Why was she bothered so much over what two strangers thought of her? Exotic dancing wasn't her life's dream. No judgement for those who chose to do so, but their opinions shouldn't have irked her like they did.

Virginia slid behind the driver's seat, and her faithful car chugged to life as she imagined herself having the starring role in Python's enormous bed. Again she silently chastised herself. She really needed to improve her sex life, or at least get a sex life.

———

Python stared at the door for a few seconds after she left. Virginia Swanson. Sounded like some old movie star name. Classic. Classy. Just like her. He'd been with a lot of women in his thirty-five years. Most of them the same in one way or another. He guessed the way he looked attracted a certain type of girl. Usually they were on the edgier side, with baggage and a story—always some kind of a story—a deadbeat ex who didn't pay child support, or a drunk boyfriend who beat them up.

His last girlfriend hit the trifecta. She had four kids from four different guys and had gotten fired from her job as a mud-wrestler because she was stealing money to support her gambling habit. Even though the guys ragged him about it, he liked helping those women and trying to fix them. It made him feel wanted.

What brought on all that deep thinking? As soon as Python moved into the apartment over the club last month after they'd fired the previous manager, he'd installed a bar. Thank fuck for that, because right now he needed a drink. He poured two fingers of Jack and gulped it down, then poured another and filled the glass with ice.

Even Virginia's crazy babbling was cute. Not a word he often used for the women he knew, but Virginia was definitely cute, and she also had a nice voice. Smooth, like she'd gone to one of those good schools where they'd taught her how to talk right.

He lowered himself onto the couch, then kicked his feet up on the coffee table and smiled, picturing the look on Virginia's face when she'd stepped into his bedroom. Shock, surprise, and then something else, maybe it even turned her on. Then there was the funny way she tried to make a smooth exit and smacked herself into the doorjamb as if she couldn't get out of there fast enough. Maybe she was afraid that if he'd coaxed her, she would've stayed and joined in.

Python would've gladly gotten rid of the other two 'cause Virginia was the kind of girl he'd want to enjoy alone. He pictured himself wrapping his fist around that straight platinum hair, then pulling her lips to his while he shoved into her from behind. Ohhh, fuck yeah.

The sound of someone knocking on his door brought him out of his sextasy. He pushed down on the bulge in his sweatpants as he stood. Maybe she decided to have that drink after all. A smile crossed his face. This was turning into one hell of a fuckin' birthday.

He yanked the door open and stared.

"What's wrong with you?" Cobra pushed past him into the apartment.

Python had been so sure it was Virginia that it took him a few seconds to regroup.

"What?" Good news, his hard-on was gone.

"I saw the way that reporter—*what's her name?*—ran outta here."

"Virginia?"

"Great, you got her name. I guess that's a step up for you. Usually you don't bother with names."

"The fuck are you talking about?"

"I set up this interview so we can get some decent publicity after the shit storm that went down last month. I told her boss she could drop in anytime. And what do you do but scare the piss outta her."

"A little heads up would've been nice. How was I supposed to know who she was? And I didn't scare her."

"Oh great, so you fucked her."

"No." Python grabbed up his cigs from the coffee table, knocked one out of the pack, and lit up.

"What then? 'Cause things usually go one of two ways with you and women. You either scare them with your kink, or you fuck them. Which was it?"

"Neither. And the one you should be ragging on is Rattler. That wiseass sent her up here acting like she was gonna join my birthday party."

"And when you say birthday party?"

Python sipped at his drink. There was no good way to spin this. "You wanna drink?"

His luck, she'd probably go back to her desk and write an article about Ecstasy being a sex club.

"Am I gonna need one?"

Python twisted his lips and poured Cobra a shot of Jack.

"So I was up here with the two new girls, Crystal and Tina or Tanya ... or Tara."

"And that's another thing. I thought we said the girls who work here were hands off."

"Technically they don't start till tomorrow night, then they're off limits."

"You're a real prince."

"I know, I'm a real perv. Fuckin' two willing women in my own bedroom. Shit, I don't know how I sleep at night."

Cobra smirked at his sarcasm. "Finish the story."

"Anyway, I'm up here enjoying my birthday and Rattler texts me. Says he's sending someone up. So of course I assume it was another addition to the party."

"Of course you would, because you're you." Cobra downed the shot.

"So she comes up, kinda catches me with the other girls, and freaks out a little bit."

"And then what happened?"

"When she told me she was the reporter, I told the others to leave, and I settled her down."

"And nothing happened between the two of you?"

"She didn't even have a drink."

"Well, I saw her practically running out the back door like the whole fuckin' place was on fire."

"I didn't do nothing. As a matter of fact, once she calmed down, I think she might've liked me."

"You got enough crazy in your life."

"That's just it. This one ain't crazy. She seems normal."

"Good to know." Cobra poured himself another shot. "Tomorrow, you go over to that television station where she works. You answer all her questions about Ecstasy, and you make us sound like we're goddamn knights in shining armor. Talk about the people we employ here, the health benefits we offer, and the charity fundraisers that are held here."

"Yeah, yeah."

"And here's the most important part: then you walk outta there and you never see her again."

Python shot Cobra a look. "You're telling me who I can—"

"No, I'm telling you who you can't fuck." Cobra slammed his glass onto the granite bar. "C'mon, like you were seriously thinking about you and her?"

"What if I was?"

"Yeah right, a girl like her. Quit screwin' with me, it's late." Cobra headed for the door. "Oh, and happy birthday."

Python mumbled his thanks, then locked the door. He'd had enough visitors for one night.

CHAPTER THREE

Virginia drained her coffee cup and contemplated refilling it from the ancient coffeemaker in the break room. She stretched her arms over her head hoping the movement would get her blood flowing. It was only noon, yet she could barely keep her eyes open. That's what happened after a night of tossing and turning, where the little sleep she did get was plagued with dreams of a certain biker in her bed. Normally Virginia slept so soundly that she never remembered her dreams, yet the huge man covered in tattoos stuck out in living, freaking color.

She yawned for a second time, and of course Nicole noticed. How could she not; they practically sat on top of each other. Their small work spaces were crammed with two monitors each and a few laptops. Everything that up-and-coming, not-quite-there-yet news reporters needed.

"I'm not going to ask why you're so tired"—Nicole grinned—"or how your interview went with a gangster biker who belongs to a gang."

Virginia narrowed her eyes. "I'm so glad, but if you did, I'd have to remind you that the proper term is *outlaw biker* and they belong to a *club* not a gang." Yes, she'd done her research. She might be lacking in the real-life department, but she was a whiz at gathering facts and keen observation.

Over the last months she'd questioned her decision to move to another state, away from everyone and everything she knew, but vivid memories of her father's controlling ways or her mother's archaic ideas regarding women put the small cubicle she shared with Nicole into perspective. Who needed a window office when you had your self-respect?

"Gang, club, who cares. Was he hot and dangerous like those shots we saw online?" Nicole asked.

Nicole was referring to a grainy online photo of a line of bikers at a gravesite a month ago. Cobra's brother died suspiciously and oddly enough, the body of a Vegas mobster, Vinnie Black, was found not far from Ecstasy's parking lot. No solid evidence had surfaced, but it'd cast a shadow over the Serpents.

After some digging, Virginia found out that the Serpents had some pull with the upper echelon at KLAS, so when they asked for a favorable story, they got it. With the devastating drop in tourism after the Coronavirus, Vegas needed all the positive press it could get. The last thing community leaders wanted was gossip circulating around that outlaw bikers were running wild and piling up bodies.

Virginia's boss basically told her what to write even before she visited Ecstasy. His patronizing tone annoyed her, but she wasn't in a position to argue. She promised to focus on the Serpents' charity donations around the city, but Virginia also hoped to uncover the real dealings of the club in an exposé that would be her stepping stone to stories that mattered.

"Oh. My. God." Sharon, their receptionist, leaned over her partition with an animated expression. "There's a super-hot guy out in reception asking for you. He's big and just—hot."

"Your biker." Nicole leaned over her side of the partition, bombarding her on the other side.

"Yes," Sharon whispered excitedly. "That's exactly what he looks like." She glanced at the clock. "And it's lunchtime. I'll bet he's going to take you to lunch."

"On his motorcycle," Nicole added.

"He's definitely fuckable," Sharon said, exaggerating every syllable.

"And when was the last time you had a date?" Nicole asked, then threw in an annoying, all-knowing expression.

Nicole and Sharon were always coaxing her to go out with them to happy hour, but Virginia usually stayed late at her desk working. Most times she ignored their ribbing, but the thought of Python out in reception had her palms sweating.

"First of all, he's not my biker." She shot a glare between them. "And will you two please just stop." This was what she got for having an Aries and a Cancer as best friends. "You sound like high schoolers."

"Probably the last time you got laid." Nicole waggled her perfectly waxed brows.

"Not true, Miss Know-it-All." Virginia hadn't had sex in high school at all. Going to an all-girls private school and never attending any of the mixers didn't leave room for much opportunity with the opposite sex—not that she'd ever admit that to Nicole. In truth, she'd had her first sexual experience on a dare. Her best friend at the time told her that she couldn't reach her twentieth birthday as a virgin. So one week before her birthday she had sex, and it was as exciting as watching water drip from a faucet.

Virginia pushed back from her desk and headed for reception with Sharon close behind like a yappy chihuahua. "You have to tell us every detail ... what he says, what he—"

Virginia cut her off with a deadly glare, then entered the reception area and froze. Squeezed into a plastic molded chair that barely contained a normal-sized person was Python. She closed the distance between them while he thumbed through a five-year-old copy of *People* with Caitlyn Jenner on the cover. He flipped the magazine shut, then stood. Wearing her sensible work shoes, Virginia was much shorter than in her spikes. Damn, the man was tall.

"Hey." His deep, guttural rasp sent a zing through her, but because Virginia knew Sharon was at her desk only a few feet behind her, she schooled her reaction.

"What are you doing here?" Her voice was level, controlled. Very good.

"Came to see you."

That was obvious unless he knew other staff at KLAS. She remained quiet, forcing him to elaborate.

"Things got fucked up last night."

"Just a misunderstanding."

"So, I thought we could do that interview."

"Now?" Virginia's mind flew off in all directions. Her minuscule workspace wasn't even big enough for her, and then she'd have Nicole hanging on her every word. She glanced at the huge clock on the wall behind him. "I have forty minutes for lunch."

He paused, then said, "Sure, lunch."

The word *lunch* seemed to throw him. Maybe bikers didn't eat lunch, although that wasn't in her research. Oh, good God, she needed to stop her brain.

"I'll be right back." Virginia hurried back to her desk to snatch her purse and was back in the reception area before Nicole could ask any questions.

She turned to Sharon, who had a ridiculous smile plastered on her face. "I'll be back at twelve forty-five."

Virginia swore she saw Sharon bouncing in her seat. This news would travel like wildfire, and the question and answer period when she returned would be excruciating.

They left the ground floor of the two-story building and she eyed her car in the parking lot. She wondered how this would play out until he placed his hand on the small of her back and led her to his motorcycle parked at the curb. Of course it was a Harley—a Fatboy to be exact—low to the ground and supposedly growly sounding. Virginia's research extended to what most bikers rode, and that in itself was an education.

His silence unnerved her, and she bit the inside of her cheek until it hurt to keep herself from babbling about the RPMs, gas mileage, and related minutiae she'd gathered about Harley motorcycles.

Python unlocked a back compartment and handed her a helmet. "You like Mexican?"

"Who doesn't?" Her flippant response seemed to confuse him.

Without another word, he straddled the bike and motioned for her to do the same. It took her two tries to get her legs right. When they were situated, he turned to her. "You ever ridden before?"

"No, is that going to be a problem?"

"Just stay tight, and move with me."

He kicked the motorcycle to life and her riding tutorial ended with a loud roar and a vibration between her legs that was noteworthy. Thankfully, she'd worn her normal work attire of black pants, this time with a beige shirt.

The April day with its clear blue sky and light breeze made riding on a motorcycle exceptional. The slight chill of winter had gone and the oppressive heat of summer hadn't yet appeared.

Python drove like he was one with the massive machine. He followed all the traffic rules and not once did she feel afraid. His advice to move with him was an added benefit and a definite bonus. Molding herself against the broad, taut muscles of his back let her drink in his scent—spicy cologne, motor oil, and a hint of smoke—very masculine, very earthy, very Python. Calvin Klein should clearly make this his next cologne launch.

The ten-minute ride ended much too quickly as they eased up to a small, sienna-colored adobe building. She'd passed the restaurant many times on her way to work but never eaten there. The parking lot was already jammed with cars, and Virginia worried about her lunch timeframe. Of course, she could always tell her boss she was working, but she wasn't quite high enough on the workforce chain to be allowed exceptions.

They dismounted, and again his silence played with her insecurities. She reminded herself that he'd come to see her, and that the Serpents needed her article as much as she needed them.

She cut a quick glance to his somber expression and easily saw how he could intimidate, and as hot and sexy as she found him the night before, she had to remember that he wasn't some Netflix character playing a role, he was the real deal. A one-percenter who was the sergeant-at-arms for an outlaw club, and inadvertently involved in an alleged murder, as well as many other shady deals. But she couldn't deny it, he made her heart race and her blood run hot. So different than anyone she'd ever known. Not many bikers running around the hills of Beverly unless they were on their way to MGM Studios.

They reached the door and the gentleman biker opened it to a flurry of customers and waitstaff. With the same firm hand on her back, he moved her forward through the crowd. More like he moved his bulk forward and she went with him, which was easy to do since he was at least four to five inches taller than the tallest person in the room.

He stopped at the reservation desk manned by a short,

round woman. Her face lit up as she embraced him in a hug until she started to spit out rapid-fire Spanish, which Python returned just as quickly. Virginia stood with what she expected was a dumb smile until the woman grabbed up two menus and herded them to the back of the dining room.

Python continued the steady stream of Spanish until they were seated. Then the woman looked at her as if seeing her for the first time, smiled, and said in English, "She's cute."

They faced each other as Virginia played with the menu. All Python's animation left with the sweet lady who seated them. His silence surrounded them, but one lesson her communications professor had taught her was: whoever spoke first lost when trying to get information. Even though her reporter instincts clambered with a myriad of questions, she met his gaze with silence. She used the quiet time to examine his Caribbean blue eyes and the intricacy of the serpent earring that wound its way up his lobe.

He bit his bottom lip and she sensed a break.

"I brought you here because I fucked up last night."

God bless Professor Morrison.

"The night didn't go as planned, but not really your fault."

"Cobra didn't give me a heads up, and with it being my birthday and all ..."

"Your birthday?"

"Not a big deal." He waved his hand around.

"Where I come from, birthdays are a big deal."

"Where I come from, they don't mean shit."

That could be a story in itself, but she didn't want to deviate. This wasn't a personal exposé, this was a fact-finding mission about Ecstasy.

The waitress came over and placed a large glass of water in front of each of them, then pulled out her pad to take their order. Python said something to the waitress in Spanish and then looked at Virginia. "Do you trust me?"

What a loaded question.

"To order for both of us?" he added.

"Yes, I'd prefer it." She closed the menu and handed it to the waitress. Choosing food in a restaurant always baffled and confused her. Too many choices.

Python rattled off in Spanish what sounded like a lot of food.

"I take it that you come here often."

"Good food, and I helped the owner out one time."

Another cryptic sentence that launched a hundred questions.

"Why don't we just move forward from here like last night never happened?" she suggested.

Like she could ever get the vision of him sprawled out naked on that giant bed with not one but two women draped over him. Heat crept up her neck at just the memory. She had to rein in her brain. Normally, she was almost robotic when interviewing, hitting every point, leaving no stone unturned.

"The Serpents need some good publicity," he said.

Right, and she was using them to hopefully further her career. His honesty didn't move her to her own revelation, but it did stir a tiny bit of conscience. Especially if he inadvertently dropped some significant piece of information at her feet, something so juicy that it shot her to the top, assuring she'd never have to cover another beauty pageant, restaurant opening, or biker with startling blue eyes.

She asked him a series of generic questions about the workings of Ecstasy. How the girls were hired, how many girls they employed, and all the nuts and bolts of keeping a club like that running and competitive. Python filled her in on all the rules regarding the girls and their customers and how they were put in place to protect them.

Although he didn't give away any juicy secrets, she was

enlightened to the workings of a very intricate business with many different aspects.

When their food came, she shut off the recording on her phone and laughed. "Is someone else joining us?"

"Figured I'd hit on a little bit of everything." His expression relaxed a bit. "And I'm hungry."

Simple explanation, but she imagined feeding a man of his size was a full-time job.

The server angled the plates and bowls in order to fit them all on the table. He'd ordered tacos and enchiladas along with other dishes she'd never eaten, and she had to admit that it looked delicious.

He wasted no time filling his plate and then digging in.

"Now that we're off the record, why don't you tell me where you learned Spanish?" she asked.

He paused mid-forkful, and his eyebrows knitted together.

"The question's not part of the interview, so you don't have to—"

"I learned it in San Luis."

He made the simple statement like it explained his life story.

"Arizona?" She filled her taco shell with grilled chicken, lettuce, and chopped tomatoes. "Is that where your family's from?"

He shrugged, but stayed silent.

Python's grim expression made Virginia regret her question, so she busied herself with the contents of her taco.

His eyes never left her, but he didn't elaborate. The newswoman wanted to forge ahead and ask questions that might be intrusive, but the girl that rode on the back of his bike couldn't do it. They'd crossed some quasi invisible border between reporter and subject, but it was more than that. She sensed a profound difference from the man last night to the man that sat across from her now. Ironic, because catching him in bed with two other women should've caused way more awkwardness than sitting in a Mexican restaurant in broad daylight.

———

Sure, he heard her question and saw how she leaned in, but he kept his past secrets on lockdown. The last time he cared about a woman his whole world fell apart. Zelda. Fragile, damaged and too broken to fix. She was the main reason he never got too close to a woman. No, he never talked about his past before the Serpents, and he wasn't about to start now with this delicate flower, whose deepest wound was probably a paper cut.

Virginia would be a hard no. He could break her without even trying, but he loved staring into her big brown eyes. She had such a tiny face, which made her eyes look even bigger. Everything about her was tiny, even her hands when she fiddled with the recording device on her phone. He wondered how those delicate fingers would feel caressing his chest or squeezing his—

Exactly what Cobra told him not to do, but Cobra couldn't tell him who he could screw even if it was the worst idea ever.

She concentrated on her food for a few minutes, then met his gaze over his cheese enchilada. "You seem so different today."

"How?"

"You didn't have to come to my office today, and yet you did, but at the same time, you're kind of acting like you don't want to be here."

Big joke on her. If she only knew. He'd gone to her office because Cobra wanted it done, but now he wanted way more from her, and that was wrong on so many levels. A guy like him and what he did for the club didn't gel with relationships. He had and knew too many secrets. Secrets that either kept people alive or got them killed. "I guess you could say I'm doin' it for the club."

"I see." She finished off her taco and wiped her lips with the napkin. Her mouth was pretty exceptional too. The way her lips puckered into a perfect circle, plump and—She couldn't have been more than twenty-five. Too freakin' young to get involved with his shit show of a life.

"You have to get back to work, right?" Make it about her. Don't let her see how he wanted to reach across and touch her delicate skin.

"Right."

He slapped some cash on the table, and when Virginia slung her large purse over her shoulder, she caught the edge of the glass, sending water down the front of her beige shirt. She jumped as ice cubes bounced off her while she lunged for a napkin.

He mashed his lips together, trying to swallow down a laugh, but she was so damn cute trying to act like she wasn't soaked from the waist up or that the water hadn't made her bra completely visible.

"Go ahead, laugh. I know you want to."

He let out a chuckle that ended in a loud guffaw. "Sorry, but you gotta admit, you're kind of a klutz."

She tried to scowl but ended laughing too. It was a nice sound, not shrill and screechy but more soft and sweet.

"Only when I'm around you."

"I make you nervous?" He waggled his eyebrows.

"Not at all." The glint in her eyes told him otherwise.

Liar, he wanted to shout, but this teasing and testing road they were headed down could get them both in trouble, so he kept it together and angled her toward the door, noticing how she hugged her purse in front of her see-through blouse. Again, cute. Most of the women he knew would've stripped it off. He said his goodbyes to Marta, and they walked in silence to his bike. He was grateful for the short ride back to the TV station. Less time he'd have to torture himself with her sweet body pressed up behind him.

Python pulled up to the curb in front of her building and purposely stayed on the bike, keeping the motor running. She handed him the helmet, and he leaned back and stored it away.

"Thanks for lunch and for coming down here to do the interview."

"Sure." Python had the brushoff part of a relationship perfected—no emotion, no conversation. His hand gripped the throttle and he gunned the engine, then angled the bike toward the street and got gone.

CHAPTER FOUR

Later that night Python filed into the back room of the Gold Mine, an old, western-style bar a few blocks off the Strip, with the rest of the Serpents for church, the biker equivalent of a weekly board meeting. He and Cobra bought the building from an old-timer who claimed Bugsy Siegel would stop in for a drink whenever he was in town.

The story sounded good, whether it was true or not, but the bar and the rooms upstairs were a financial asset that sat on a very valuable piece of property.

Cobra claimed his spot at the head of the thick wooden table with the etching of a snake slithering up the middle. All the brothers dropped their phones in a box by the door and took their seats. Since they were still without a VP, Python sat to Cobra's right with Rattler, their treasurer, on his left and then Boa, their road captain, and the rest of the patched members and prospects.

Python lit Cobra's smoke, then his own as the others settled in.

"Lots of shit goin' on," Cobra said around the exhaled smoke. "Looks like the Desert Rats are trying to move into our weed business. They think since Vinnie's gone, it's open season."

"Also heard the Rats hijacked some underage girls and are using them to run their farms," Python added.

"Never fails. Squash one roach and five more appear," Rattler said. "Only instead of roaches, it's Rats."

"It's clear how this has to be handled." Cobra looked to Python.

Python looked across the table at Rattler and two of the prospects. "We'll take a ride out to the desert."

As sergeant-at-arms, he took care of all the muscle. From hiring and managing the bouncers at the Gold Mine and Ecstasy to stomping on heads and breaking bones when assholes got greedy. Python loved crushing his fist against another man's face, the adrenaline, the rush. The only thing better was laying a bet or having a woman under him.

"Next Saturday, the Forgotten Kids event over at Sunset Park." Cobra shot a look to the two prospects. "We all set?"

Every year the club ran the charity event for foster kids: food trucks, games, rides.

"Another way to show the city what upstanding citizens we are," Cobra said. "Plus, it's a good time for the kids." Cobra and Python exchanged a look.

"And the rides are fuckin' awesome," Rattler chimed in.

"What're you, twelve?" Python sniped.

"And what're you, an old man?" Rattler shot back.

Cobra rolled his eyes at their exchange. Python couldn't get it together since he'd seen Virginia that afternoon. He had a lot to do regarding the Rats so he needed to get his head out of his ass and start thinking straight.

Cobra discussed more club business, and a half hour later they adjourned.

Python could almost taste that nice cold beer sliding down his throat when Cobra nodded his head to stay back.

When the others left, Cobra lit up another cigarette, and Python waited, not quite sure what his president wanted. Back in the day, they'd started the Serpents after most of Python's former club got hauled in by the DEA. The only reason he wasn't nabbed was because he wasn't at the club-house that night. He'd been sitting vigil in a hospital hoping against all odds that the woman in the bed would pull through. Women—his curse and salvation wrapped up in one complicated package

"What's up?" Python said, not liking Cobra's serious expression.

When they formed the Serpents, they both agreed on their ranks. Python liked smashing heads, and Cobra was a natural for president. Smart, cagy with just enough edge. And right now, it was that edginess that had Python's jaw tight.

"You'll never guess who stopped by the Gold Mine today," Cobra dragged deep on his smoke.

Now there was an open-ended question. Python stayed quiet and Cobra continued.

"Harry."

Yup, Harry didn't need a last name. Those who were anybody in the underground world of Vegas knew who Harry was: loan shark, bookie, crazy fucker. Python played it out even though he knew exactly how the rest of this conversa-tion would go.

"How much do you owe?"

Python lit up his own smoke and took a long drag, hoping the question would magically answer itself.

The two men stared at each other. Python had about two inches and thirty pounds on Cobra, but they'd never thrown down.

"Fifty large," Python finally mumbled.

Cobra reared back. "Fifty-thousand fuckin' dollars?"

"It kinda got away from me." And that was the truth.

When he was playing cards, shooting craps, or betting the horses it all slipped away. He was blessedly detached from all the bullshit and the doubt that swam around inside him as if he were sitting on some huge euphoric cloud.

"Ya think?"

"I'm gonna get it together. I got a sure thing coming up." That even sounded lame to his ears. The next thing he'd be saying was that he could quit anytime, like the junkies wandering around downtown. Even he knew that was one big lie. He couldn't quit 'cause he didn't want to. Gambling kept him alive—or let him live.

"So, you're gonna bet more money you don't have to pay off what you already lost." Cobra screwed up his lips. "That makes sense."

"I just had a bad run." Python knew it was getting ahead of him, even tried to rein it in a few times but—

"A bad run is a couple hundred bucks." Cobra huffed out a sarcastic laugh. "Fifty-thousand is a clusterfuck."

"I said I'll take care of it. Everything's cool. Harry and me got an arrangement."

The stubborn fucker wasn't gonna give this up. Cobra could be a persistent pain in the ass, wanting his own way and usually getting it. Great quality for the president of an outlaw MC, but fuckin' annoying as a friend.

Cobra ground his cigarette out in the metal ashtray. "There's a reason they call him Harry Houdini."

"I know. 'Cause he makes people disappear."

"He's also tied to the Rats."

Python threw up his palms. "Why you wanna tell me shit I already know?"

"'Cause I don't think you get it. We already got it goin' on with the Rats. I don't want anything to screw with that big shipment going out the end of the month."

"I get it."

"I don't think you do. Finding Vinnie's body last month in the tunnels behind Ecstasy left us wide open."

Python shrugged. "We didn't shoot the fucker."

"I know, I was there," Cobra deadpanned.

"I'm just sayin', it was some bad luck they dumped him there."

"Well, that's something you know about."

"Very fuckin' funny." Python scrubbed his hand over his jaw. "I've been thinking of cutting back for a while. Good time to start."

Cobra shot him a look that said he didn't believe him. Funny, he didn't believe himself either.

"You go talk to that reporter chick today?"

"Virginia. Yeah, all worked out. Gave her the behind-the-scenes on Ecstasy. Everything everybody wants to know about running a strip joint. I was like a regular Chamber of Commerce."

"Good, one less thing to worry about."

Not for him. Python hadn't been able to get the little blonde off his mind all day. Even reminding himself that they were probably at least ten years apart in age didn't help. That kinda revved him up—not too whacked in the head.

———

"Great, just great." Virginia stomped into her cubicle, but Nicole didn't react. She'd been annoyed when Virginia wouldn't share all the details of her lunch with Python.

Virginia acted aloof and secretive to save face because there were no details. The hot biker took her for a ride on his motorcycle to a Mexican restaurant, they ate, she drenched herself with water, then they rode back—end of story, all she wrote, good-bye.

Python probably thought she had trouble with her fine

motor skills. He couldn't get away from her fast enough. Embarrassing, and if she was being honest, disappointing.

Virginia made some more noise shifting papers on her desk while rooting around in her chair. The area they shared was so small that you could hear someone change their mind, so Nicole was most definitely ignoring her frustration on purpose.

Virginia leaned up in her chair enough to see over the three-foot partition that divided them. "I'm sorry I didn't give you the great story you wanted before, but sadly there is no story."

"A crazy-ass hot biker comes to take you to lunch, and there's no story." She harrumphed.

"You didn't even see him. You have no idea what he looked like."

"Sharon did, and she's very good with descriptions."

Virginia believed that. Sharon could make a soap opera story out of the kid that delivered their lunch.

"It was all business. We went to that Mexican restaurant down the street called Lindo something, I did the interview, he answered the questions, we ate and then came back."

A wave of disappointment washed over her.

"I know that place, Lindo Michoacan. Good food, authentic decor. Very cute. As a matter of fact, the word *lindo* means cute in Spanish."

Interesting. Python had called her cute that night in his apartment, and he did speak Spanish. Maybe that's why he took her there. Now she was reaching.

"Maybe you should take over the food critic job." Aside from men, Nicole loved to talk about cooking and food, so maybe she could veer her off the subject of Python.

"Did he at least say he would call or that he wanted to see you again?"

So much for the diversion. "No, and that would go with

the part where I said nothing happened. So, you see, I wasn't holding back, I just had nothing to tell."

She purposely left out her conflict with the water glass. Even a man like Python, who flirted with danger regularly, was probably afraid to be near her.

Nicole's face flattened and her animated expression faded. "I'm sorry."

"Don't be. It was nothing. It could never be anything." Virginia cocked her head. "Me and an outlaw biker?"

"You never know. All the romances I read always have the very bad boy with the virginal girl. Hey, get it ... *virginal?* ... *Virginia?*"

"Right, like I've never heard that one before." Her name was the butt of so many jokes at Miss Hines Academy that she'd seriously considered changing it.

"All right, I'm done." Nicole motioned to her. "So what's got you so upset?"

"After my unremarkable lunch, I wrote up my piece on my bad-boy biker and his strip club, even added my own brand of humor and banter, then sent it to Larsen with the hopes of a good assignment, and what do I get? The Forgotten Kids event this Saturday at Sunset Park."

"You got something against helping children?"

"Of course not, but I wanted something edgy, something where I can prove myself and my writing. An assignment where I have no chance of running into a badass biker." Virginia dropped into her chair.

Nicole's head popped up over the partition. "Did you say badass biker?"

"The event is run by the Serpents. Larsen said since I already met a few of them, they'd be more apt to answer more questions about the event."

"Great, I'll be home cleaning my apartment, and you'll be eyeballing hot biker guys."

"You could always come with. I could use the moral support. Seems like every time I'm around a certain biker, I become a bumbling fool." She was just thankful the ride back on Python's bike dried most of her blouse.

"Yes." Nicole combined a fist pump while making a kissy face.

Nicole might drive her crazy with her constant questions, but she was a good, supportive friend, always in her corner or making her laugh. Sadly, she didn't receive that kind of encouragement from her own family. When she defied her father by not taking the executive job in his multi-media company, he threw every obstacle in her path, but she was determined to show him she could survive without his money or influence in California.

She'd make it on her own in Vegas even if she had to live on dry cereal and Ramen noodles. And yes, of course she could get a second job, but it was much more than that. She used her spare time writing her version of the next great romance novel. It was a dream she'd had since high school, and one she wasn't about to give up on. But dreams didn't come cheap, so if she wanted her big break, she had to make it happen for herself.

A half hour later, Nicole leaned over the partition. "It's seven o'clock. You ready to leave?"

Virginia was already deep into researching a new story. "No, you go ahead. I have a few more things to wrap up."

"Okay." Nicole shrugged. "See you tomorrow."

The cell phone buzzed on her desk and she checked the screen and sighed. Virginia didn't need to hear the disappointment in her father's voice; she was disappointed enough for the both of them. As the vibration of her phone on the metal desk continued, she decided she might as well get it over with because her father never gave up and was known to keep calling her until she finally relented.

She drew in a deep breath and puffed out her lips with a frustrated exhale, then swiped at the annoying device.

"Hi, Dad." She forced a cheery, upbeat voice.

A pause meant to intimidate, then he asked her, "Have you come to your senses yet?"

Yup, that was her father—right to the point, grab the bull by the horns, a low blow to try and throw her off her game.

"Regarding?" Two could play at this game. She'd make him pay for passing along those intelligent genes that enabled her to graduate Magna Cum Laude from USC.

"Regarding coming back to California where you belong, taking the job I offered you, and living the life you should be living."

"You mean living in that museum you call a house, working where everyone knows I'm your daughter, and basically existing in a fake life?"

"Let's not play word games, Virginia."

"I'm not. Just clarifying what I already know."

"This is not a pleasant side of you, Ginnie."

Great, now he reverted to the childhood nickname she hated. Not a smart move at all, Dad.

"You're right because I'm not going to be bullied or intimidated into coming home and living in the shadow of your name."

"And you'd rather live in a tiny apartment in the middle of the desert than reap the benefits of my advice and prestige?"

"I'm determined to make it on my own." He just didn't get it.

"Hmmm."

"Without your help," she added, quite proud of herself for standing up to the man that could discourage her with a look.

She'd been so caught up in her show of independence that she missed the signs. As owner and CEO of one of the largest media networks in the country, he'd learned to negotiate, wait out his opponent, then dangle the preverbal carrot.

"Then I have no choice than to lock up your trust fund until you come to your senses and return home. As of today, you will get your wish and be the master of your own destiny."

Virginia remained quiet. The meager monthly amount her father doled out barely covered her food, but it was something. Now, she'd definitely have to cut back, but she refused to give her father the satisfaction he so dearly wanted.

"I'll be fine," she said in a steady, strong voice.

"Time will tell."

Virginia gripped her phone long after the call disconnected. For a second she considered pitching it across her desk, but she certainly couldn't afford a new one. She gathered herself up, more determined than ever to succeed on her own.

Her father's smug voice rang in her ear, but she wouldn't give up.

If KLAS wouldn't give her the breakout story she wanted, she find it herself.

CHAPTER FIVE

Nothing compared to the freedom of riding his bike on an open desert road, whipping down the highway with the sun on his face. A new day, a fresh start, and all that bullshit, which also included another job, and another beatdown. Duty calls.

Python and Rattler headed out to Searchlight on their bikes with two prospects following behind in an SUV. The old gold-mining town with a population of a little over five hundred proved the perfect spot for the Rats to set up shop. Only one problem, Searchlight was a part of Clark County, and only the Serpents ran weed in Clark County.

They veered off the main road and traveled single file along a gravel road to what looked like an abandoned house surrounded by scrubby bushes and a few scraggly trees. If Rattler's intel was right, and it usually was, this place housed two floors of plants cared for by six underage Asian girls and two guards. The Rats kept the young women basically as slaves. Fucked up all around.

They cut the engines on their bikes and coasted down the remainder of the dirt road.

"This should be easy," Python said over the heavy-metal music blaring out of the rundown shack. "The guards are inside watching the girls. The Rats are so cocky, they'd never expect a hit."

Rattler motioned to the two prospects to go around the back.

Get in, get the girls, and send a message to the Rats. When the prospects disappeared around the back of the house, Python and Rattler drew their guns. They did a short countdown, then Rattler booted the flimsy door, sending it off its hinges. The two Rats' prospects reached for their guns, but it was over before it started.

"Lay them on the floor nice and easy," Python said as Rattler covered him. "Along with your cell phones."

The entire first floor was gutted to make room for rows and rows of plants. The young teens tending them stopped what they were doing and stared wide-eyed above their face masks.

"We're not gonna hurt you," Rattler assured the girls.

The prospects laid their phones and guns on the ground, then the one closest to Python whipped his hand into his boot. Python picked him off, shooting the gun right out of his hand, then stepped closer and drilled a bullet into his right kneecap.

The man screamed out in pain, fell to the floor, then curled into a fetal position while the other prospect stood with his mouth gaping open.

"Stupid fucker." Python sneered.

"Stay with these two." Python ordered the Serpents' prospects, then he and Rattler marched up the stairs.

The dormer was filled with bare, filthy mattresses side by side. They'd ripped out the bathroom for more plants, and as far as Python could see, the only running water was used for the product.

"I'm all about making money"—Python's gaze swept over the stifling, dank room—"but this is fucked."

"Way different than the way we do business."

They clomped down the wooden stairs, and the guy Python shot was moaning with the other guy kneeling over him.

"Give me my phone, man," the prospect said to Python. "He needs an ambulance."

Python leaned down and fisted the prospect's straggly hair, then cut his glance to his buddy on the floor. "He should've thought of that before he drew on me."

Then he pressed the barrel of his gun against the prospect's temple. "You tell Demon not to let this happen again, and if he does, I won't be so nice."

Python grimaced as he wiped his hand on his jeans. "What the fuck do you put in your hair?"

Python jerked his head toward the door, and they filed out. The young women huddled together, speaking Mandarin with big, saucer-like eyes, as Rattler herded them to the SUV. Some of them were only teenagers. Young teenagers.

"Drop them off at the women's shelter on Flamingo, but don't go in." Python said to the Serpents' prospects. "They're definitely illegals, but we can't get into that shit. Someone there will know how to help them."

"What about this place?" one of the prospects asked.

"Torch it."

"What about the weed?"

"Ain't our product." Python smirked.

"And the two inside?" Rattler asked.

"He'll pull his buddy out. I'm just sending a message; I don't wanna start a war." Python patted his pockets for his smokes. "And to show what a humanitarian I am, I'll even call an ambulance for the bastard when we get back on the highway."

When the first torch hit the house, Python could hear the girls cheering from inside the SUV.

First a popping sound and then the crackling of dried out wood, and a few seconds later, flames shot out of the first-floor windows, followed by billows of thick smoke.

Rattler sucked in a deep breath. "Now that's what I call getting high."

"Let's get the fuck outta here." Python and Rattler mounted their bikes as the prospects hopped into the SUV.

———

Later the same night, Python, Cobra, and Rattler sat at the bar in the Gold Mine.

"Productive day." They all clinked beer bottles to a job well done. Hopefully, the Rats would get the message. It was bad enough they owned part of the Shangri-La in North Las Vegas, but letting them grow and run product was a whole other issue.

"You never filled me in on your birthday celebration."

Rattler left the statement open-ended. Nosy fucker wanted to hear all the gory details.

"I gotta say, the last one I sent up was cute." He waggled his eyebrows.

"I give this guy"—Cobra jerked his thumb at Rattler —"something to do, and he fucks it up. You couldn't tell that she wasn't his usual variety of snatch?"

Rattler shrugged. "I figured she was playing the naughty librarian bit."

"Are you two done?" Python took a long pull off his beer.

Rattler slapped Python on the back. "Three women. Not bad for an old man."

"Nothing happened with the other one, and who are you calling old?" Python slammed his beer bottle on the bar with more force than necessary. Calling him old was one thing, but making him think about Virginia sucked big time.

Rattler threw up his palms. "Hey, I'm impressed. How old are you anyway, forty?"

"Fuck you." Python flipped him off. "Thirty-five, and I can still get more pussy on a bad night than you."

Rattler was about six years younger than him and loved to raze him on every birthday, but he made a great Road Captain, and he was one of the best riders in the club. He claimed he'd been riding since he was a kid, but his personal history changed with the amount of booze he consumed. Didn't matter though, he knew his stuff.

"Yeah, okay, but you still haven't told me what all you got up to."

And Python wasn't about to either. Sure, some of the guys made a documentary about all their conquests right down to the who, what, and where they stuck their dick, but Python wasn't that guy. Nor was he about to divulge any information about Virginia. Let Rattler think what he wanted to think, but Python sure wasn't adding to it.

"Use your imagination. Or has the younger generation forgotten how to do that?" Python and Cobra exchanged a fist bump.

Rattler laughed and called for more beers from the prospect tending bar. "When the dust settles, we should scope out Searchlight and the surrounding area for our own. Sleepy little town between here and Laughlin." Python swigged at his beer. "Good stop off place halfway in the middle."

"Probably what the Rats were thinking," Cobra said.

"Demon might be bat-shit crazy, but he's not stupid." The president of the DRs spent most of his days spun on some synthetic substance, but he was as smart as he was unpredictable.

"I'll definitely check it out," Rattler said.

Cobra and Python knew he would 'cause Rattler took his job seriously. Didn't matter if it was their weekly rides to the weed farms or a four-day run to a biker event, he had everything organized and mapped out.

"Haven't been outta Vegas in a few weeks." Python grabbed his cigs off the bar. "Don't get to ride enough in the wide-open spaces." He missed the long runs they used to go on before the Serpents settled in Vegas.

"That don't bother me." Rattler nabbed Python's cigarettes. "I kinda like weaving in and outta traffic, freakin' out all the tourists."

"You're a sick fuck," Python said. "I don't like being caged in."

Python had enough of that as a kid. Sharing a dormitory with eight or ten other guys didn't leave much room for privacy or open space.

"I'm a city boy," Rattler said. "All that land kinda freaks me out."

Python's phone lit up on the bar and he was happy for the diversion. Last thing he wanted to talk about was his fucked-up childhood—or rather, his nonexistent childhood.

"Yeah," Python grunted into the phone.

"We need to meet." Python knew that psycho voice.

"Why?"

"Why the fuck you think?" Demon snorted into the phone. "I'm at the Shangri-La."

Python stayed quiet, and Demon continued, "We need to iron this shit out."

"I'll be there in twenty." Python stubbed out his cigarette.

"Where will you be in twenty?" Cobra asked.

"The Shangri-La."

Both men pushed off their bar stool, and Python shook his head. "I'll go alone."

"Not smart," Rattler warned.

"What's he gonna do to me in a strip joint full of people? He just wants to cry like a whiny fuckin' baby. Then he'll offer me some half-assed deal. And that's the part where I laugh in his face." Python cocked a brow. "It's like free entertainment."

"Good luck, brother." Rattler flagged the prospect for another beer.

"Text us if shit gets deep," Cobra added.

Python knew they both had his back. Both loyal to the end. They'd stood side by side plenty of times. Cobra's sinewy, ropy muscles made him powerful and precise, and Rattler's long reach made his jabs quick and agile. Nothing like throwing fists in a good fight.

———

Python pulled into the lot alongside the Shangri-La, which was wedged between a hot-sheet motel and a Taco Bell. Booze, boobs, and burritos—convenient.

Only one bike with the Desert Rats insignia was parked in the lot. Demon was alone just as Python suspected. He didn't trust Demon or any of the Desert Rats, but the Serpents were much higher on the food chain so an ambush would not be in their best interest.

It all came down to protocol. Had the Rats been higher on the echelon, Demon would've insisted on meeting with Cobra, not his sergeant-at-arms. Just like any business meeting, there were rules to be followed. Granted, most meetings on Wall Street didn't end in bloody gunfire, but business was business.

The bouncer waved him through the door, and Python gagged on the damp, unfiltered air and the stink of smoke, sweat, stale beer, and—piss? What a dump. Just last month they were hit with a twenty-five-thousand-dollar fine by the gaming commission for gang violence, hiring illegals, and suspected prostitution. This would've been the next stop for the girls who he and Rattler freed today at the weed farm. A far cry from the way he ran Ecstasy.

Python let his eyes adjust to the flashing strobe lights. He hated that shit; it gave him a headache. He refused to have it at Ecstasy, but after getting a closer look at the dancers, Python understood the need for a diversion. Most of them looked like they should've retired five years ago. The whole place looked worse than he remembered. They must've paid the health department a lot of cash to keep this dump open.

The small, tightly-packed area made it easy to pick out Demon sitting at a table in the back, off to the side of the stage. Three dancers approached him in the two minutes it took to cross the room, but he kept moving. He wouldn't fuck these girls with someone else's dick.

"Wasn't sure you'd come," Demon said as Python sat down.

"Just wanna make sure you understand how things are," Python said.

A waitress came over and Demon lifted his chin. "What do you want?"

"I'm good." He also wouldn't drink the water in this place.

"We need to talk."

"There's nothing to talk about. You were told to stay outta Nevada and then you open up shop right in Clark County."

"That prospect you messed with will probably never ride again."

"Who are you kidding? You don't give a shit about your patched members, much less your prospects."

Demon twisted his lips and smirked. "Still fucked up. You hit us hard."

"What aren't you gettin'? You were in our territory, growing product without permission. That's a 'fuck no.' You're lucky I didn't smoke 'em both."

Python wouldn't be surprised if Demon didn't ice them himself. The Desert Rats didn't allow screw ups, and mistakes were handled quickly and efficiently.

"Hmmm." Demon grunted. "Maybe we can work out a deal."

"No deals. Just stay outta our territory."

"Even if I got Harry to lower your debt."

Python leaned across the narrow table, putting him right in Demon's face. "What the fuck did you say?"

"I know you owe him fifty large, and I also know he's getting impatient. So, maybe you do a favor for me and I do a favor for you."

Python sucked in a deep breath and slowly exhaled. He knew the Rats and Harry were partners in this place, but Demon knowing about his debt wasn't good.

Demon pulled out his smokes and Python gazed around the room to buy himself some time. The strobe lights flashed, and he caught sight of a familiar face across the room. He stared harder, not able to believe what he was seeing.

"You listening to me?" Demon asked.

"What?" Python strained to see through the flashing strobe lights.

"What are you looking at?" Demon turned in his seat.

"I gotta take a piss," Python said.

"Now?"

"You got a problem with that? Maybe you wanna come hold it for me."

"Fuck." Demon waved his hand at him. "Hurry up."

CHAPTER SIX

Python pushed away from the table and stormed to the back hall, then slammed into the ladies' room.

Virginia jumped away from the sink and spun around to face him.

"What are you doing here?" Python barked.

"You do realize this is the ladies' room."

"Answer me," he demanded. "What are you doing here?"

"Not that it's any of your business, but I'm doing research for a story I'm writing."

"On what, the top ten sleaziest strip clubs in Vegas?"

"Why do you even care what I do or where I go?"

Yeah, why did he care?

"The last time we saw each other, you acted like you couldn't get away from me fast enough."

True. The whole lunch, his mind played some back and forth bullshit game that confused the hell out of him. His dick brain wanted to reach out and drag her onto his lap, wrap her legs around him, and have her sink onto his throbbing cock in a crowded restaurant at lunch hour. His practical brain told him to act cool and put some distance between them, because thinking about her that way was all kinds of wrong. Practical brain won by shutting everything down, knowing it was the only way to save her and him.

"And now you're worried about my welfare?" She jutted her chin out, and again the word *cute* came to mind. "A little hypocritical, don't you think?"

She had a point, but he couldn't let her stay here. A few weeks ago there was a shooting right out in the parking lot. And she was right, but if he mentioned that every time he thought of her his dick got hard, he'd sound like a complete perv.

"And for your information, I've taken self-defense classes and I know how to protect myself."

In one swift move, he spun her around and slammed her against the tile wall with his forearm braced across her chest. He wasn't hurting her; he was making a point. Most of those self-defense classes were a joke. Unless you were conditioned for violence or practiced every day, the split second you hesitated would slip you up every time.

He arched his eyebrow. "Use one of your fancy self-defense moves, and I'll walk outta here."

She struggled against him, but they both knew the outcome. The position of his forearm pinned her arms to her side, and the position of his feet totally blocked any movement of her legs.

"And in case you're wondering, I can do this to somebody my size too. Only with a lot more force and a shit ton of pain."

"You've proved your point," she huffed out.

He lowered his arm, but he wasn't ready to let her go yet. She tried to move around him, but he blocked her way, then jammed the metal garbage container under the door.

"Good, because it's not safe for a woman like you to be here."

"A woman like me?"

All right, so he'd used the wrong words, but a lot of shady shit went down here, and he knew she couldn't handle it.

"Look, I'm all about equality. Your body, your decision. But all you gotta do is look around to know this place ain't safe. Almost every guy in here is either connected or a gangbanger."

"Which one are you?"

He glared at her and she inched back a step. "Don't try to sass your way outta this."

"And all these dancers are women," she threw back at him. "The woman that just came off stage was as small as me."

He barked out a laugh. "The woman that just came off stage has been working the Strip since she was sixteen. She could probably take me down."

"Fine. Considered me warned. You can go back to whatever business brought you here with a clear conscience."

That'd be a trick in time travel. He hadn't had a clear conscience since he was about eight.

"And who is that guy you're with?"

"Again, none of your business."

She inched along the wall, but he threw up his arms and caged her in, then he shot her his "don't fuck with me" look. Very effective since they were only a few inches apart and he towered over her. She heaved out a frustrated sigh, and he almost expected her to stamp her foot. Cute. There was that word again.

"A cameraman from the studio."

"Oh, that's great. The hoods who run this place will love you takin' pictures."

"I already talked to the person who runs it. His name is Demon. What is it with you guys and the weird names?"

"You talked to Demon?"

"Yes, he said I could take pictures of the outside, but not the inside to preserve people's privacy."

"Right, especially since most of his dancers are illegals."

"He was a little jumpy, but he didn't do anything wrong. I don't know what you're getting so worked up about. He was wearing the same kind of cut as you."

"Oh, fuck no. That bastard and his club are nothing like me or the Serpents." Python braced his hand against the wall a few inches from her head. "I'm not playing, Virginia. Stay far away from him 'cause that guy wouldn't give a second thought to taking whatever he wants from you."

"You can't tell me what to do." Her brown eyes flashed with indignation.

"All right, then I'll go out there and tell that guy you're with what an asshole he is for bringing you here." He cocked an eyebrow. "Only I might have a hard time expressing myself without using my hands."

"If Demon and this club are so bad, then what are you doing here, and how do you fit in to all this?

"I make no excuses for who I am or what I do, but I've never hurt a woman physically. That you can believe."

"Fine." She pushed at his chest, but the action was laughable. "I'll leave after I observe for a little longer."

She angled her body and tried to slip under his bicep, but he wrapped his arm around her waist. "No fuckin' way. You're leaving now."

Even in this dump, she smelled like sweet candy, all fresh and just ready for him to take a big bite. Sure, he tried to tell himself that he could walk away from her, that it was better to never get started, but he didn't do good with denying himself. He was a balls-deep-or-nothing type of guy, and right now that was all he could think about.

Feeling her move and writhe under him, calling out his name or straddling his hips with that beautiful blonde hair draped over his thighs, he'd take her every way he knew how, making her wet and needy ... making her want him.

She'd just become his newest goddamn addiction—much scarier than dice or cards, much riskier than the horses. This addiction could wind him up and spit him out without a second look, and he didn't care.

The old saying of wanting what we couldn't have screamed in his ear. He wasn't a man who deprived himself; number one reason why he got into shit and owed his bookie big time, but this gnawing itch couldn't be scratched, not until he got a taste of her, and he guessed even then he'd want more—much more.

Python leaned up against Virginia, molding her body to his, then lowered his head and took her perfect mouth. His tongue played along the seam of her lips, and she welcomed him in. He'd thought she might resist, but they were on the same damn page. She wrapped her arms around his neck and flexed her hips. Best fuckin' feeling ever.

———

Oh. My. God. What am I doing?"

She'd managed to divert his questions and avoided telling him that she was investigating the seedy underbelly of Vegas, especially since his club and the people they associated with might be the main characters. Sure, she promised her editor the puff piece about Ecstasy, but being at the Shangri-La had nothing to do with that and everything to do with boosting her career.

Although, savoring the way Python's body pressed up against her had nothing to do with her career and everything to do with sending her life straight to hell.

From the second he barged into the bathroom, she saw it in his eyes and knew they would end up like this because there was no way to deny it. Virginia wanted him, needed him in some primal way that she didn't understand. She could deny it all she wanted, but whatever simmered between them couldn't be ignored any longer.

Even the way he trapped her against the wall. He knew just where to place his body to make his point, how far to go without hurting her physically. She never felt threatened bodily; although, mentally, Python short-circuited every alarm, bell, and siren that shrieked, *danger ahead—proceed at your own risk.*

They stared at each other. Virginia knew what would come next and she wanted it—badly.

His hands traveled down her back, rounded her hips, and cupped her ass, then he lifted her off the floor until they were eye to eye. Python cocked his head and licked his gorgeous lips, then pressed them against hers and sealed them together. He jostled his hold on her, braced her against the wall with one hand while his other hand twisted into her hair.

He broke the kiss, his beautiful blue eyes hooded, his lips parted. "Fuckin' love your hair." He threaded his fingers through it, then wound it around his fist. "So soft."

Taking her mouth again, she parted her lips, letting their tongues tangle in an erotic dance of swirls and twists. Python's body pressed flush to hers as his hips rhythmically ground into her pelvis—but it wasn't enough. Virginia shifted, trying to angle her body until it was right where she needed him. From his pants and groans, it seemed like he needed her too.

Python's lips traveled down her neck, tugging her hair just enough to get better access while his warm mouth had her moaning into his ear and she inhaled his scent—smoke and spicy male. When he shoved his jeans-covered thigh between her legs, she finally had him where she wanted him. Some relief, but not enough. It would never be enough until he was inside her, spreading her, filling her up.

Reality hovered around the edges of her brain, her logical brain, the one that graduated with honors from USC and made her leave her parents' Beverly Hills mausoleum to carve out her own life. The one that told her she was about to have sex with a hotter-than-hell outlaw biker in the bathroom of a sleazy strip club. A strip club that she should be observing, not participating in, but the way his sinful body molded to hers made her eyes roll back.

Python's hand slipped between them, then she heard the metal of his belt and the warmth of his abs against her stomach. "You got me so damn hard."

When his fingers glided into her thong, she gasped. He easily found her spot like they'd been doing this for years. This man knew what she wanted and how she wanted it.

"Right here, baby?" he asked as he tortured her core. "You're already hot and wet for me, huh?"

His slow teasing rhythm combined a throbbing ecstasy with a yearning torment.

"I'm guessing you were thinking about me today and that's what got you all worked up. Maybe you were even thinking about how I would feel inside, spreading you, making you ache."

Oh, god, he was right. She'd thought of him many times today. His persistent fingers kept cadence with his words. Her head fell back against the tile wall and her eyes slid shut with the pleasure of it all.

"Nah, baby, eyes on me. I want you to see who's making you feel this good."

Python's confident, unrelenting desire amped her up even more. He kept stroking her until he heard her panting breaths. His mischievous smirk said he knew she liked it and got off on the power to control her body with a flick of his fingers.

She thrust and gyrated onto his hand, and his grin widened. "You like that, huh?"

He shifted her again and she heard the rasp of his zipper. "You with me, baby?" he mumbled against her lips, pulling her shirt out of her pants. The cold tile wall hit her back as he shoved at them.

"Yes, God, yes."

He flicked a look from side to side. "You deserve better than this, better than me."

His concern broke through the lust and it added to his hotness knowing that if she backed away, he'd let her go. Crazy, but in the moment she trusted him, and backing away was a definite no.

"I don't care about that. Please." She thrust her hips against him to punctuate her point and he groaned.

"We're doin' this, yeah?"

"Absolutely." Her assurance spurred him on. In a flash, he dug his hand into his pocket and fished out a condom.

True, this was not her normal. Never had sex outside of the bedroom. Vanilla described the only kind of sex she'd had in the past. So wasn't it about time to break out, and what better way than with an outrageous stud of a biker in the bathroom of a seedy strip club.

Python shifted his hips, ripped the silver package open with his teeth, and then the door banged inches from her head.

"Hey!" A woman yelled from the other side of the door. "What the fuck?"

They froze. Virginia's arms were entwined around his neck, her shirt open, and her legs anchored to Python's waist while his jeans hung off his hips with a condom still clenched between his teeth.

"Shit," Python hissed, then he put his finger over her lips to be quiet.

After some more banging, a kick rattled the trashcan that Python had braced under the door.

"Open the damn door. I gotta take a piss before I go."

Virginia widened her eyes, but he shook his head.

Then another kick to the door. "I'm getting the bouncer if you don't open this damn door."

Virginia heaved out a sigh, unwound her arms and legs and settled herself on the floor.

The banging and yelling got louder.

"All right," Python yelled back through the door as he straightened his jeans and threw the condom in the trash.

Virginia fumbled with the buttons of her blouse, then righted her pants. She ran her hands through her hair and tugged at the tangled clump at the nape of her neck from Python's fist.

Python stepped away from her and the full griminess of the bathroom returned along with the blaring, uncovered overhead bulb.

He glanced back at Virginia. "You together?"

She nodded and reality hit her in the face.

Python moved the trashcan, and the loud woman barged through the door. "What is it with you people that like to fuck in the john?" She eyed the both of them in her five- or maybe-six-inch stilettos, a g-string, and nothing else. This woman's rail thin body seemingly defied gravity—a direct contrast to her enormous breasts.

"What the hell are you staring at, honey. Haven't you ever seen tits before?"

"Ease the fuck up," Python growled.

Miss Tits gave Virginia the once over and huffed out a laugh. She closed the distance between her and Python, then rubbed up against him like a cat in heat. "Stick around later, and I'll give you a private dance."

Amazing, Miss Tits acted like she wasn't even there. This woman's high heels put Virginia at eye level with breasts that were the size of her head. She probably should've felt uncomfortable, but the writer in her found it fascinating. This woman would make an interesting case study.

Python stepped away from the stripper, then pushed Virginia in front of him and out the bathroom door.

When they walked out in the hallway, he stopped and turned her toward him. "You all right?"

"I would love to interview her."

"Why?" Python pulled a face. "To find out what made her a bitch."

"Everyone has a story."

He shrugged, then led her out of the hallway and stopped at the edge of the main room. He scraped his hand through his hair, keeping distance between them; what a complete turnaround from two seconds ago when their bodies were seared together.

Virginia glanced at the empty table where she'd been sitting with Brian, the cameraman. Her escape into her biker fantasy must've taken longer than she thought so he left. Great.

"Just promise me you'll stay away from Demon."

Virginia's short interview with Demon left her on edge and wary and wanting a shower. The man exuded sleaze, and although she wouldn't admit it to Python, Demon had all the tendencies of a dangerous criminal.

"About that," Python jerked his thumb toward the restrooms.

The stripper interrupted them and saved her from jeopardizing her story. It was totally unprofessional to get involved with someone she was investigating.

Python grunted something, but the loud music drowned him out.

"There you are."

Virginia pivoted to see Brian standing behind her. The two men eyed each other, but she had no intentions of introducing them or explaining where she'd been for the past however many minutes. There was no good way to say she'd had her thighs wrapped around the hips of a wicked biker and two minutes away from having an uncontrollable orgasm.

Brian surveyed the situation, then leaned into her. "I found out some interesting information."

Virginia flicked one last look at Python, then grabbed Brian's arm and led him away before he said anything in detail. His mundane, average looks were unremarkable, making it very easy for him to blend in and go unseen. He also had an innate ability to find out information, which made him invaluable on a project.

When they got to their table, she looked back to where Python was standing, but he was gone. She surveyed the room, but between the crowd and the flashing lights it was impossible to focus on anyone, a definite asset when socializing in a criminal hangout. Anxious to hear what Brian had found out, she suggested they leave so they could talk without screaming.

———

Virginia led the nerdy cameraman back to their table and Python watched the sway of her hips as she did. Those same hips that were pressed up against him not two minutes ago. The way she clawed Python's back told him she was into it as much as he was. If it hadn't been for the bitchy stripper, he'd be blowing apart right about now. How Virginia pulled herself together made him wonder if she was almost relieved

—as if the interruption saved her from a big mistake—meaning him.

Python trudged through the club and regained his seat across from Demon, who was staring mesmerized at the redhead on stage. He couldn't believe Virginia dealt with this scumbag ... telling her he'd give her an interview. Yeah, Python knew how that would go. The last woman who got near him ended up in the hospital, and the one before that disappeared. Demon liked to play rough, and if the women didn't go along with it, too bad. The sick fuck probably liked the fight, like a predator who played with its victim until he killed it.

Demon's shifty eyes slanted to Python. "Where you been?"

"Had something I had to take care of." True enough, although he hadn't taken care of it. Just like the last time, Virginia had him edgy, tense, and strung out—the same craving as he got just before a bet.

The stripper from the bathroom strutted over and stopped at their table. She leaned in with her fake tits in his face. "Don't forget to come see me after my set." Her hand slid to the front of his jeans and squeezed, then she straightened up and pranced toward the stage.

Demon twisted his lips. "You left a meeting to get your dick wet?"

Python leveled him with narrow eyes, then shot a glance over his shoulder to where Virginia had been sitting with her cameraman. Empty. They must've left out the back. What the hell had he been thinking trying to screw a girl like her in the bathroom of a strip joint? A shitty strip joint. Even the bitchy stripper knew he and Virginia were mismatched. Ridiculous.

"You listening to a fuckin' word I'm saying?" Demon shouted over the music.

Python spun around and faced Demon. "What?"

"What the hell is the matter with you?" Demon dragged deep on his cig, his beady eyes shining through the smoke and strobe lights.

"Nothing." He had to get his head back in the game. Here he was sitting across from a deadly scumbag and he was thinking about Virginia's soft—

"I said I can help you out if you help me out."

"Forget it. I don't need your help."

"Harry doesn't see it that way. You let us have a little territory just south of Vegas and he's willing to cut your debt in half."

Right, all he had to do was sell his soul and his club out to the fuckin' devil.

"It could just be a deal between you and me. Cobra and the rest of the Serpents don't have to know about it."

Typical Rat move. No loyalty just greed. No wonder their club was imploding from the inside out.

"Fuck Harry and his deal" Python knocked his knuckles on the table. "And you keep your Rats outta Serpents' territory."

Demon lowered his eyes to the table, then slowly gazed up at him. "Not smart." He stubbed out his butt. "Definitely not healthy."

"You asked your questions and you got your answer." Python slapped his palms on the table and stood. "We're done." He sensed Demon's eyes on his back as he sauntered out of the club like he didn't have a care in the world.

Now all he had to do was figure out how to get fifty grand together. Actually, with the vig he was up to fifty-one thousand. The last sure thing he told Cobra about really wasn't that sure of a thing. Horses ... You just couldn't depend on them.

CHAPTER SEVEN

The sweet aroma of frying peppers, onions, and garlic surrounded Virginia as she made her way around the variety of food trucks lining the fairgrounds of Sunset Park. The warm, clear April day set up the perfect atmosphere for an outdoor event.

This assignment was neither earth shattering nor career enhancing, but an order from her editor, as in—do the job or step aside for the ten other people who would gladly take her position. She'd kept her thoughts to herself, though, because the information that her cameraman had obtained at the Shangri-La would round out her story very nicely. Virginia's current outline was mixed with grit, human interest, and a bit of drama, all the ingredients she hoped would advance her to the next level where her stories would be taken seriously.

Thankfully, Nicole promised to meet her here as a favor, so at least she wouldn't be alone when she inevitably ran into Python.

Just his name skittering through her brain brought on a hot flash that circled her neck and slithered down her spine. *Slithered like a snake ... a python.* Oh God, she needed to stop obsessing about a man she couldn't have, one who she didn't want and certainly wasn't good for her, just like the sleeve of Chips Ahoy cookies she polished off last night. Great, an eating frenzy brought on by thoughts of Python and their bathroom escapade at the Shangri-La. Not good, not good at all.

She drew closer to the center of the carnival, impressed by the turnout. The usual amusement rides dotted the area, but the amazing lines to play the arcade games astonished her. Her surprise wore off when she noted each stand was manned by scantily clad women, presumedly from Ecstasy.

As they said in the newsroom, sex sold. These women weren't doing anything other than running the usual games of chance, yet their skimpy shorts and tight tank tops had people lining up for the pleasure of throwing a plastic ring over a milk bottle or popping a water balloon in a clown's mouth all for a good cause. The Forgotten Children's banners were all over, and Virginia was sure this weekend's profits would be impressive.

Great public service announcement for the Serpents, although as she observed, it might be more than that for them. She watched as the big bikers ran the rides, joked with the kids, some with families of their own. These big tattooed men seemed to really be enjoying themselves. Perhaps she was missing the smaller story within the big one. The one that said families came in all shapes and sizes, and although the biker life was unorthodox, it certainly seemed like they were having a good time while giving back to the community.

Virginia reflected on her own sterile childhood and almost laughed out loud picturing her stick-in-the-ass father going to a local carnival.

"I've been looking all over for you," Nicole said.

"I just got here." Virginia scanned the area, but no sign of Python. He had to be here somewhere.

"So, have you seen your biker?" Nicole asked.

"Will you please stop saying that." Creepy how Nicole read her mind. "He's not my biker."

"But you wish he was." Nicole waggled her eyebrows, and of course Virginia laughed. There was something infectious about Nicole's honesty.

"They got a great turnout," Virginia said. "Let's check it all out."

They moved further into the center of the grounds, passing the kiddie rides and a tent with a fortune teller.

"You should go in." Nicole pointed to the fortune teller. "Find out if a biker is in your future."

"I'm regretting telling you about the other night." Virginia had confided in Nicole about the interlude in the ladies room of the Shangri-La in desperation to sort out her feelings. Of course, Nicole found the whole episode erotic and used it as proof that they were made for each other. *Not*.

"I don't understand why you keep fighting it. Just go with it and do something crazy for once."

Virginia shrugged, but it didn't stop Nicole.

"You haven't had a date in what—*ever*."

"That is not true." They stopped at a cotton candy stand, another one of her weaknesses. "Just last month I met that guy on Tinder."

"Right, you had coffee for twenty minutes and decided he wasn't for you. That's not a date, that's a drive-by." Nicole stepped back and eyed her critically. "And what is that you're wearing? My mother wears shorter shorts."

"What's your point?"

"My point is, it's eighty degrees, you're twenty-six years old, and you look like you're going on safari. You have a slim, adorable figure, yet you wear clothes that look two sizes too big."

"I'm here to cover the carnival, which means business attire."

"Business attire, fine, but those shorts look like they swallowed you alive, and could that t-shirt be any boxier? You need to break out and wear something daring, or at least do something daring."

"And getting with an outlaw biker and wearing clothes that constrict my blood vessels would solve that?"

"It sure would make for some interesting conversation for a change."

Virginia laughed at her friend and took the cone of cotton candy from the vendor, then turned back to the crowd. The sound of people squealing on the rides, children running around, the smell of hot dogs, fried foods, and sweet treats all swirled around her until she suddenly stared, frozen in place.

"That is an impressive sight," Nicole said into her ear and then sighed dramatically.

"It certainly is," Virginia agreed.

Two stalls down, Python commandeered a basketball shooting booth.

"Go over and check it out." Nicole nudged her from behind. "Better yet, go over and check him out."

Virginia dug her sneakers into the gravel. She wanted to ogle him from afar first.

Sinking baskets was the obvious object of the game, but Python brought new meaning to full-court press. His black leather cut hung over a white wife-beater, accentuating those magnificent, swirling tats on display in living color. She was also treated to a glimpse of his abs when his low-slung jeans separated from his t-shirt. Now if she could just keep from dribbling.

Python looked like a big, overgrown kid with the most amazing smile, wide and genuine as he handed the kids the balls, cheered them on, and even helped a few faltering balls make it into the basket. A paradox completely foreign to the man who had threesomes and headed security of an outlaw biker club by throwing fists and breaking heads.

He even reached over and hoisted the smaller kids up and let them stand on the counter to get a better shot. It seemed like every kid left with some kind of prize, but the sheer delight on Python's face softened the harsh edges as he enjoyed himself as much as the children.

She hadn't missed the look of sheer bliss on the mothers' faces of those children or any other female who crowded around his stall. Jokes were always made about certain people being magnets for the opposite sex, but Python's attraction bordered on an electronic force field. Yet he just rolled with it without showing the arrogance of many men who were far less attractive. The man overflowed with confidence and swagger but never acted conceited.

"Are you just going to stand here and stare?" Nicole prodded.

Virginia had contemplated just that. Stay at a healthy distance because the last time they were together ... No, she wouldn't go there. After all, she was assigned to write a segment about the fundraiser, and since his club was the sponsor, she'd act like a professional and do her job.

She'd taken about ten steps in his direction when the statuesque brunette from Python's threesome slipped into the side of the booth and joined him. Virginia's jaw dropped at the woman's cheek-baring short shorts and the hot pink tank top scandalously squeezing and clinging to every curve. The brunette ran her hand over Python's chest, and when she planted a big fat kiss on his lips, the crowd erupted with cheers and whistles like some PG-rated porn show.

Virginia stopped so short that Nicole almost plowed into her from behind.

"Don't let her stop you. Go talk to him."

"Is that the way you think I should dress?" Virginia asked sarcastically.

"It would definitely get his attention."

Men now joined the crowd of women clustered around, making the basketball booth one of the most popular games at the carnival. The brunette set up the balls, collected the money, and flirted with the fathers, while Python engaged the children and entertained the crowd with his antics. They looked like two perfect specimens of an exhibition displaying the human race at its finest.

Virginia craned her neck to where Cobra stood selling raffle tickets for a brand-new Harley-Davidson. She'd just go interview him. Much, much easier.

"Where are you going?" Nicole asked.

"Away from them." She jerked her head in Python's direction.

"Don't let that fake Barbie intimidate you. Look, I was wrong before. You have more smarts in your—"

"Please, Nicole, I don't think anyone is interested in my brain right now."

She pulled out of Nicole's grasp and turned in the opposite direction with a tad too much force. She lost her footing on the loose gravel and reached out to balance herself. Unfortunately, she grabbed on to the pole holding up the awning at the hotdog stand. In the next second she, the pole, and the awning hit the ground with a loud crash.

She closed her eyes and prayed to the God of Embarrassment to let her sink into the gravel, but of course that didn't happen. She heard a commotion of voices and opened her eyes. The striped awning partially covered her, and for a split second, she considered hiding under it, but of course two men dragged it off her. She recognized one as Rattler, from her night at Ecstasy, along with another biker whom she didn't know.

"Geez, are you all right?" Rattler asked, as he roughly yanked her up by her arms. "You went down like a fuckin' brick."

She brushed off her butt, then looked down at the gravel, dirt, and hay stuck to her bare legs. Yes, as usual, her grace under fire blew up in her face, and how nice of Rattler to point out that fact so loud and clear. Anyone who might've missed her journey into humiliation was now informed.

One question flashed through Virginia's brain. How did these things happen to her? Nicole fussed around her and the hot dog vendor asked if she was hurt, then balled up the awning and put it behind the cart. She hoped he'd be able to salvage it and was just happy that he wasn't charging her for damages. Her moment of klutziness could turn expensive.

When the dust cleared, literally, she brushed the rest of the gravel off her legs, straightened up, and turned right into a brick wall of muscle and swirling tattoos, her nose in direct line with the middle of Python's massive chest. Yes, it was confirmed, God had truly forgotten about her.

Virginia craned her neck because, yes, he was that freaking tall, and glared into his half smirk, half smile. Like a kid who'd been told not to laugh in church, Python was bursting to let out a huge howling guffaw. He handed her the sunglasses that had flown onto the gravel and tried unsuccessfully to wipe the smirk off his face. Her gaze wandered to his side and there sat Kobi, mouth open and tongue hanging out like he was laughing too.

"Thank you," she mumbled while hoping for any natural disaster to interrupt this moment.

As if seeing him naked with two women less than a week ago wasn't bad enough, she'd doused herself with water, then was interrupted by a stripper while having almost-sex in a grimy bathroom. Extreme embarrassment and this man seemed to go together.

"There are easier ways to get my attention." His snickering and deadpan delivery had her fingers balled into fists.

She took two steps back to put some distance between them and because her neck was beginning to ache. "Seems like you have all the attention you can handle."

A millisecond later, she wanted to shove the catty words back down her throat. Her snide remark gave away the fact that she was watching him and now acting childish. Bravo for behaving like an ass while trying to be cool and making an already mortifying situation worse.

Then he annoyingly smiled wider, enjoying her descent into acting like an elementary schooler on the playground.

"You look like you could use a cold beer." He draped his arm over her shoulders, then looked to Nicole. "How about you?"

"No, I'm good. Thought I'd check out the rest of the carnival," Nicole said sweetly as Virginia pierced her with death glare daggers.

Python shrugged and led Virginia over to the beer tent with Kobi trotting along at his side. The tent was out of the late afternoon sun and at least ten degrees cooler. Between her flaming face and rising blood pressure, a little shade was definitely in order. A makeshift bar and picnic tables were set up under the tent. Python jerked his chin at three guys sitting at a table and they promptly vacated. She looked between Python and the men, then sat down.

A few minutes later he returned with two ice-cold beers, which she practically grabbed from him, and pressed the cold bottle against her cheek.

Python held up his bottle. "Here's to the three most fucked-up ways I've ever had with a woman."

She cocked her head not quite sure what he meant.

"Our first meeting involved you and a threesome you weren't involved in. Our second meeting was in the bathroom of the sleaziest strip joint in Vegas, and now here at a biker benefit for foster kids where you try to single-handedly tear the place down."

She wondered briefly if he was able to read her mind, then laughed long and hard at his summation of their encounters. It absolutely relieved the tension and prevented her from taking herself too seriously. She laughed so hard she had to put her beer down. On a high note, she didn't do a spit-take, although Kobi was staring at her.

"To be fair, I only demolished one hotdog cart." She waved her hand around. "The rest of the carnival is fine."

"True, but I think I better keep an eye on you, 'cause there's no telling what else you'll get up to."

"What about your basketball booth?" Virginia bit the inside of her cheek to keep from blurting out another bitchy remark about his bed partner.

"I think Crystal can handle it. Probably bring in more money than me. Every guy in the place will be trying to make that basket."

"Anything for charity." She sipped at her beer, enjoying the heavenly, icy liquid that slid down her throat. "I do have some questions I'd like to ask you about the event."

Fifteen minutes later he'd filled her in on all the reasons why the Serpents got behind the charity as well as a pretty in-depth account of what happens to foster kids in the system and how they are aged out at eighteen.

"That's terrible. I hate to admit it, but I never thought about the consequences of that situation. What teenager is ready to be on their own at eighteen? Even kids from a solid background would flounder without support or further education. It's outrageous, and ..." She realized her voice had risen, and Python was just staring at her like she was crazy. "I'm sorry, it's just seems so unfair."

"That's why we do the charity every year."

His simple statement rang in her ears and the sadness in his eyes told her their yearly charity meant more to him than helping kids sink a basketball or good publicity for the club.

"All kids need a chance ... need to think that someone gives a shit," he added.

She stared at him for those few extra seconds that usually made both people self-conscious. Averting her eyes, she played with the label on her beer bottle while he patted his pockets and came up with his cigarettes. He knocked one out of the pack, lit it, and blew the smoke upward.

"It's a good thing ... what you and the club are doing, and I'll be sure it's the featured topic in my story."

"Got a minute for an old friend?" A man of medium build stood at Python's side.

The transformation of Python's expression chilled her. He glared at the stranger, then stood.

"I'll be right back," Python said to her, then moved to the other side of the tent with a man who did not look like a friend at all.

Kobi stood and nudged his snout into Virginia's lap. She aimlessly stroked the animal's ear as they both watched the body language of Python and this mystery man. She couldn't hear a word they were saying, but the message was clear. Python had a good four inches on him, but the shorter man with the face of a ferret was in charge.

Python's face remained granite hard, his anger seconds from bubbling over, while Ferret Face berated him, flayed his hands around, then poked Python in the chest with his index finger to accentuate his point. Any minute she expected Python to blow up, but the explosion never occurred. Instead, he mashed his lips together and took whatever this man was saying. The whole scenario didn't make sense. The writer in Virginia asked: How did this non-biker, non-threatening person cow Python? Or better question, what did this seemingly understated man have on Python?

Last week at the Shangri-La, while she'd been exploring her erotic fantasies in the bathroom, her cameraman, Brian, chatted up the bartender. After he bought her a few shots, he found out the Shangri-La was owned by the Desert Rats and a guy named Harry. Just Harry. She had plenty to say about the Desert Rats, none of it good, but nothing about Harry.

This person dressed in khaki pants and a golf shirt was definitely not a friend or a biker. Asking Python about this mystery man would be a dead end, so Virginia made believe she was taking selfies while snapping shot after shot of the stranger instead. She'd refer to them on Monday when she perused the station's database because a story was definitely there.

Virginia's phone buzzed in her hand and she jumped. As soon as she saw it was her mother calling, she let out a frustrated sigh. Her parents were like a tag team. First one, then the other, lecturing her over all the reasons she was throwing away her inheritance and her life. The phone continued to buzz, and just like her father, Virginia knew her mother wouldn't give up. Vera Curtis headed every fundraiser in Beverly Hills, and her power of persuasion was legendary. Might as well get it over with while Python was occupied.

"Hello, Mom."

"Virginia, how are you?"

Odd, her mother asking about her well-being. Normally her mother's only concern was herself.

"I'm fine, Mom." Virginia's senses perked up. Where her father was blunt and to the point, her mother usually had a hidden agenda.

"I'm so happy to hear that. I understand you and your father had an unpleasant conversation the other day."

"It was only unpleasant for Father because he didn't get his own way."

"Your father can be stubborn, but that's what's made him a success." Her mother's dramatic sigh. "And he's worried about you, as am I."

"There's nothing for either of you to worry about. I'm fine." Virginia's patience was wearing down. She just wished her mother would get to the point and start carrying on about her like she usually did.

"I'm glad to hear that, but I do miss you." Her mother paused. "I've been thinking about the fun things we used to do when you were little."

Virginia fondly remembered those sunny days sailing around the inlets of Balboa Island, along with the skills her mother shared with her on the tennis court.

Those skillss helped Virginia win almost every amateur competition in California. Then Virginia became a teen, and as crazy and ridiculous as it sounded, her mother became jealous of her accomplishments.

"I was thinking that maybe you could come home next weekend, and we could revisit some of those good times."

Virginia's heart kicked up. Her mother certainly sounded sincere, and she did miss those times they'd shared.

"Don't let your father keep you away. I miss you."

Virginia's gaze swept to Python. The ferret-faced man walked away, and Python was on his way back to her.

"Please think about it," her mother added. "I'll send the jet and you could be here in forty minutes," her mother enticed.

"All right, call me midweek with the details."

"Oh, wonderful, we'll have the best time, just like the old days."

The phone disconnected and Virginia's chest tightened

with a desire to recapture those days—a desire to feel her mother's love again.

A few seconds later, Python stood at the edge of the table. His scowl had softened a tad, but she noted the tick in his jaw.

He snagged her hand. "C'mon, let's go for a ride."

"Don't you have to stay and work the carnival?"

"I've been here since early this morning. They'll be fine without me for awhile." He turned the key and glanced at her. "You ready?"

Those two simple words brought up so many scenarios. Yes, she was ready for a renewed relationship with her mother, and yes, she was ready for an adventurous, wild ride with a man who occupied her thoughts for the better part of this week.

He slapped his hand against his thigh and Kobi obediently followed. She noticed for the first time that the dog wasn't on a leash. Python obviously had taken the time and effort to train the animal. Virginia hustled to keep up with Python's long strides and Kobi's four-legged advantage.

Python stopped next to an immense roofless black jeep— the kind with the large tires and removable doors. Luckily, the doors were attached, but the vehicle was massive. Python chirped the locks, then opened the back door as Kobi hopped in and immediately sat in the middle seat. Python had to give Virginia a hand up to the running board and then into the jeep.

He turned the key and glanced at her. "You ready?"

Those two simple words brought up so many scenarios. Visions she'd spent the better part of this week suppressing at work, on the ride home, or any time at all. She'd even gone as far as to replace the bedmates she'd seen him with on his birthday with herself. Of course, for that one she needed her vibrator, but ...

"You all right?" he asked.

"Yes, yes. Yes, of course." She needed to get ahold of her repeat responses.

The truck growled to life, not quite the same sensation as his bike vibrating between her thighs, but ... Oh God, she needed to stop. One last thought: being with Python beat her vibrator, hands down. Okay, done.

CHAPTER EIGHT

A half hour later, Lake Mead came into view, and after a few twists and turns, they passed a restaurant and a boat marina. Python guided the jeep off the paved road to a narrower gravel road, and after a few more turns, he eased into a quiet cove secluded far from the bustling marina.

Virginia missed the wind in her face, but the scent of heat and Python surrounded her. Her eyes slid closed making a memory. The slamming of the driver's side door shook her back to reality and she managed to alight from the jeep all by herself. Python opened the rear door, and Kobi eagerly jumped out and headed straight for the water.

"You ever been down here?" Python asked.

"No, I've been to Boulder City but never all the way down to the lake." His question made her wonder. Since she'd arrived in Las Vegas, work predominated her time with little left for entertainment. Maybe Nicole was right. She needed to get out more and just have fun.

He pulled a blanket out of the rear of the vehicle, then he snatched up her hand and they headed toward the water. The quiet, secluded area showed off the beauty and the massive size of the crystal blue lake. Medium-sized rocks made up the beach, but as they grew closer to the water, the rocks became pebbles.

He stopped a few feet from the shore and spread out the blanket. They both sat down, and again, Virginia's mind spun with questions.

"Nice here, right?" Python said.

"Beautiful." She pointed to Kobi who had already waded in. "Seems like he's been here before?"

"We come down to the lake whenever I can get away. Quiet. Nobody ragging at you." He shifted to face her. "I like to get outta the city, away from all the lights and noise."

"So, you're not a city boy?" An open-ended question, and she couldn't wait to see how the self-contained biker answered.

"Not really."

"Yet you live and belong to a club in Las Vegas."

He shrugged. "Just where I ended up."

Geez, she'd have a better chance getting a backstory from Kobi.

"When we had lunch you mentioned Arizona was where you learned Spanish."

"Right." Python focused on Kobi playfully splashing in the water.

"So, you're from Arizona?"

He untied his boots and toed them off. "Let's wade in and join him."

Okay, so that was some drastic subject change, but she wouldn't push. As a reporter, she was used to people not answering questions. Although, she had to admit, the more he held back, the more intrigued she became, and it went far beyond her being a reporter. It dealt with the extreme opposites and the conflicts that made Python one of the most interesting people she ever wished to know.

The cool water felt heavenly, so good that she waded in to where her shorts met the top of her knees. Nicole was probably right, she could've worn something a little shorter and more fitted.

Python threw a rubber ball to Kobi, and the dog easily swam out to retrieve it. Virginia watched Python continue to throw the ball with Kobi, catching it mid-air a few times, while puzzling over this complicated man. She gazed into the clear water, able to see every rock, as if looking through shimmering glass.

She turned and playfully kicked some water at him. A sly smile tugged at his lips, but he didn't retaliate, so she did it again. This time she could see the spots of water on his jeans. He turned away from the water's edge and headed for the blanket.

Huh, I guess bikers don't like water.

He pulled off his cut, folded it and laid it on the blanket, then balled a fistful of his t-shirt and dragged it over his head. He still had his back to her so she could gawk without fear of being caught at the Serpents insignia from shoulder to shoulder. The first night in his apartment he'd been totally naked, but her senses had short-circuited with all the other diversions, namely the 3D porn show. Then, after those women left, she purposely diverted her eyes from his outstanding body to save herself the further embarrassment of staring.

He tossed his t-shirt over his cut, turned, and yes, the front view was as impressive as the rear view. Especially the rings piercing both nipples. He stalked toward her with a smirky grin on his face, and she was grateful for the cool water because her core was on fire. Of course, with their height difference the water was only to his calves, but still enough to drench the bottom of his jeans.

He rested his hands on his hips. "Was somebody out here splashing water at me?"

He moved closer to her and she backtracked. The water rose to her thighs, but he stalked closer—all muscle and scruff with the sunlight shimmering off his multiple piercings. She'd noticed all the Serpents wore the silver serpent earring, but Python also wore a cuff in his right ear and at least five silver studs in his left ear.

"Where're you goin', babe? Trying to get away from me?" He teased her.

Virginia picked up her pace, but as she exhibited at the carnival, she had enough trouble walking forward, so going backwards in thigh-deep water spelled sure disaster.

As a sharp rock dug into her heel, she yelped, then tried to regain her balance but fell backward into the water. She saved herself from going completely under but was soaked just the same.

Python, the big fool, threw his head back and howled with laughter.

She struggled back to her feet and scooped two big handfuls of water in his direction, drenching his jeans. He continued to laugh, then lunged and dragged them both down. This time she went under the water, and when she surfaced, Python's large hands circled her waist.

She sputtered and spit out water, then pushed her hair out of her face. He shook his head like a dog sending water every which way, then he flipped over on his back, keeping her on top of him, and kicked them into deeper water.

Virginia wrapped her arms around his neck like he was her personal life raft. When he stopped swimming and stood, her legs automatically wrapped around his hips and his arms circled her waist. The water came to just below his shoulders so she knew there was no way she could stand.

They stared at each other, only inches apart, wet and clinging to one another. His hand slid under her t-shirt and cupped the swell of her breast, brushing his thumb over her nipple. It pebbled tight from the cool water, yet hot from his touch.

"How is it we always end up like this?" she whispered, as she gripped his shoulders.

"Something keeps throwing us together."

"Fate."

"Don't believe in that kinda bullshit, but—"

"Then you explain how we both end up in a strip club I've never been to before, or how at a crowded carnival with hundreds of people we seek each other out."

"When you put it like that, it is freaky."

He attacked her lips without warning, then pressed the tip of his warm tongue inside her mouth until they were teasing and tempting each other. Virginia's eyes flickered open to the beautiful blue sky and the miles of clear, calm water surrounding them. Truly a perfect day, a day she'd want to remember.

She shivered slightly and he broke the kiss. "You cold?"

"A little."

He scooped his hands under her ass and easily treaded out of the water, then sat her on the blanket and jogged back to the jeep and returned with a few towels.

Virginia wrapped one around herself, then pulled at the material of her cargo shorts, and the thick cotton of her t-shirt. Yes, Nicole was definitely right, this heavy fabric would never dry.

Kobi joined them, shaking his wet fur and drenching them with beads of water. Python dried him off, then laid the towel out and the dog snuggled into his side. "You big baby," he said.

Python toweled off his torso, and again her eyes were magnetically drawn to the tats, the rippling muscles of his arms, and the scruff along his jaw. As the magazines said, this man was the whole package, and to make matters worse, he was modest. Even with all the badassery, he exuded kindness.

"You must have some exciting stories belonging to a biker club in Vegas."

He cocked his head, his face flattened out, and for a few seconds she had no idea what he was going to say. "Not as much as you might think."

She marveled at how he diverted the conversation or just let questions about himself hang out there unanswered. Most men she knew loved regaling women with their whole life story whether they wanted to hear it or not.

"You should consider politics," she said.

He scrunched up his forehead.

"You have a talent for not answering a question or just ignoring the question totally. The makings of a great politician."

"Just don't need to be the next story on the eleven o'clock news."

"You think—no, I'm asking about you because *I'd* like to get to know you better, not for the station."

"That was the original deal though, right? You were doin' a story about Ecstasy, and then somehow you and I had ..."

"True, but complete your sentence. What exactly do you and I have?"

"Fuck if I know."

Not exactly the answer she wanted, but again, his brutal honesty both impressed and annoyed her because his blunt words rang with truth.

"Like you said before, it seems like something is shoving us together."

He twisted his fingers into the towel she clutched, then leaned in so his luscious lips could cover hers. This man had the art of kissing down pat. She wouldn't have expected his kisses to be so soft and gentle yet demanding at the same time—just the right amount of passion and lust mixed in with a heavy dose of dirty.

He broke away from her lips and mumbled. "So, what do you think we have?"

"Fuck if I know." She mimicked his words.

He smiled against her lips. "Exactly."

One fact she did know: It would be very hard to be objective when she wrote her final article. Python turned out to be nothing of what she expected. Plus, she'd broken the cardinal rule: Never get involved with your subjects.

His gaze lowered to the wet material of her t-shirt glued to her body. He licked his lips, then pushed the wet fabric to the side and nuzzled her breasts. His warm tongue flicked over her nipple and she moaned. The sound surprised her, but his tongue and the gentle sucking had her angling herself closer to him for better access. His hands traveled along the smooth skin of her stomach then toyed with the waist of her shorts. "Wanna touch you, taste you."

He might've had trouble talking about himself, but when it came to sex, he knew exactly what he wanted. She found his stark, direct expressions refreshing.

"Yes," was all she could mutter because his fingers already undid the button and zipper of her shorts.

His fingertips ran over her abdomen and her muscles flexed. He tugged her shorts and panties lower and traced along the inside of her thigh, then up over her abs again. He kept his eyes fixed on hers, making it impossible to look away.

Her breath caught in her throat when his two fingers teased her, but she never broke eye contact. He ventured further and his lips twisted into a smirky grin.

"I'll bet you taste so sweet."

Bam! There it was again. His innate honesty and she loved it.

She turned her head from side to side and laughed when Kobi mimicked her actions by standing and moving his head in both directions.

"Just wanted to make sure we were alone."

He spread her thighs wider. "You got me so wound up, I really don't give a fuck."

She could believe that. Although this would be her first outdoor, somewhat public, experience, she could only imagine all the places public and private he'd done it.

Kobi stood guard and Python laughed. "Don't worry, if anybody gets too close, Kobi will take a bite outta them."

He shifted, spread his legs and positioned her between them. Her back to his front.

"Feel good, babe?" he whispered into her ear as he circled her clit.

"Mmm, yes."

He teased her a few more times, then dipped in without warning. First one finger and then two.

She drew her knees up and the feeling intensified. He pushed further until the heel of his palm massaged her clit, then tilted her chin up and dragged her lips to his. She twisted slightly and his fingers never stopped thrusting.

Faster and faster he curled them inside her while keeping her lips captive in a drugging kiss. She'd give up breathing to make this insane, intense sensation never stop.

Her hips kept perfect time with his hand, and she lost herself in the moment and allowed this tattooed, outlaw biker finger fuck her into oblivion. Her breathing came in little pants, and in one swift motion, Python removed his fingers and pressed the rings adorning his knuckles against her nub.

A noise she'd never uttered escaped her, and she collapsed against him, panting—her shorts around her ankles, her legs splayed wide, and a wild exuberance flowing through her.

Python pushed away Virginia's hair and sucked on the side

of her neck as the aftershocks rolled over her, his warm tongue laving the sensitive skin at her nape.

He slid his hand against the skin of her abdomen and she ached at the emptiness. Then he sucked his fingers into his mouth and licked his lips. "I knew you'd be sweet."

Again, his raw, primitive reactions engulfed her.

She shivered and grabbed for the towel. The late afternoon sun had shaded them and the dry air off the lake chilled her.

"Why don't we pack up and take this party inside."

She didn't exactly know what he meant, but it sounded like he wanted to spend more time with her. This man's fingers just brought her to a place she'd never experienced with full-on sex, so she couldn't wait to see what else he might have in mind.

He tugged on his dry t-shirt, then slipped on his cut and laced up his boots. Unfortunately, her clothes were still wet. She buttoned and zipped her shorts and managed to stand. Her shaky legs pushed her feet into her sneakers.

He gathered up their wet towels, then stopped. "I like you."

Again, his simple words floored her. He had a knack of saying ordinary words in an extraordinary way.

"I like you too."

Then they trudged back to the jeep with Kobi alongside them. She wasn't looking forward to the ride back to Vegas in wet clothes.

He stuffed the blanket and towels in the rear, then pulled a black leather jacket from the back seat. "Put this on so you don't freeze your ass off. It gets cold in the desert once the sun goes down."

She slipped on the heavy leather and laughed. The band of the jacket practically hit her knees and the sleeves fell way over her hands. She had to admit though, it was warm, and best of all, it smelled just like Python. Leather, smoke, and something spicy.

Kobi jumped into the jeep, then stared at her intently.

"Today was nice." She gazed up at Python's tousled, damp hair.

He mashed his lips together, his expression serious. Then he gripped her hips tight, lowering his head until they were only inches apart. "I'm not done with you."

"I know, I'm not done with you either." In a moment of boldness, she reached around and cupped his ass through his wet jeans.

He smiled against her lips. "I like you like this."

"Like what?"

"All wild and sassy. Spreading yourself wide for me."

How could his words make her wet all over again? She'd just had one of the best orgasms of her life and yet she was ready to have him right there, right now.

"I like me this way too." She nipped his lower lip. "You better be careful or I'll attack you right here."

"As much as I love outdoor sex, I think we're gonna need a little privacy for what I got kicking around in my brain."

"Sounds interesting." He opened the passenger side door, and again, he had to help her up and into the vehicle.

"Just one thing." He slammed the passenger door and went around to the driver's side.

She honestly had no idea what would come out of his mouth next. Perhaps another description of how he would ravage her body, or an out of the way indoor place that was risky, like the restroom at Walmart or the parking garage at the Bellagio?

"You mind if we go to your place?" he asked, then slammed his door.

Her mind had spun in so many crazy scenarios that she paused and stared at his mundane request.

"You're not up with that?" he questioned.

"No, no, that's fine." She congratulated herself for not adding the third no.

"You sure?"

"Yes, no, I mean, yes, that's fine." Damn, and she was doing so good.

"I'd go back to my place, but it's my night off, and if Rattler knows I'm just upstairs, he'll annoy the shit outta me with every stupid question he doesn't feel like dealing with."

Virginia motioned to Kobi. "Any idea why he's staring at me?"

"You're sitting in his seat."

"I'm sure I'm not the first one to steal his seat." She could only imagine the assortment of women who must've seen the inside of this vehicle. Right, she didn't want to think about that.

"Yeah, you are."

"You're telling me you've never had a woman in this jeep before."

"Never had a woman in this jeep or on the back of my bike."

And she'd done both, but still his statement didn't make sense.

"So, you go out with a woman and—"

"And nothing. I don't do that either. I either meet them somewhere or they come to the club." His crystal blue eyes showed nothing but honesty, and crazy as it sounded, she believed him.

"And the women who were helping you celebrate your birthday?"

"Were in my bed. Completely different."

She didn't get it but knew if she dug any deeper, she'd be just as confused or he'd just shut down, so she nodded like she understood. It wasn't that she had such high regard for sex or even equated the act to love, but she certainly held it higher than allowing someone to ride in her ancient Toyota. Must be one of the biker codes that she overlooked. 'Thou shalt never allow a woman to ride in or on motorized vehicles.'

"There's just one thing; my building doesn't allow dogs, and my nosy landlady is always looking out the window. I think sometimes she's just looking for an excuse to throw me out."

"No problem. We'll drop Kobi off at my apartment. I gotta feed him anyway and let him run around out back."

"In the parking lot?"

"Behind the parking is an empty field where he gets his exercise."

"Aren't you worried something will happen to him or someone will take him?"

"An all-black German shepherd who weighs in at ninety pounds? Believe me, nobody is gonna mess with that dog."

She gazed over her shoulder again, and Kobi had laid down, taking up most of the seat, but he still had eyes on her. She had to admit, he looked as confused as her.

"All that swimming must've wore him out." Python reached into the back seat and tousled the dog's fur, then patted him on the head.

———

Amazing, this woman never stopped surprising him. She was concerned about taking Kobi's seat in the Jeep and him running around in the lot alone. He guessed that was a normal reaction, which brought more attention to the fucked-up one-sided relationships he usually had with women. He leaned into the passenger seat, cupped the back of her head, and covered his mouth with hers, pressing his tongue deep, letting her know what was to come. He smiled at the glazed look in her eyes.

They had to be the oddest couple ever. The petite, brainy news reporter and the outlaw biker, but for now ... at this moment ... he could be what she wanted even though that was the biggest lie ever. Tonight he could be anything she needed, even if it was all some kind of fucked-up fantasy, a short-term reality that could never last. Two people hurtling toward the edge of the cliff, the biggest disaster of his life and he welcomed it.

CHAPTER NINE

"Hello, Mrs. Carson." Virginia waved at her landlady peeking through the shade of her first-floor apartment. It snapped shut and Virginia laughed. "By tomorrow you'll be the talk around the pool," Virginia said over her shoulder to Python as they climbed up the outdoor staircase to her second-floor apartment.

She could only imagine the impending stories the older woman would gossip about while poolside, especially since the length of Python's leather jacket made it look like she was naked underneath, and Python looked—there were really no adjectives to describe the six-foot-five badass biker with the python tattoo winding around his neck. She'd be lucky if Mrs. Carson didn't call the SWAT team.

The modest two-story rectangular building boasted a small pool and an even smaller courtyard, typical of many of the rentals in the Paradise section of Las Vegas.

"I hated leaving Kobi, he looked sad," Virginia said as she unlocked the door.

"You're sweet."

She gazed up at him, not expecting him to say that. They

entered her small one-bedroom with a view of the pool. That bit of creative advertising originally attracted her to the space until she realized to see a view of the pool you had to crane your neck out the bathroom window. In other words, you'd have to be a contortionist.

She'd decorated the apartment in a combination of the best deals offered by Wayfair and Target with a touch of early century Amazon. The seven-hundred-square-foot space accommodated her nicely until now with Python taking up too much of her living room. He looked out of place, his broad, muscular, tattooed body too rough and raw for her delicate decor.

His eyes did a quick assessment, taking in every room except the bedroom, which was located down a short hallway. He turned back toward the door and for a second she thought he was leaving; instead, he fiddled around with the locks, mumbled something, and turned to face her.

"Your locks are shit," he said plainly. "I'll get somebody here tomorrow to install something decent."

The calculator in her brain erupted, and she waved her hand at the door. "No, really, it's fine."

He frowned. "It's not fine. A twelve-year-old could break into this place."

"Well then, I'm safe. This is an adult-only building." She smiled at her wit and was greeted with a deeper frown.

"I'm not playing, Virginia. This area can get a little sketchy at night."

"I appreciate your concern, but locksmiths aren't cheap." A fact she knew firsthand when she locked herself out three months ago. Where was that twelve-year-old then? "KLAS pays the newbies only a little more than their interns, so I think I'm going to have to put security on the back burner for now."

He ignored her protests. "I'll get somebody here tomorrow. No charge."

"I don't think it's necessary to—"

He closed the distance between them and lifted her chin with his forefinger. "How would it look for the sergeant-at-arms, the guy who's all about security having his woman living in an apartment with locks that are shit easy to bust?"

Every other word in that sentence disappeared except "his woman." Her heart kicked up and she didn't know why. She didn't even know what "his woman" meant in biker lingo. Her research told her bikers had ol' ladies, the equivalent to wives; sweet butts, the equivalent of friends with benefits; and club whores, the equivalent of—that one spoke for itself. Never once had she seen the term "his woman."

"Babe? Where did you just go?"

"Nowhere." She cleared her throat, hoping it would also clear her mind. "What were you saying."

"I said, are you hungry?"

"I am." She hadn't eaten since the cotton candy and the beer at the carnival. She'd definitely missed some food groups. He kept staring at her and she figured she might as well tell him now that cooking wasn't her forte. "I'm not much of a cook, so—"

"No, sweat. I don't expect you to cook for me. Most nights I eat in the kitchen at the club."

"So you probably would like a home-cooked meal." Now she felt bad. Cooking remained one of life's mysteries, and growing up with a full-time cook on staff didn't give her much time to practice. Her mother only stepped foot in the kitchen to complain. Main reason they blew through three cooks a year.

His brows furrowed together as he rubbed at the scruff along his jaw. "I don't think I ever had a home-cooked meal."

"That's impossible. What about when you were a child at home?"

He scrolled through his phone, ignoring her question. "How about Italian?"

"Take out?"

"Sure."

"You got to change into dry clothes at your place." She ran her hair threw her damp hair, now in clumps from Python's open-air jeep. "But I've got to take a shower and wash my hair."

"Why don't we do that shower thing, then I'll call the restaurant." He shrugged off his cut, laid it on the couch, then pulled his t-shirt over his head. "Both of us wet ... Me soaping you up, oh yeah."

She squeezed his hand and led him into her tiny bathroom. He tugged her t-shirt over her head and flung it behind them, then she leaned in and turned on the shower. He released the front closure of her bra and the garment slid down her shoulders.

Python stared at her as he ran his finger down her neck. She cocked her head slightly, expecting him to say something, but he remained silent.

Her anxious fingers popped the button of his jeans, then slid down the zipper slowly like she was uncovering some lost treasure. She had to admit to curiosity. Although she'd seen most of Python's body the first night in his apartment, the details were a blur. Now she could take her time over every intricate detail—like the way the ink on his abs accentuated his tight six-pack, and the sexy-as-hell *V* with a smattering of light hair, or how erotic she found the small rings of his nipple piercings. Plus, she'd finally know if the man lived up to his name.

She'd seen his tongue piercing and the thought of what it

could do sent a shiver to the soles of her feet. A height of ecstasy she'd never experienced.

He nudged her hand lower while his hooded eyes and parted lips egged her on, and when he licked those full lips, a molten lava replaced her blood and coursed hot through her veins.

She separated his jeans, then paused. Of course, the man went commando. He sprang to life, and yes, Python was an apt name. A clichéd adage flickered through her mind, but his feet and hands were huge too. Oh God, why wouldn't her brain take a vacation?

He stuck his hand behind the shower curtain to test the water. "It's warm. Let's get in."

The small space barely accommodated her no less this beast of a man. He shuffled under the water and wet his hair. When she bent for the shampoo, their hips bumped and he laughed. She squirted some in his hand, and he washed and rinsed his hair, then shook his head.

"You look just like Kobi when you do that."

"A wild, mangy loner and his dog."

She smiled at his joke as he jostled her sideways until she was under the water, and then squeezed some of the shampoo in his hand. "Turn around, let me wash your hair."

She savored the way his fingers massaged the soap into her long tresses, but her brain stalled when he called himself a loner. That description didn't gel with a man who belonged to a biker club or had multiple sex partners. His fingers dug deeper into her scalp and a moan escaped her lips. She never imagined he'd be so good at this.

"I love your hair."

She tilted her head into his grasp. "You're very good at this."

He rinsed out the soap, massaged in some conditioner, then rinsed that out too. Sweeping her hair aside, he sucked on the side of her neck. "So fuckin' sweet," he murmured against her wet skin, and when he nipped along her collarbone, she knew he left a mark.

Virginia turned to face him with the liquid soap in her hands. "Now it's your turn."

She could feel his gaze drilling into her, and when she peeked up at him, they held one another's stare for a few seconds. Her hands worked the soap over the colorful python etched across his chest, and when she slid them lower and made small circles around his abs, those muscles flinched, and she knew she found the perfect pace.

After reaching his hips, she paused, and then dropped to her knees. She rubbed her cheek against his thigh, then peeked up at him. Python's body shivered and vibrated against her face. Bracing her hands around his thighs, she lowered her mouth to him.

When her lips drew him in, he hissed in a breath and rocked his hips. This wasn't her first blowjob, but it was her first one in the shower with a man this size. There would be no way she could take him all, but where her mouth left off, her hand took over until she had the perfect rhythm. His fingers dug into her hair urging her on until she wanted this as much as him—maybe more.

She'd had sex partners but never one as endowed as Python. Apprehension mixed with exhilaration at the thought of him taking her, stretching her, possessing her. She'd dated men for months and never experienced this freedom. The wild abandon of his acceptance. She knew nothing about him and yet their needs were in perfect sync. She continued to pull and suck him in, quick and deep, her excitement and pleasure spurring her on. He bent from the waist slapping his hands against the wet tiles, bracing himself, with his head hanging between his arms as if she was sucking the very strength right out of him. A heady exuberance intoxicated her as she controlled this powerful man.

Python's body stiffened, and he pulled himself free of her mouth, spilling himself along the cleft of her breasts. She peered up at him, and his look of sheer satisfaction told her he found another way to mark her as his. Python hugged her to him, then reached around her and shut off the faucets.

"That was un-fuckin-believable." He pushed her wet hair away from her face and tilted her chin up to meet his lips. "Hmmm, love tasting me on your lips."

He unwound his arms and shuffled to the side just as she was about to pull back the shower curtain. Virginia's foot slid behind his, and she slapped her hand against the wet tile, but it was too late. As her other hand groped for the shower curtain, Python tried to steady her, but a second later they both crashed against the shower wall. He maneuvered her so his body broke the fall into the tub with the pole and shower curtain crashing down on top of them.

"What the fuck, babe?" His deep laugh filled the small bathroom as she wiggled against him. He spun her around, but when her knee brushed up against his dick, he quickly stilled her movement. "Geez, don't hurt the good stuff."

"Oh, my God, are you all right?" She twisted herself around, straddling his thighs.

He tried to push himself up and his hands slipped. "This tub is a deathtrap."

Uncontrollable laughter bubbled up along with an acute case of embarrassment. Python tossed the shower curtain and pole onto the floor, and after a few failed attempts, they stood. "I think you're trying to fuckin' kill me."

She pulled two clean towels out from under the vanity and handed one to him.

"You're very dangerous for a little thing." He dried his hair, then rubbed the towel over his torso, and when he wrapped it around his waist, it left most of his thigh exposed. Impressive, like some exotic Roman toga.

"I'm not usually this clumsy." A mini-movie of her slamming her head into his door jamb, as well as dragging down a hotdog cart flashed across her brain. "Well, maybe a little."

"I think it's cute how you get all flustered and jittery."

"Cute is usually not one of my favorite words, but—"

He pulled the towel out of her hands and drew her to him. "I mean it as a compliment." Then he scooped her up in his arms. "Where's the bedroom?"

————

Python loved the feel of Virginia in his arms and the way he could cuddle her little body into him, like he wanted to hold her tight and never let go. Even though he felt the need to protect her, it came from a different place than with other women. She wasn't needy and clingy, and her life wasn't screwed up like most of the women he knew. She was strong, independent, and fierce, even if she was a little klutzy, bringing the whole freakin' shower down on top of him. It was probably all of those things that made him call her his woman, but it even surprised him when it slipped out. Another first. He also hadn't missed the confused look on her face or the way she stared at him. Either way, she seemed just as puzzled as him.

He carried her into the bedroom and stopped. "That's your bed?"

"Yes, why?"

"It's so freakin' small."

"It's a full-sized bed." She laughed.

He sat on the side of the bed and she straddled his hips. "We can make it work." Then she pushed him back and crawled up his body. When she got to his nipple ring he half expected her to purr, but as her tongue played with the metal hoop, he thought he might instead.

Python lifted himself up on his elbows 'cause he didn't wanna miss one minute of this show. Virginia came off all sweet and innocent, but there was a hellcat inside her. It might've gone to sleep lately, but he'd seen it peek out at the lake. He heard her moans, and he knew she liked getting it on outside with that hint of danger.

She switched to his other nipple, and fuck if his dick didn't throb. The shower and her sucking him off was hot, but he wanted in, and he wanted in now. She squealed when he flipped her over, her eyes wide as he hovered above her.

"Gotta have you, babe."

She reached between them and stroked him, then spread her legs wider, arching her back to welcome him.

He lowered his hips and rubbed himself against her center, then sucked in a raspy breath and froze.

Her eyes flew open at the same time. "Condom."

Python rolled off her, shocked by his own actions. He never forgot to wrap up. He was the king of condoms who bought them by the carton—strips of them all over his apartment, in his pocket, in his wallet, in his bike and jeep, and even stuffed in his desk drawer at the club. What the fuck did this woman do to him?

He jackknifed off the bed. "Be right back."

He found his jeans in the bathroom, dug the condoms out of his pocket, and returned to the bedroom.

He held the strip up and smiled. "I told you I believe in being prepared."

She seemed relieved, and his mind went in all different directions. She didn't keep them in her apartment. At first, it amped him up, like she didn't do this on the regular, but then —would this be too special for her? Would she expect more than he could give her?

When she leaned up, cupped his balls and squeezed, his questions exploded like a cartoon bubble, and while her delicate fingers helped him wrap up, he couldn't even remember what they were in the first place. Fuckin' scary.

She spread herself wide, and this time he didn't hesitate, he drove into her hard. and the way she squeezed him had him clawing at the sheets. He stilled for a second to gauge her reaction. Not to brag, but he knew he was big, yet her body fit him perfectly.

"Don't stop," she gasped out.

"You all right?" He had to hear it from her, to know she was with him. All in.

"I will be once you give me what I want."

This was happening. Anticipation jacked up his heartbeat as he cupped her ass and drew her closer, angling her hips higher. She moaned out and he knew he was hitting her spot. When he gripped her hips tighter, she flexed and arched herself into him.

Python wasn't going to hold out much longer, but he wanted her with him. He wanted to jump off that cliff with her right beside him ... or under him. He leaned forward and braced himself on the mattress, then lowered his lips to her nipples, sucking one deep and then the other until she was writhing beneath him. Reaching between their bodies, he found her clit. The sounds she made when he rubbed over the sensitive flesh made him catch his breath. Keeping pace with their thrusts, her whimpers increased until they were full out moans.

"Ahh, Virginia. Your body was made for me."

How her tiny figure took him all in set off a flame burning hot through his veins.

Suddenly, her tongue licked her parted lips, and he knew she was close. He leaned in on shaky biceps and caught the tip between his teeth and nipped at it. Her gasps and pants vibrated through him, and he hoped he could hold out because this woman had him wired to blow.

Pain jolted through him as her nails dug into his back, leaving their mark, then her fingers threaded through his hair and tugged—hard. When she bucked beneath him, he was a goner. She met him, and moved with him, both of them searching, punishing each other.

When he circled her clit with his thumb, she made the sexiest fuckin' sound ever. Their bodies moved together in a desperate push and pull. He kept the pressure going until her body went slack, then he slowly drew himself out and slammed in one last time.

"Fuck, me," he growled two seconds before he blew. His choppy breaths filled the room as he collapsed over Virginia, her uneven gasps warm against his neck. He tried to roll his weight off her, but she held him to her.

"Don't move," she whispered, then hugged him tight. Such a simple, pure act.

Her honesty and sincerity blew him away, and at the same time scared him. She had no ulterior motive, no agenda. Usually after sex the women in his life were asking him for a favor, like sex was some kind of fucked up bargaining chip. He'd gotten so used to it that Virginia's honest emotions confused him. Not too screwed up.

At first he'd worried about this being too special for her, reading more into it, and wanting more than he could give, but now he worried it was too much for him. The crazy thoughts floating through his mind had no right being there. A head-breaking, outlaw biker had no right to think about the future, had no right to want a future, and sure as fuck not with a woman like Virginia.

CHAPTER TEN

Virginia gazed up at him, her eyes all soft. "You are a beautiful man."

She was fucked-dumb for sure if she thought he was beautiful.

Python furrowed his brow. "That's a first. I've been called a lot of things, but never beautiful. Should I be insulted?"

"Absolutely not." She paused with a faraway look in her eyes. In the short time they'd been together, he recognized that look. Her mind had taken over and who knew what she'd say next.

"You are the perfect mix of hot and sweet—like the way you take care of Kobi, and gave me your jacket so I wouldn't be cold in my wet clothes. Sweet. Then there's the tough guy edge to your face, your swagger, and the two orgasms you just gave me right here, plus the one at the lake makes three. Hot."

"Two, huh?" Yeah, he was a prideful bastard, and he loved to hear how he got her off.

"That's right." He slid to her side and she flicked his nipple piercing, and goddamn if his dick didn't twitch.

Getting sucked off in the shower, mind-blowing orgasms, shooting his load hard, and the damn thing wanted more of her.

"Let's see if we can improve on that number." He waggled his tongue. "I saw you eyeing my piercing before."

———

Virginia bit her lower lip as her heart hammered with anticipation.

He slid himself down her body, a sly grin firmly in place. When he lowered his lips to her sensitive flesh, a sound bubbled up in her throat and her legs spread wider. He took her invitation and hooked his hands under her knees and dove in. Python's strokes were unrelenting, and what he did with his tongue piecing was sinful, but oh-so good. He brought her up, then eased off, pacing himself, keeping track of her, and knowing exactly what he was doing. Stroking her thighs and drawing her closer, she was a gourmet meal set out just for him.

He nipped at the flesh of her inner thigh and she moaned. She squirmed and wiggled and he caught on to her game.

"You tryin' tell me something, sweet thing?"

"Don't tease me," she gasped out. She ground and flexed her hips as he commanded her body.

"Ahh ... teasing is the best part." He went back to her inner thighs and when he sucked deep she knew she'd wind up with another mark and she didn't care. Right now, she didn't care about anything but this magnificent man bringing her to another time zone.

He finally licked his way back to her core, his magic tongue dancing over her clit right before he nipped and then sucked on it—hard. Pain and pleasure at its purist.

When he added his thumb and pressed against her, she

bucked violently, teetering on the edge of ecstasy, but still not quite there. His thumb moved in small circles as his tongue lapped at her, and when his teeth nipped her this time, she broke apart and shattered into pieces of someone whom she didn't know, someone who'd let her anxiety and inhibitions fly free. Virginia jerked her hips again and again and vaguely wondered if she was hurting Python, but her body had taken over and all sense and reason disappeared.

Her eyes slid shut as she floated on this delicious cloud. He shifted, and a second later his lips tugged at hers. She tasted herself on his tongue and the erotic sensations fired her up all over again as she dug her fingers into his hair and pulled until he broke away and looked at her.

"That was ... amazing."

"My pleasure."

"Oh no, the pleasure was all mine. Literally." She smiled at her little joke and wrapped her arms around his neck. "You are extremely talented."

"Pays to have piercings in all the right places." He nuzzled her neck.

"I don't think you understand. That's the first time—" When he furrowed his eyebrows she regretted her moment of honesty.

"First time ... what?"

"The first time a guy has ever done or gone down ... there."

"You're shittin' me."

She chuckled at his words and his shocked expression, then bit her lower lip and shook her head. "First time."

"Wow." Then he scratched his head like he was trying to figure out time travel. "So all the other guys you've been with never ..."

"To be fair, there haven't been that many."

"I didn't mean you had a lot of guys, I just meant—wow."

"Anyway, I just wanted you to know how great it was and how much I ... well, what can I say, another outstanding orgasm with a very hot guy all works for me."

"I knew the first time I saw you in my apartment that you'd be hot."

"You mean when I walked in on your ménage à trois? That first time?"

"You make it sound almost exotic."

"You had enough to occupy you, so I doubt you noticed me."

"Nah, not true. You had that whole naughty librarian thing goin' on. Innocent, a little scared, a lot turned on, and sexy as fuck."

Amazing, he'd just capsulized her exact feelings.

"I was a little turned on by what I saw."

"I know. Reading people is my business, babe. I gotta know what the other guy is gonna do way before he does it."

"So, you knew this"—she motioned between them—"was going to happen?"

"Not gonna lie. I was surprised when you left and then I was surprised when you didn't come back."

"Geez, what an ego on you."

"I didn't plan on it going this way, but I hoped. You're different—independent and smart. There's no challenge in a woman who's willing to spread her legs without putting in some work." His blue eyes examined her for a few seconds, then he ran his hand over her thighs. "But you deserve a lot more."

They lay quiet listening to each other's breathing. It was a comfortable silence, peaceful, no pressure. She leaned up on her elbow and ran her fingers through the close-cropped, soft curls falling over his forehead.

He covered her hand in his. "Would make my life much easier if all I wanted to do was fuck you."

Virginia stared at him, stunned by his words. The bluntness she admired about him now confused her. She knew guys thought like that, but somehow hearing it out of his mouth while they were still in bed after multiple orgasms was just weird—*and wrong?*

"You know you just said that out loud, right?"

He sighed deep, then he rubbed at the stubble on his jaw. "I don't even really know you, and you sure as hell don't know what I'm about. We're as different as two people can be."

"If this is the positive part, you're going to have to work a little harder."

"I'm just sayin'—"

"I don't know where this is going either, but I'd certainly like to get to know you better. It just seems that whenever I ask you about yourself, you shut down, so I stopped asking."

"Some things are hard to answer."

"Let's begin with something easy. The first night we met —yes, that night. You said it was your birthday. So, how old are you?"

"See, even that's hard."

She frowned. "You don't know how old you are?"

"No, smartass. I'm afraid if I tell you, you'll freak out 'cause I'm much older than you."

"Okay, I'll go first. I'm twenty-six."

"That's what I thought." He rubbed at the stubble on his chin. Seemed to be a thing he did when he was uncomfortable. "I'm nine years older than you."

"You're thirty-five?"

"Your math skills are astounding," he deadpanned.

She thumped him on his bicep. "Now who's being a smartass?"

"I'm being a wiseass to deflect you from my age in case you might be thinking I'm too old."

She cocked her head, then waved her hand over his body. "If this, and what you just did for me in bed is old, then sign me up for social security."

He barked out a laugh and pulled her to him.

"And those two girls I saw you with the other night looked even younger than me, so I don't know what you're worried about."

"That was different. They were just entertainment, a quick fuck and—" His lips twisted. "Too honest again?"

"I never thought I'd find honesty a negative in a man, but you've brought a whole new meaning to telling the truth."

"Okay, so we got the age thing out of the way. Now it's your turn to tell me something because you haven't been exactly laying it out there for me, either."

He had her there. Maybe this game of truth or dare she started would backfire on her.

"I graduated from USC, I'm an only child, and I'm originally from California." It was a safe and honest answer, cleverly leaving out her media mogul father, the founder of Century Communications, her spoiled, indulgent mother, and growing up in a house most would consider a mansion. "And I came to Las Vegas for the job at KLAS." After she turned down an executive position at Century and an office space bigger than her apartment.

"That's cool. We do runs into Cali sometimes."

Virginia didn't know what he meant, but since she assumed it concerned the club, she wasn't going to waste her question.

"How long have you had Kobi?"

"I found him five years ago roaming around down by the tunnels behind Ecstasy."

"The tunnels?"

"The storm drains running under the city."

"Right, I've read some very interesting articles on the people living in them."

"It's a whole underground world." Python tugged at the sheet. "They call themselves Mole People. Shitty how some people have to live."

"And that's where you found Kobi?"

"Somebody must've abandoned him, probably 'cause they couldn't afford to feed him anymore." Python smiled. "And the way he eats, I'd believe it. He was all skinny and mean, full of fleas, baring his teeth. First time I went near him, he took a bite outta me." Python twisted his forearm to show her a jagged scar on the inside of his arm. "I knew right then he was for me."

"Because he bit you? I would think that would be a definite deterrent."

"I knew he was a fighter. Probably only bit me cause he was scared."

She admired his compassion and foresight.

"It wasn't until I took him to the vet I found out black German shepherds are pretty rare."

"How did you get from him biting you to taking him to the vet?"

"Easy. We make a mean Kobi slider at the club, so every day I'd put a few out for him. Before long, he was hanging around the back door of the club." Python laughed. "Cobra told me to either stop feeding him or take him in 'cause he was scaring the shit outta the customers."

"That's a nice thing you did, especially since your relationship started out a little rocky."

"He was just fighting back the best way he knew how. Like I said before, him and me are a lot alike."

His honest admission tugged at Virginia, making her throat tighten. Something about this huge bear of a man telling a heartfelt story about a stray dog. Almost a cliché, but somehow, coming from a tatted biker whose job description included bodily harm, it made it genuine.

A part of her guessed he was talking about his own life as much as Kobi's. This was the story she wanted to tell. Pull back the layers and show the real people behind the Serpents. Show their human side.

"Once he ate regular and had a warm place to live, he calmed down." He scrubbed his hand over his jaw. "I guess I got a thing for strays. Lost causes."

"He certainly seems happy now."

"Now, it's my turn." He paused. "Did you always wanna be a reporter? Is that what you studied in college?"

"Since I was little. Actually I envisioned myself as the next best-selling author, and although I still fantasize about that, I love digging in and getting a story. Doing the research and finding out about what makes people tick, why and how they do the things they do. It's fascinating. So when this opportunity at KLAS came up, I jumped at it."

"That's cool. You knew what you wanted and went after it." His finger idly traced over her stomach. "You said you were an only child, so how did your parents feel when you moved away and came here?"

Interesting, she wouldn't have expected such an introspective question from him, but once again, her biker kept her off balance. *Her* biker?

"They were okay with it." She shifted away from him slightly, as if afraid he'd sense such an outrageous lie. After keeping her job offer a secret for weeks, she finally had to come clean and tell her father that, no, she wouldn't take the position at Century Media and, yes, she was moving four hours away to Las Vegas.

"Nah, I don't buy it. Your face says they were pissed, and

the way you got that sheet balled up in your fist says you had some issues too."

"Wow, that's very good."

Her father made his disappointment known, then ignored her like she didn't exist, while her mother yelled and screamed up until the day Virginia drove away in her rented Toyota. Her father's last resort of forbidding her to take her BMW convertible as leverage had failed miserably.

Python ran his finger along her jaw. "They were probably pissed 'cause they were gonna miss you."

If only that were true. Their anger was fueled by how the repercussions of her declining such a prestigious job would look to her father's fellow board members, and her mother's tennis partners. After all, who would give up such an opportunity? Who would be so stupid and naïve? Easy answer. Someone who wanted to live their own life and escape the stifling existence and the narrow minds of those who lived on Stone Canyon Road.

Virginia rubbed her hands against the sheets to eliminate the sweat that thinking about her father produced. "Enough about me. How long have you been in Vegas?"

———

He sucked in a deep breath. "I came up from Arizona in my early twenties. I'd been in and out of trouble since my teens, and I thought Vegas would be a good change. One problem, unless *you* change, it don't matter where you go. Bad shit just keeps following you."

"Is that when you met Cobra and formed the Serpents?"

"Not right away. When I first hit Vegas, I hooked up with the Desert Devils MC. Real bad group of dudes." Those guys made him look like a boy scout. "It wasn't long before the DEA hauled most of them away in a raid."

"But not you?"

"I wasn't around that night." It was a night that still haunted his dreams—*Zelda*—sitting by her hospital bed, hoping for the best but expecting the worst. He'd tried to help her, tried to get her away from Grinder, but they both knew it was futile. In the end, she paid with her life and the life of her baby.

Virginia waggled her eyebrows at him. "Don't tell me, you were with a woman, right?"

He plastered a smirky grin across his face because that's what she expected, and it was way easier than wading into the crazy emotions swirling around from his past.

"Women really are your kryptonite."

"Gotta admit, they are my weakness." The only way to explain the debilitating guilt that still slithered through his gut.

"That's the gentle side of you coming out."

"Gentle? I'm thinking you are either seeing something in me that isn't there, or you're seeing something no one else sees, 'cause another word never associated with me is *gentle*."

"That's you on the outside, but inside—"

"I'm just an old softy." A trait that had almost gotten him killed.

"The way you were with those children at the carnival this afternoon, you can't fake that. You genuinely enjoyed being with them and they liked being with you."

"I like kids ... all ages. They're honest. They either like you or they don't, and there's no bullshit about them."

"They also sense when someone is fake," Virginia added. "And they knew you were the real thing."

This time his smile was genuine, telling her he agreed.

"Okay, my turn." She leaned up in the bed. "Do you have any brothers or sisters?"

"Ahh, no."

"See? We have something in common. We're both only children."

"I actually don't know if I do or I don't." He paused and mashed his lips together. "I grew up in the system, like from when I was a baby."

"Oh." She stared at him willing him to continue.

"I don't have any family history."

A sadness crept over her face, but the last thing he wanted was her pity.

"I see why the Forgotten Kids carnival is so special for you."

"You know we never did eat." He rolled away from her and threw his legs over the bed.

Enough with this memory lane bullshit. He'd already revealed more about himself than he wanted.

———

An hour later they sat on her bed with discarded takeout containers littering the floor. Not being able to decide and compromise on food choices, they ended up ordering mussels, stuffed eggplant, clams casino, garlic bread, a cheese calzone, and a pepperoni pizza.

He laid an empty plate on her bedside table, and a notepad fell to the floor, scattering little pieces of paper all over the carpet.

He bent over to retrieve them, then studied them. One was a list of names, another of places around Vegas, and the last few were lists of crimes—one of them murder.

"What is all this?" he asked, as she grabbled them away from him.

"Nothing." Then she sighed deep and leafed through them. "Some notes for a book."

"A book?"

"You know, words on a page all bound together." She stuffed the papers back in the notepad. "Or words on a page backlit on a tablet."

"Yeah, smartass, I get it." He laughed. "I thought for a minute, you were some psycho planning out my death."

She leaned over him and shoved the pad into the nightstand drawer.

"Writing a whole book, that's huge."

"It would be even better if I could get past the first chapter." She groaned. "I've been staring at the same twenty-five hundred words for months."

"You probably just need some time to get it done. It can't be easy putting down all those words after working all day."

She squeezed his forearm. "You're sweet."

"Sweet, gentle, and beautiful all in one night." He shook his head. "Yup. Fucked-dumb." Her eyes were glued to him as he popped the last piece of garlic bread in his mouth. "What?"

"I don't believe I've ever seen anyone eat as much as you." She waved her hand over the mostly empty takeout containers. "It's amazing because it certainly doesn't show on your body."

"You're helping me work it off, like before when you were bent over the kitchen cabinet taking out the plates."

Her all bare-assed and bending over was too good to be true. So, he spun her around, propped her up on the counter, which happened to be the perfect height, and got balls deep right there between the toaster oven and the electric can opener. She shook and shivered and squeezed his dick till his eyes crossed.

She snuggled into Python, and he sensed she wanted to ask more about him, but as great as this was, he wasn't ready to give up anything further regarding his fucked-up history. He didn't know where this was going, but for right now, he had two truths. He wanted to spend more time with Virginia, and wanting to spend more time with her shocked the shit out of him.

————

The next day Virginia was awoken by a shrill buzzing. It took her a few minutes to identify the sound—a weed-whacker attacking the overgrown flower beds below her bedroom window. They had to be the only complex that employed gardeners on a Sunday. Knowing Mrs. Carson, it was probably cheaper.

She stretched, then rolled over and opened her eyes to an empty bed, listening to the silence in her apartment. If Python was still there, she would've heard him. Nope, he was gone. She'd been in such a sound sleep, she had no idea when he left.

He probably fled before she could ask him any more questions. She'd had other guys accuse her of asking too many questions, so why should he be different. Maybe she could blame it on being a writer, but she'd always had a natural curiosity about people. It was what drove her to be a reporter.

Virginia ran her hand over the sheets, then mushed her face into her pillow and inhaled. Python had the most intoxicating scent—woodsy, musky, smoky. She couldn't put her finger on it, but it was definitely Python.

She scanned the room and the floor and all traces of him were gone. Maybe it was all a sex dream: the cool water of Lake Mead; the heat of Python's skin against hers; hot shower sex; and his magnificent tongue making her lose all control. No, the images were too clear. It really happened. It just wouldn't be happening again.

What did she expect? He hadn't promised her anything or

told her any lies. By his own admission he was a man who lived outside the rules, and even though he alluded to her being different and maybe special, he could never be tied down to one woman. He was wild and free and that was the way he liked it.

How did she think this would've played out? She'd take him to the annual holiday party at the station? Or he'd take her to some wild biker party where the women paraded around naked and having group sex was encouraged. His leaving was for the best. They'd had fun. A fling, and now she could concentrate on writing her breakout piece for her editor without any guilt or second thoughts because of Python.

She'd fondly think of this weekend in the future as her wild weekend with a badass outlaw biker.

Her confusing thoughts were interrupted by the buzzing of her doorbell. She flipped a look at her phone for the time. Who would be at her door at nine thirty in the morning? She rolled out of bed and ran her hand through her hair. Probably Mrs. Carson wanting to know if she'd joined a biker gang. Crazy lady needed to get a life.

She yanked on a pair of sweats she'd thrown over her chair and a baggy t-shirt. Whoever it was would have to take her as she was this morning. Who knew great sex could give you a hangover? What had Python said, "fucked-dumb"? Yup, exactly.

Virginia looked through the peephole and a man's face peered back at her.

"Can I help you?" she asked through the door.

"I'm here to fix your door," a gruff voice said through the door.

"I think you have the wrong apartment."

The body stepped back and looked over her door, apparently at her apartment number. "Nah, right apartment."

"But there's nothing wrong with my door."

"Python sent me. Said I gotta fix the locks."

"Are you kidding me?"

"No, darlin'. Now let me get this done so I don't have to listen to him ragging on my ass."

Virginia released the lock and was greeted with a man as wide as the door. "I don't think this is—"

The large stranger wedged between her and the door, then examined the two locks. "Python was right, these are shit."

"You don't have to do this, I mean—"

He ignored her, rummaged through his toolbox and began to take apart her lock.

"Did you hear me?"

He turned to her and she took a half step back. He was shorter than Python, but his massive chest and gut made him impossible to ignore.

"I heard you, but I do stuff for the Serpents all the time, and Python wants this done, so I'm doin' it."

Certainly sounded logical, except when you factored in that she told him it wasn't necessary and yet he sent someone anyway.

"When did he call you?"

"I don't know, around four this morning. Gave me your address and said he wanted the locks fixed on his woman's apartment." He threw his meaty palms up. "So here I am."

There were so many parts to be dissected in that one sentence, but she was still too groggy. Fucked-dumb, right.

"I was about to make some coffee. Would you like a cup?"

"That would be great. Been up all night doin' shit for Cobra."

And there were a million more questions. She headed into the kitchen and busied herself with the coffeemaker as the questions kept coming. Had Python left her apartment at four and called this man? And what was a locksmith doing all night for Cobra? But most intriguing was this man using the phrase "his woman." Python obviously referred to her this way.

She flipped the lid closed on the coffeemaker and listened to the water sizzle through the machine, then pulled two mugs out of the cabinet and stuck her head into the living room.

"Do you take anything in your coffee?"

"Just black."

She could've guessed he wasn't the type for fancy creamers, but as Virginia had found out, people were full of surprises, especially bikers whom she'd only just met sending service people to her apartment for minor repairs. Yikes!

She poured the coffee into the mugs, went into the living room, and held out the steaming mug. "I'm Virginia."

He took a large gulp, immune to scalding temperature. "Lenny."

She settled on the couch, and Lenny took another big gulp, then placed the empty cup on her end table.

"Are you a member of the Serpents too?" He didn't wear the leather cut and "Lenny" wasn't a snake name, but things weren't always as they seemed, especially in the world of bikers.

"Nah, I'm just on call for them. Do jobs for them when they need it."

She doubted those jobs were as innocuous as repairing some locks on a twenty-year-old door.

"Would you like some more coffee?" she asked.

"I'm good." He nodded to the shiny new lock. "Almost done."

She took his cup into the kitchen and refilled hers, then unloaded her dishwasher and straightened up the kitchen. A few minutes later, Lenny filled the doorway of her galley kitchen.

"All done," he announced.

"Great. Thank you." She reached for her purse on the kitchen chair and pulled out her wallet.

He waved her away. "No money."

"Let me give you something for coming over here on a Sunday."

"If Python ever found out I took money from his woman he'd kick my ass."

"Well, we surely wouldn't want that."

He handed her the new keys, then collected all his tools. "Thanks for the coffee." He jerked his chin at her and was out the door.

She examined the new lock and had to admit it was much sturdier then the old one. She swiped her phone to Python's number when there was another knock on her door.

Lenny must've forgotten one of his tools. She opened the door and was faced with two men in gray delivery uniforms.

"Can I help you?"

"Are you Virginia Swanson?"

She nodded as she read the shorter man's name tag. Sleepy-Time Bedding.

"Yes."

"We have a delivery for you, if you'll just sign here." He shoved a clipboard at her and a pen.

"A delivery of what?"

He narrowed his eyes and pointed to his name tag. "A mattress."

"I didn't order a mattress."

He stepped back, looked at the number over her door, and pointed to the clipboard. "Order came in last night online for a Virginia Swanson at this address."

"And you're here the next morning?"

"That's our motto. 'Sleepy-Time mattresses delivered within twelve hours,'" he said proudly.

"That is impressive, but—"

Her phone buzzed in her hand and she swiped at it.

"Hello."

"Hey, babe, was Lenny there yet?" Python asked.

"Yes, and now there's someone here with a mattress and—"

"No shit, they really do deliver within twelve hours," Python yelled over the roar of a motorcycle.

"Yes, but I didn't—"

"No way I can sleep on that small mattress you had," he huffed out.

"You sound like you're out of breath."

"I gotta go. Just wanted to make sure it all came." She heard the revving of a motorcycle, more like many motorcycles. "Oh, and I'll come by and pick you up at seven. There's a party at the Gold Mine later."

"But I—"

"Babe, really gotta go. See you later."

The phone disconnected and she stared at it, then looked up to see the two delivery men staring at her.

"Look lady, we've got a lot of other deliveries, and we like to keep on schedule, so if you'll just sign, it's all been paid for." He pointed to the clipboard again, and she scribbled her name at the bottom.

She watched, mesmerized, as they trooped into her bedroom, dismantled her old bed and then returned with a new king-size mattress, box spring, and frame. In less than a half hour, the transfer was done.

She eased herself onto the couch and flipped through the brochure announcing her as the owner of a Sleepy-Time, Dream-Cloud comfort mattress with multiple levels of firmness and a gel-infused memory that contoured perfectly to every body. Apparently, this mattress was rated in the top five for spine-friendly support.

Her gaze wandered to her newly installed lock and then her mind wandered to tonight's entertainment. A biker party, at a biker bar with a biker whom she had crazy, hot sex and who just spent hundreds of dollars on improving her apartment.

Nothing strange about that, except they'd only known each other for a little over a week and ... she had no idea what to wear to a biker party.

———

Python made the call short and sweet. He went with what always worked, telling instead of asking. Successful tactic when he was trying to get something done for the club, although it might not be the best way to handle a woman.

Of course, he wouldn't know about that since he'd never had to work at getting a woman before, they were just always available. And whatever this was with Virginia confused him and set him on edge. Not a pleasant sensation.

"Do you think you could join in the conversation?" Cobra glared at him, his cobalt-blue eyes snapping him out of his daydream. "Especially since it looks like the Rats fucked with us again."

Python stuffed the phone into his jeans pocket and stifled a yawn.

"What's the matter?" Rattler taunted. "We get you up too early this morning?"

"Took him five rings to pick up his damn phone," Cobra scoffed. "Now what could make a man that tired?"

Python flipped them both off. "Maybe because it was four in the fuckin' morning when you called."

"As my sergeant-at-arms, you're on call twenty-four seven. Or did one of your harem women fuck you into a coma last night?"

Python tired to keep Virginia a secret, but inviting her to the party tonight left him wide open. He'd have to prepare himself for Cobra and his other brothers giving him shit about how seeing Virginia was a bad idea, especially since he already knew it.

Cobra leaned against his bike and the others formed a tight circle around their president. Python pulled a cigarette out of the inside pocket of his cut. "We had to ride to the Cali border in the middle of the night to find one of our weed houses burned to the ground." Python flicked his lighter and lit up. "The Rats gotta be stopped. Like now."

That sobered their razzing. The Desert Rats torched it in retaliation for what Python and Rattler did in Searchlight. Then in true Rat fashion, they beat it back over the border to California where they couldn't be touched unless the Serpents wanted an all-out war on their hands with the other California clubs.

No one got hurt and it was one of their smaller places. They were able to pay off the local fire department of the small town to keep it quiet, but Python, Cobra, and the rest of the Serpents weren't fooled. This was Demon sending a message of what was to come.

"One of our lookouts on the border says the Rats got plenty more underage girls doing much more than running their weed farms. They got them working in their meth labs, and selling pussy and drugs. They give them *Little Mermaid* fanny packs filled with all kinds of goodies and have them make deliveries. Two advantages: nobody suspects kids with a Disney fanny pack, and if the cops get suspicious, they can't search minors, and on the off chance they do get busted, there's plenty more to take their place." Cobra scrubbed his hand over his jaw.

"Bad all around, but thinkin' they can get away with this in Nevada is fucked up," Rattler added.

"Demon is an efficient bastard." Cobra added. "He's got them fucking, sucking and selling, all-in-one. Multitasking at its lowest."

Nobody was happy, least of all Python. Demon called him last night with another threat: allow the Rats into Nevada or they'd be sorry. Python told Demon to go fuck himself, and twenty minutes later, Cobra called him with news about the fire at the distribution house.

"The time for talking is over," Cobra said. "No more negotiating. We set up a plan of action, now."

"And when you say action?" Rattler asked.

"I mean smoke their asses. Ride out to that shithole they call a clubhouse and blow the thing to hell."

That sure would eliminate Demon and his threats and phone calls.

"But before we do that, I say we pull the Rats apart first." Python's suggestion had their full attention. "His prospects hate him, shit, his patched brothers ain't thrilled with him." The others nodded their agreement. "I'll contact that prospect from Searchlight and see just how eager they'd be to patch over to a real club. A club that has their back."

Cobra's face stilled and Python knew the man's wheels were turning. Cobra thought first, then acted, an attribute that made him the perfect president.

"Undermine them from within first. Less blowback when we attack."

"Exactly," Python added. "And having the pleasure of sticking it to Demon with his own people. How fuckin' sweet would that be?"

The others agreed with nods and grunts.

"All right," Cobra said. "Make your contacts and then we'll move forward."

"I'm also gonna hit up Joker again," Python added. "He came through for us with Vinnie and the East Coast mob, and we could use his cool head." Python twisted his lips. "I don't believe his bullshit reasons for wanting to stay outta the MC world."

Cobra shrugged. "We could use him, no doubt, but seeing his son shot up back in New York rattled him."

"Can't hurt to ask again."

The brothers all agreed, and Cobra zeroed in on Python. "You get it all together, and then we move. No more bullshit from these assholes."

"Absolutely." They tapped fists, but Python couldn't shake the guilt. Fucked up all around since he felt responsible. Cobra wouldn't say it in front of the other brothers, but they both knew Python's gambling debts gave Demon the leverage to think he could strike on them and push back. Pulling this together for the Serpents would ease some of the guilt even if it didn't settle his debt. Another fuckin' problem he had to sort out.

Cobra straddled his bike and throttled his engine. "Let's get back to Vegas."

Python pitched his cigarette into a muddy puddle of water from the fire hoses, and the butt sizzled out. He fell into formation, and as their bikes tore up the asphalt, Python's mind spun with ideas of how to get the money he owed Harry. Sure, there were a few ways to do it, but all of them could put the club in jeopardy.

CHAPTER ELEVEN

An hour after the delivery guys left, Virginia was still in her sweats and t-shirt discussing her unusual morning with Nicole on the phone.

"So you don't think the guy who installed your locks was a real locksmith," Nicole said.

"He said he does work for the Serpents."

"Right, he's probably a safecracker." Nicole joked.

Virginia laughed at her friend's vivid imagination, but the thought had crossed her mind too. She just didn't want to say it out loud.

"The crazy thing is, he arranged all this at four in the morning when he apparently left my apartment. I was in such a sound sleep, I didn't even hear him leave.

"Fucked-dumb, huh?" Nicole teased.

Virginia regretted sharing that phrase with Nicole, especially since now she taunted her with it.

"The time isn't that unusual," Nicole said logically. "He probably contacted 'Thugs-R-Us: open twenty-four hours.'" Nicole giggled at her little joke.

"I fail to see the humor in that." Virginia used her chastising mother voice.

"Fine, but you have to see the humor in you going to a biker party later at a biker bar. Now that's hilarious."

"No, that's scary. I have no idea what to wear or what to—"

"I'll come over later and we'll figure it all out. I'm assuming he's picking you up on his motorcycle?"

"*Yes* to the motorcycle and *no* to me needing help with an outfit." The last thing she needed was Nicole picking out some outrageous combination of clothes.

"I'll bring over a few of my things that might work. Oh, I can't wait to see him up close and personal."

"Did you hear the part where I said I don't need any help?"

"I heard you. I'm just choosing not to listen. Anyway, without my help you'll go out wearing your usual black pants and white top. They'll think you're part of the waitstaff."

"That's completely inaccurate, sometimes I wear a beige top."

Nicole blew a frustrated breath through the phone. "Like I said, half the time you look like you're going to wait tables."

Virginia's mind flashed to Rattler's comment about her wearing a server's costume the first night she went to Ecstasy.

"All right, you can come over, but I'm not wearing anything outrageous, and you will be long gone before he gets here."

"You are no fun at all," Nicole grumbled.

An hour later, she'd showered and blown out her hair, and conceded to keep an open mind at whatever outfit Nicole had in mind.

Her phone buzzed and she groaned. Why did her father have the absolute worst timing?

"Hello." She gripped the phone tighter than necessary.

"Virginia?"

"Yes." The question in his voice confused her. Who was he expecting?

"I think it's time you come to your senses."

"Dad, please let's not do this again. I told you the last time I'm staying in Vegas at KLAS and you can do your worst —cut me off, never talk to me again—you can't scare me into coming home."

"It's you who's scaring me, Virginia."

Great, now he was going to talk in riddles.

"Do you have any idea who you've been consorting with?" The indignation in his voice always amazed her.

"I don't know what you're talking about."

"I'm talking about your choice of friends."

Yes, Nicole could be a little offbeat sometimes but—

"A biker gang, really?"

Oh, my God, how did he know about the Serpents?

"I'm doing a story on them, so it's part of my job. Wasn't it you who always said that the job came first?" She'd listened to that litany all her life: How her father couldn't take a vacation, couldn't go to school functions. It was a great alibi until her mother caught him at the Beverly Hills Hotel with his secretary in a push-up bra and fishnet stockings.

"Is it part of your job to be on the back of some thug's motorcycle and then to let this criminal into your apartment?"

"Are you having me followed?"

"Of course I am," he arrogantly admitted. Only her father could make outrageous, intrusive behavior sound normal.

"Your mother's worried sick."

"She is?" Wow. The only thing her mother ever worried about while Virginia was growing up was the measurement of her waist and thighs, and if her new tennis instructor would bring her to the next level. Virginia had always hoped her mother was talking about the game.

"What if something like that got back to the members of the country club. It's bad enough you've moved to an uncivilized city, but then being seen with someone from a gang."

"It's a club, not a gang." Virginia rolled her eyes into the phone. Leave it to her father to pigeon-hole a group of people he knew nothing about.

"What?"

"It's a motorcycle club, not a gang. They find it offensive when you—"

"I don't care what these thugs find offensive, I want you to stop affiliating with them."

Virginia would've loved to tell herself her father's recriminations surfaced because her parents were worried about her welfare, but that wasn't the case. They were more concerned with gossip or the horror of not being able to get a golf game or a good table at an exclusive restaurant as a result of their daughter's nefarious connections.

"As I said, I'm doing a story, and I'm not about to alter it to please you and Mother."

"I've done some digging, Virginia, and these men are criminals in every sense."

She'd done the same research and, yes, he was right, but there was more to Python than met the eye. Plus, her attraction for the overbearing, over-the-top, sometimes sensitive man couldn't be denied. She thought about him when she wasn't with him and dreamed about him long after he was gone.

"Virginia, did you hear me?" Her father's tone was laced with impatience.

"Yes, Dad. Fine." She had no idea what her father had said, but agreeing always worked in the past.

"Good, I'm glad we understand each other."

The phone disconnected. Her father ended conversations as abruptly as he began them. It creeped her out how he was having her followed and his knowing about Python and her connection to him. Although she wasn't sure what their connection was, so how could her father? Much too confusing.

A knock on the door jarred her from her thoughts. She checked her phone. Nicole was early and probably loaded down with outrageous outfits that Virginia wouldn't be caught dead in.

"Okay, this was all I could carry, but I have more out in the car." Nicole burst into Virginia's apartment with her natural exuberance and single-mindedness. She made a beeline for Virginia's room, dumping all the clothes on her new Sleepy-Time mattress.

"Is this new?" Nicole motioned to the mattress as she picked through the jumble of material.

"From Python." Virginia said

"Is that considered a first gift in the biker world?" Nicole grinned, then moved on to putting together four outfits. One more outrageous than the other.

"Very funny."

"Pick one." Nicole waved her hand over a denim skirt small enough for a child, a sheer white tank top, jeans with so many rips and holes they hardly qualified as clothing, halters tops, and extremely short shorts.

"I'm not wearing any of those."

"I know this isn't your usual, but you have to break out a bit," Nicole coaxed. "After all, you're going to a biker party with a badass outlaw and—"

"Please don't remind me." Virginia was way past having second thoughts; she was already on to her fourth about this bad decision.

"You'll be fine, but there's no way you can wear your usual

boring black pants and white or beige shirt. I got some great ideas from *Biker Babes*, it's a website for hot biker chick clothes."

Virginia groaned and Nicole shot her a death glare, then dug into the duffel she'd flung on the floor and laid out another outfit. "How about this?"

When Nicole stepped aside, Virginia moved closer to the bed. "At least this doesn't make me look like a—"

"Don't be judgy." Nicole cut her off. "Put it on. You'll rock it with your tight little figure."

Five minutes later, Virginia stood in front of the full-length mirror attached to back of her closet door and had to admit that she didn't look bad. Actually, she looked pretty good—sexy even.

"So?" Nicole prodded.

"I like it." Virginia did a half turn and checked out the rear view. "Not bad."

"Not bad? You look hot. I don't know why you don't show off your figure more often. Your legs are long and slim, your stomach is flat, and your boobs are just the right size. Not too big, not too small."

"Thank you, I think." Most of Virginia's twenty-six years were spent dressing to please her parents, their friends at the country club, or the small circle of acquaintances she's acquired through tennis. Because of their wealth, her parents always cautioned her on getting too close to people for fear of them using her or worse. One of her main reasons for leaving California centered on breaking away and breaking out, and what better way than with clothing.

"He is going to freakin' come in his pants when he sees you." Nicole swatted her on the ass.

Virginia laughed at Nicole's graphic description, but she had to admit the white, frayed shorts, red tank top and calf-high motorcycle boots definitely made her feel liberated.

"Now, that we've settled on an outfit, let's do something with your hair and makeup."

"What's the matter with my hair and makeup?"

"Absolutely nothing if you're going to church, but you're not. You're going to a *biker party!*"

Nicole rolled her eyes, then whipped out a makeup case worthy of a Hollywood studio and wouldn't let Virginia look in the mirror until she was finished. When Nicole used words like *edgy, breaking out* and *seductive*, her heart-rate amped up, so as soon as Nicole plugged in her curling iron, Virginia sucked in a deep breath.

The flurry of activity diverted Virginia from the anxiety of going to the party until Nicole finally let her see herself in the mirror. Virginia leaned into her reflection to get a better look. She stared, mesmerized, at the smoky shadow Nicole artfully applied, making her brown eyes smolder along with the bronzer under her cheekbones. She'd painted her lips with a frosted pink lipstick, making them pouty and full. The look was vastly different from her usual makeup routine, which consisted of tinted moisturizer and a little mascara.

"Amazing." Virginia heard the awe in her own voice as she fingered the large soft curls Nicole had woven into her hair.

"You're a sexy, hot woman, Virginia, but for some reason you don't use it."

Virginia felt like those women in the makeover shows. "Thank you." She stood and embraced Nicole in a fierce hug that had more to do with her liberation than the revamping of her hair and makeup.

"Now, you're ready to go let loose and have fun." They hugged again and separated. "What time is he coming?"

"Soon, and you have to leave."

Nicole pulled a face, but no matter how grateful Virginia was, there would be no way she'd let her stay and inspect Python.

Nicole begged and pleaded but Virginia pushed her out the door with the promise of relaying every gory detail the following day.

When Nicole left, Virginia closed the door and twisted the deadbolt of her new lock. Was she fooling herself about her feelings for Python? He'd shown her his gentler side in the way he played her body, knowing exactly what she needed. After the way they'd met, his sexual expertise shouldn't have surprised her, but it was more than sex. His playfulness and easy banter tugged at her, conflicting with the facts she knew to be true about him.

She'd taken this assignment reluctantly, then saw a way to make this story into much more than a five-minute news segment. It stirred even deeper ideas, making the dream of writing her book a reality.

She needed to get back on track and focus. As much as she'd enjoyed this crazy weekend, she had to put the brakes on whatever this was between them. She needed to squelch her fantasy of living on the wild side, because having feelings for someone so different from herself could never work.

As soon as he came to pick her up, she'd tell him she couldn't go to the party tonight.

Then she'd make it clear she wouldn't accept any more gifts from him. Virginia wandered into her bedroom and stared at the pristine white pillow-top king-size mattress. It did look comfortable, but she'd insist that he take it back. From now on, their relationship would be purely business. It was all too much, too . . .

A knock on her door dragged her back to the present. Probably Nicole with one last accessory for her outfit.

She flung the door open and sucked in a breath. An ominous stranger towered over her, then pushed his way into the apartment, slamming the door behind him. She instinctively reached for the doorknob to flee, but he stepped toward her and grabbed her arm, jerking her into the center of the living room.

"You remember me?" His rough voice sent an icy spike through her, like the steel bars piercing his face.

In the split second since he'd cornered her against the coffee table, it all fit together. Demon, the sketchy owner of the Shangri-La, was here in her apartment and standing not two feet away from her.

He leered at her with a twisted smirk. "I can see why Python keeps you locked down. Pretty piece like you he'd want all to himself."

Any other time Virginia would've had on a baggy t-shirt and sweatpants. The way his eyes roamed over her scantily clad outfit made her feel dirty. How dare he make her feel less with just a glance.

"What do you want?" Virginia used her anger and forced her face to stay expressionless while her stomach churned and her heart raced. Showing fear would not be good.

"What do I want?" Demon reached out to her, and when she reared back out of his grasp, he laughed. His face stilled and he stared at her. "Such a loaded question. I want the Serpents to play fair and share their good fortune with the rest of us instead of being a bunch of greedy fucks." His low, level voice simmered with rage like the subtle growl from a lion getting ready to pounce on its prey.

He licked his lips. "Hmm, you are fine." He waggled his tongue, showing her his piercing. "You're much too sweet for Python. That motherfucker might break you."

She sidestepped along the coffee table, and he tracked her, keeping the distance between them unnervingly close.

"Your man owes a shit load of money, and I've offered to help him, but he's a stubborn fucker. Even put his club at risk today 'cause he didn't take my offer." Demon drew in a deep breath. "Next time you see him, you tell him about my visit, and that if he doesn't cooperate, I'll be by to see you again." He slid his fingers through her hair. "We'll have a real good time. I'd like breakin' in a sweet ass like yours." He twisted the strands around his fist and yanked Virginia's head to the side. Her hand flew to her scalp as her eyes watered with the tingling pain.

Demon released her and laughed, then in three strides he was out the door and gone. Virginia flipped the new lock, realizing the irony. Her wobbly legs made it to the couch, where she slumped against the cushions, spent and keyed up at the same time. His quick appearance and departure made her wonder if she hadn't imagined it. How could an encounter lasting less than five minutes have such a devastating effect?

At the Shangri-La, Virginia knew Demon was someone to be wary of—but in the confines of her small apartment, he was horrifying—a sinister force with cold, dead eyes reflecting no regret or conscience.

She rubbed her sweaty palms against the couch cushions and tried to control her choppy breathing. It was one thing to write about and investigate criminals, but it was another to stand face to face with them. Demon radiated everything evil, and she imagined he enjoyed the violent side of the outlaw life. The same life Python lived, she reminded herself.

Demon mentioned sharing with the Serpents and money Python owed, which meant they had dealings with one another, and Virginia did see them together at the Shangri-La. She hated the thoughts spinning through her mind, yet ... She hugged herself to ward off the chill surrounding her, then dragged the throw blanket from the back of the couch over her shoulders.

Virginia tried to remember everything Demon had said and play it back so she could tell Python when— No, she couldn't tell Python. That was exactly what Demon wanted, probably to make him act out. His coming here was obviously a setup and a way to get at Python through her. She had to be smarter than him and figure this out.

Demon said Python owed someone money. She'd learned in her journalism classes all good stories were centered around money or power. Maybe this explained the disgruntled non-biker at the carnival who seemed very displeased with Python.

She jumped when she heard knocking on the door and sat perfectly still for a second; then she edged her way to the door, hating how Demon's visit triggered her fear. She sneaked a peek through the peephole and paused.

CHAPTER TWELVE

The ride back to Vegas gave Python plenty of time to think. Plenty of time to realize he'd made a mistake asking Virginia to the club party. He'd also made a mistake involving her in his fucked-up life, so when he pulled up in front of her apartment, he knew what he had to do.

As soon as she opened the door, he'd tell her if she wanted more information on the Serpents that she'd have to see Cobra because they were done. He thought he could just do his usual fuck 'em and forget 'em, but something happened at Lake Mead in the matter of feelings, sensations, and freaky thoughts of a future with Virginia, a future that wasn't going to happen. Bringing her into his life was dangerous, especially now with the Rats breathing down their backs.

He knocked on the door and covered himself in a shield of indifference, closing off the part of his mind that wanted to see her again, wanted to—

She opened the door, and his brain spun out, spiraled, and crashed. The sight of her in a fitted red tank top and little white shorts frayed at the edges showing just the right amount of leg. The well-placed rips teased him until his fingers itched to reach out and touch them. Python's eyes traveled down her tanned legs, and fuck him if she didn't have on a pair of black motorcycle boots. Every biker's wet dream.

She'd definitely dressed for him because this was light years away from the black, white, and beige, boring-as-shit outfits she usually wore.

Virginia opened the door wider and he stepped inside against his will. She stared up at him with those light brown, innocent eyes and everything he'd planned to say crashed and burned. Then a stupid smile covered his face. Shit, he was a dead man.

———

Python didn't play fair. His smile alone set her off. The genuine expression softened his edginess and made her forget he was an outlaw. He ran his tongue along his lower lip and her insides quivered. How could such a simple gesture amp her up? Not to mention the low-slung worn jeans hanging over his dust covered boots, and the black t-shirt sculpting his taut chest.

He leaned in and cupped the back of her head. "What the hell do you do to me?"

Oh God, was he reading her mind now?

He covered her mouth with his, and his wicked tongue prodded the seam of her lips. Her mutinous mouth opened for him, but when he slid his hands to her waist, she stilled.

"We have to stop." She cursed the breathlessness of her voice.

"I know." He bit his bottom lip. "But you taste so fuckin' good."

"We can't continue this." Her hands gripped his leather cut, but instead of pushing him away, she dragged him closer to inhale his intoxicating scent.

"Right."

"From now on I'll get the information I need about the club for the interview from Cobra." When she leaned up on her tip-toes and nipped at the base of his neck, he cupped her ass, and lifted. Virginia's legs wrapped around his waist without her permission, then her hips ground into him. "And I don't think I should go to the biker party with you tonight."

"I totally agree." He kissed her again, deeper, harder, melding their mouths and stealing her air.

Python continued to kiss her as he walked them into the bedroom. He broke away from her lips, looked over her shoulder, and his gaze fell to the new mattress. "Nice."

"And that's another thing, I'm not accepting any more presents from you."

"Okay." He spun around with her still glued to him and sat on the edge of the bed. He toed-off his boots and then lay back against the soft mattress, taking her with him. "Anything else?"

"No, I think we covered everything."

"Great. Now get naked 'cause if I don't fuck you in the next ten seconds my dick is gonna explode."

———

Virginia unwrapped herself from around him, then kneeled up on the bed and slowly stripped. The little grin on her face told Python she knew exactly what she was doing to him. One look at the bulge in his jeans said it all. He tugged off his cut and t-shirt, then he fumbled with his belt buckle and ripped down the zipper. Oh, fuck yeah, he had his own technicolor porn show up front and personal. Python roughly stroked himself as Virginia continued her act, but when she slipped down those little white shorts, he had to recite the alphabet to keep from coming in his hand.

Her perfect, compact body had just the right amount of curves, and when she wiggled out of her thong, his heart jackhammered inside his chest. "Ahh, babe, get down here and ride me."

She paused, a sly smile in place as she tugged his jeans down his legs. When she positioned herself between his thighs and lowered her head, her silky hair teased his abs. He flinched as tiny spasms jetted through his gut. She pushed his hand away and replaced it with hers, then licked her lips, and when she flicked her tongue against his tip, he thought his head would implode.

———

Python's thick, massive thigh muscles flexed as her small hand barely wrapped around his girth. Parting her lips, she took him in but kept her hand at his base, squeezing him in perfect tempo. He dug his fingers into her scalp as his hips kept pace with her hand and mouth. Tortuous groans filled the bedroom. In one smooth move Python reached down and pulled her up and over his chest. He grabbed for his jeans, snatched a condom out of the pocket, and held it out to her.

"Slip it on me." His blue eyes darkened like the sky before a summer storm. "Wanna come in your bangin' body."

She leaned up and fumbled with the wrapper. Finally getting it open, she rolled it over his straining cock. "What size do you buy, XL?"

"XXL," he said with a smirk.

Before she could answer, he snaked his hand between them and played with her clit. "You're soaked." She watched, mesmerized, as he sucked those fingers into his mouth. "Fuckin' sweet."

The simple gesture made her head swim.

He jerked his hips. "Now jump on and ride me. Show your biker how much you want his cock."

Her mind stalled on biker—*your biker.* Wasn't the whole idea tonight to tell him that whatever they were doing had to stop and that they weren't right for each other. It was no use —he was right—she wanted his cock and she wanted it now, like she never wanted anything in her life.

She slid down his chest and hovered over his hips. A hiss escaped her lips as he stretched her wide, but he'd gotten her so wet with his dirty talk and bad-boy attitude that he slipped right in—all of him, every blessed, glorious inch.

Python gripped her hips and roughly moved her on top of him. With his eyes hooded and his full lips parted, Virginia couldn't resist; she leaned in and sucked and nipped his lips until their tongues danced together while she played with his sinful metal ball piercing in his tongue. Dueling it out as he ground up into her, over and over again, she'd never experienced such full satisfaction, so completely in the moment.

It hit her that this freedom was what she craved, and Python gave it to her all wrapped up in this magnificent body. He let her fulfill her fantasy of breaking out and enjoying some rebellion. He continued to pound into her and she gripped his shoulders for support. Her hitched breaths and his deep groans surrounded them. He leaned up and sucked her lip between his teeth and bit down. Equal parts pain and ecstasy. Her body peaked as she dug her nails into his shoulders and shattered on top of him.

His sharp thrusts came faster, then he grinned at her. "That's right, babe, come for me, come all over me."

His words shot through her and then the unbelievable happened as her body tightened around him again and then again. The powerful releases sapped her strength and she collapsed against his chest. Python thrust up into her one last time and let out a howl. His pulsing cock competed with her orgasmic aftershocks. She shivered and he wrapped his arms around her, hugging her to him.

They lay there listening to their ragged breathing. She couldn't believe he howled like a wild animal, a wild animal who just gave her multiple orgasms again. Python enjoyed sex and had no trouble showing her how much. She'd experienced more orgasms in the last twenty-four hours than she'd had in her whole sexual life. The heady euphoria was enough to make her forget all her intentions of ending whatever they had together. Enough to make her want to do this again soon —very soon.

He shifted her to his side and silently stared at her, then a slow smile covered his face. "You got my thinking all twisted up."

"You've got my thinking tangled and a bit distorted too. And after those multiple orgasms, I'm lucky I can remember my name."

He cocked his eyebrow. "Two seconds before you opened that door I had my brush-off speech all ready."

"Two seconds before I opened that door I had a list of reasons why we were bad for each other outlined and rehearsed."

"Hmmm."

Virginia extended her arm and waggled it between them. "And yet, here we are together ... again."

"Hmmm."

"Is that a *hmmm* you agree with me or did the sex stun you speechless?"

"The sex and your tight body was fuckin' off the charts, but I also have a whole list of reasons why we shouldn't be together." His face sobered. "Number one is because it's dangerous."

The little hairs on the back of Virginia's neck stood up remembering Demon's threatening visit.

"Dangerous?" she squeaked out.

"The Serpents got some shit to settle, and I got no intentions of putting you in that path."

"But I'm not involved with that." She kept her voice level and casual, completely disguising her avid interest.

"Old outlaw code. You don't go after the enemy, you go after who the enemy cares about. Family, friends. Sure way to make an example and bring a fucker to his knees.

"Hmmm." She mimicked him because she knew he would smile, and he did. Anything to divert the fear welling up in her now that she fully understood the reason for Demon's visit. He was threatening Python through her. Ingenious. She gritted her teeth and forced down the urge to come clean and tell Python about Demon's visit. Yes, it would make her feel better, but he would surely retaliate in the worst possible way. She had to figure out another way around this mess.

"I was going to tell you to return this mattress, but now ..."

He laughed. "I guess you could say it's used. Not returnable."

She ran her hand over the pillowy softness. "But seriously, this mattress was very expensive. I'm very grateful, but it's not like we've been in a long-term relationship." She flailed out her arms like making a snow angel. "I don't need this much space."

Demon told her Python owed someone a lot of money so he certainly didn't need this added expense.

Python shrugged. "I like doin' random shit for people. Helping them out."

"Like maybe the way someone helped you out along the way?" She was fishing, but she couldn't help it. They'd been beyond intimate and yet she barely knew the basics about the man.

"No, probably 'cause nobody helped me out along the way,

except Cobra, but I was already grown by then. Probably why I hook up with lost causes."

"Am I a lost cause?" She couldn't help asking such an obvious question.

"You are nothing like any of the women I know."

She flicked her gaze to her modest bust line. "I know." She bugged out her eyes in an attempt to be goofy.

"What you got is just fine." He cupped her breast and sucked her nipple between his lips. "Do you think we could get something to eat? Or I could just eat you."

"You always use sex and food to divert me. This time you used both. Amazing."

———

Python cuddled Virginia to him. He didn't know when, but right now, he didn't want to let her go. Selfish? Hell, yeah. Crazy? Shit, yeah. Risky? Abso-fuckin-lutely.

Maybe the beast could finally get his beauty, or maybe the fairytale would crash and burn with no survivors and no happy ending, but for now, he had to believe the next hour, the next minute, the next second would be theirs and only theirs.

CHAPTER THIRTEEN

The buzzing of Python's phone jarred him out of a deep sleep. He jerked to a sitting position and tried to get his bearings.

A small hand reached out to him. "Are you all right?"

Virginia's bedroom in her apartment ... right.

He reached for his phone and the screen lit up. Four a.m. He swiped at it. "Yeah?"

"Python? It's Gina, we got a problem at the club."

Python swung his legs over the bed, fully awake.

"It's Crystal." Gina continued, "She passed out in the dressing room and—"

"Is she using?" Python barked into the phone.

"Maybe, I don't know." He could hear an undercurrent of female voices through the phone.

"I'm on my way." He swiped the call away and scanned the floor for his jeans. "Son of a bitch," he mumbled as he shoved on his boots and laced them halfway up.

"What's going on?" Virginia asked.

"I got a problem at the club with one of the girls." He tugged his t-shirt over his head.

She got out of bed and gathered up her clothes.

"What're you doin'?"

"I'm going with you."

"Why?"

"In case you need my help." She retreated into the bathroom and the next sound he heard was her brushing her teeth. By the time he had his cut on, she emerged from the bathroom fully dressed and ready to go.

She didn't have a clue what the problem was, but she wanted to help. He was right, she was way different than any other woman he'd ever known. And he reasoned if he kept her with him, he'd know she'd be safe.

———

Ten minutes later they pulled into the back lot of Ecstasy. At four in the morning, the parking lot was mostly empty. Python barreled through the back door, then into the dressing room, as Virginia struggled to keep up.

He barged past the dancers in different stages of undress, then crouched next to Crystal's limp, unconscious body. "What happened here?" His piercing blue eyes scanned each girl's face.

"I don't knows" and "you have to do somethings" echoed around the room.

Python checked her pulse. He mumbled something, scooped her up, carried her into his office, and gently lay her on the couch. Virginia and the other women followed behind him in their scantily clad costumes like some erotic parade.

He jerked his chin at one of the girls. "Turn on the cold water in the shower, and the rest of you get the hell outta here."

Virginia stayed glued in the doorway transfixed with Python's efficiency while the sound of running water filled the room. He rummaged around in his desk and extracted a box, then tore it open and pulled out what looked like nasal spray. He sprayed it up each of the girl's nostrils and her whole body jerked, then she began to shiver. Python reached for the wastepaper basket next to his desk seconds before the girl sat up and retched violently.

She continued as Python rubbed her back. "What the fuck is wrong with you, Crystal? You can't be doin' this shit." His soothing voice belied his words.

When she was done, Python gave her some tissues to wipe her mouth, then he stood, removed his cut, and laid it over the chair. He gathered Crystal into his arms and headed for the bathroom.

Emotion tugged at Virginia, as she admired Python's compassion and his take-charge attitude. He didn't ask, he acted.

One of the other dancers joined her in the doorway. "How's she doing?" The girl hugged a silk robe around herself and shivered from the overly cool air in the empty club.

"Python took her into the shower."

"That usually helps. Did he give her the Narcan?"

"The nasal spray?"

"Stuff's amazing."

Virginia understood the use of Narcan, but she'd never seen it administered, yet this girl seemed very familiar with it, as though asking if the girl was given an Advil.

"Python has done this before?" Virginia asked.

"Hell yeah. Python doesn't allow drugs in the club, but you know how that goes. If you're hooked, you're going to do it no matter what."

"And he's done this for Crystal before?" Virginia asked.

"No, it's a first for her, but there's been a few others. Python's the best. He really cares about us."

Virginia could see that. The calm, yet firm way he handled

Crystal showed he knew what he was doing. And according to this girl, he'd come to their aide many times.

"Unfortunately, Cobra will make Python fire her. He doesn't want junkies on stage or drugs in his club. Can't blame him, it's a sure way to get the cops on your ass."

Virginia could certainly understand, but Crystal obviously had a problem, and now she'd also be jobless.

"Python will help her out. I've seen him pay for rehab if the girl wants to go."

"Really?" Virginia cocked her head.

"Just last month he loaned me money to get my car fixed, but I paid him back. It was just a favor." The girl touched her forearm. "He and I don't have a thing—like we've never fucked or anything."

"Uh ... umm, sure," Virginia stuttered. "I mean, it's none of my business."

"I just didn't want you to get the wrong idea 'cause you're the girl from the carnival, right?"

"Yes."

"I was tending bar in the beer tent that day, and I saw the way you were looking at him and the way he was looking at you." She smiled. "It was sweet."

So much for thinking she was hiding her feelings. The female bartender from across a crowded beer tent picked up on their chemistry.

"Hey, Gina," Python called out. "Find something dry for her to wear." Python held a very wet Crystal against his equally wet clothing.

As he cradled the extremely pale woman in his arms, Virginia saw a man who cared, a man who wasn't as he appeared to be. Python was a man who'd seen suffering and come out the other side. Her mind traveled to his unknown past. He was far too healthy to be an addict now, but perhaps in his past, or someone close to him caused the faint glint of guilt in his eyes.

Gina hurried out of the office and Python sat Crystal on the leather couch. The girl shivered until he pulled a blanket out of a closet and draped it over her shoulders. She clutched the blanket around her and Python laid a pillow behind her head.

Gina came back with sweatpants and a t-shirt, and Python stepped away as Crystal dried off and redressed.

"You were amazing." Virginia squeezed Python's damp forearm. His wet t-shirt molded to him like a second skin with his bare feet sticking out beneath his sodden jeans. She assumed he'd put Crystal in the shower, but apparently he stayed in there with her.

He nodded toward the couch. "She'll be all right."

"Gina said you've done this before."

His face clouded over. "Addiction sucks."

Virginia might've just found the inspiration she needed to make her story relevant. Not the seedy side of drugs and crime, but the compassion of a man who helped children have fun at a carnival and women who overdosed.

"What the hell is goin' on here?" A harsh voice filled the office.

Python pushed her behind him and stepped up to the man standing in the doorway. "Who the hell are you?'

"I"m her man. I've been waiting over an hour for her lazy ass." He peered over Python's shoulder and narrowed his eyes at Crystal. "Now get the fuck up, and let's go."

The girl shrunk back into the couch, and Gina stood in full defense mode.

This irate stranger with the bad attitude glared at them with pinpoint eyes. Question answered where Crystal obtained her drugs. He bulldozed his bulky body past them, purposely shoulder-bumping Python. Even Virginia knew that was a huge mistake.

"I said get the fuck up, bitch," he bellowed.

In two steps, Python came up from behind and spun the guy around. "You better dial it down."

"Or what?" The guy pointed to Crystal. "She's mine. I'm the one looking out for her."

"Well, you've been doin' a shit job 'cause she's a full-on junkie who almost OD'd."

"Big fuckin' surprise. I can't help it if she likes the needle. Now get outta my way"—the guy tried to breeze past Python—"'cause I'm taking her with me."

"I don't think so." Python blocked him, and the little hairs on the back of Virginia's neck vibrated with doom.

The guy smirked at Python. "What the fuck did you do, take a shower with your clothes on?"

"You better get outta here before I lose my patience," Python warned.

"Just keeping an eye on what's mine."

Python closed the distance between them. "You peddling junk to any of the other girls in here?"

The guy's eyes narrowed, but he stayed silent.

"Answer me," Python demanded.

"What do you care?" He jerked his chin at Crystal. "She ain't your business."

"Everything that goes on in this club is my business."

"Are you fuckin' kidding me? This bitch costs me more than she's worth, that's why I took the deal when—"

"What did you say?" Frustration and anger were wrapped up in Python's words.

"Forget it." He pushed past Python, and when Python lunged, the guy flipped out a knife and slashed Python's bicep.

Python grabbed the guy's throat and shoved him to the

wall, sending the framed liquor license and health inspection certificates crashing to the floor. She'd witnessed an overdose and a knife fight over drugs. Had she somehow been dropped onto the set of a Quentin Tarantino movie?

Python was taller but the other guy was just as muscular and showed no signs of backing down.

"Tell me who you made a deal with, and who sent you here."

The guy fisted Python's forearms and tried to push him off, but Python squeezed his neck harder.

"Was it Demon?" Python spit out.

The guy gasped for air as his skin turned a strange tinge of blue. Virginia edged herself behind Python's desk, her hands gripping the leather chair.

"Ease up," the guy gasped out.

Python released his grip from around his neck but kept him pinned to the wall. "Did you make a deal with the Rats?"

The guy massaged his throat and swallowed hard. "He said it'd be easy. Sell to the girls, get drugs in the club."

"And then what? He was gonna get us raided?"

"I don't know. My job was to just get some of the girls using." He pointed at Crystal. "Her and that other bitch, Tara, were already juiced. One of the reasons Demon wanted them working here."

"Who else?" Python braced his massive forearm against the guy's chest, similar to the move he'd used on her at the Shangri-La, only with a lot more force and anger.

"Nobody else," the guy choked out then sagged against the wall. "You brought all this shit on yourself." The guy rubbed his throat. "Just pay up Harry, and Demon will get off your ass."

Python balled up his fist and kept smashing it into the guy's face until blood spurted from his nose. When he fell to his knees, Python dragged him up by the collar and pushed him toward the door. "I ever see you in here again, I'll fuckin' kill ya."

Crystal and Gina cowered on the couch. Python's raspy breathing filled the silent room. He rotated his arm and looked down at the blood. "Fuck!"

Python pointed at Gina. "That couch pulls out. There are sheets in the closet. Stay with her. If you need me, I'm upstairs." Then he peeled off a few hundred-dollar bills from his money clip and threw them on his desk. "Get her what she needs, and don't let her go back to that guy."

Then Python turned to Virginia. "You come with me."

Virginia flashed a quick look over her shoulder to the women, then followed Python. The blood from his bicep covered most of his right arm and continued to seep over his hand. The beating he gave Crystal's pimp couldn't have helped, yet he seemed unaffected by it.

She had to trot to keep up with him until he stopped by the stairwell door and yanked it open. She scoured his face for some indication of his feelings, but all she got was a nod of his head, so she passed through the doorway and headed up the stairs. His heavy boots clomped behind her, and at the top of the stairs she wrestled the door open because, well, he had a huge gash in his arm.

He unlocked the door to his apartment, then headed for the kitchen. After rummaging under the sink, he came up with an oversized First-Aid kit. He flipped it open and Virginia was impressed. From the look of the contents, Python could perform minor surgeries. A medical kit this extensive was probably mandatory if you were sergeant-at-arms of an outlaw biker club.

Kobi padded into the kitchen and she scratched him under his ear, happy for the diversion. The animal examined Python, and then whimpered like he knew his master was injured.

"It's okay, buddy," Python said over his shoulder.

Virginia stroked the dog to reassure him, then turned back to Python. "Are you all right?" His silence was killing her, and there was nothing in the big plastic box to remedy curiosity.

"I'm fine."

She detested that word because usually, when someone used it, it meant the exact opposite.

"You're not fine. Some guy just stabbed you." Her logical brain said that would make sense, but maybe this was more macho biker crap.

"That guy was a punk. And he didn't stab me, he slashed me like a pussy. Big difference."

"Okay."

"I'm not mad at him, I'm mad at me." He stuck his hand and the lower half of his arm under the kitchen faucet and washed away the blood, then he cleaned out the gash with sterile pads until the bleeding slowed.

"Please let me help you with that." she said.

"I got it." He tore the wrapping on the bandages apart, cut a few to size, then applied them like a pro, like he'd done this many times before.

His expression and body language were foreign to her, almost robotic, like he'd completely shut down, and it scared her. She knew what the club was about, but for the first time she saw the side of Python that made him a Serpent.

"Still doesn't explain why you're mad at yourself."

He taped the last bandage in place, snapped the First-Aid kit closed, and nailed her with this sky-blue eyes.

"Drugs in Ecstasy are a hard *no*. That means no for the customers and no for the dancers. The last thing we need is the DEA sniffing around because those fuckers will shut you down without a second thought. Everyone who works at Ecstasy knows the rules."

"From what that guy said, they set you up with those girls on purpose."

"And that's on me too. Crystal and Tara hung out with me for a few weeks before they applied for the jobs."

Virginia clearly remember both women from Python's birthday. At the time she'd envied their blatant sexuality not realizing the demons they fought.

"And because of that I didn't vet them properly. Maybe if I hadn't been thinking with my dick, I would've seen they had a problem."

"You can't blame yourself for their addictions."

"I know that, but because I wasn't paying attention, Demon was able—" He shoved the First-Aid kit under the sink, then whipped around to face her. "You were ragging on me the other day for not telling you about myself." He spread his arms wide. "So now you know, that's the type of guy I am."

"You're being way too hard on yourself."

"Babe, I get you think you can handle my life, but believe me, you can't. This isn't some HBO mini-series. This is the real fuckin' deal where strippers OD, and their pimp boyfriends sell them off to the highest bidder, then slash the outlaw biker." He pushed away from the counter and paced the kitchen. "You shouldn't have been in that office tonight. You shouldn't be in a strip club with a biker and some crazy-ass pimp trying to knife him."

"If you think that's all I see, then you don't know me. You're so much more than that."

"Nah, I'm way outta your league. You should be—"

"Drinking a Bellini on a terrace overlooking the golf course?" She threw him a sarcastic glare. "Been there, done that. Not as exciting or glamorous as one might think."

"I thought by keeping you with me I could keep you safe, but it's the exact opposite. This is why I don't get involved past one or two nights. I should've never let you get this close to me. I tried to stop this thing between us." He heaved out a heavy sigh, then stared down at her. "I tried to hold back . . . from that first night when you walked in my bedroom. You knew it and I knew it, but that don't make it right."

"You didn't even know me then."

"I knew I was gonna have you."

"Sounds a bit archaic."

"Why you gotta use those fancy words?" His voice was sharp as a bite. "You may not wanna admit it, but you knew too."

"Maybe." She bit the inside of her cheek to keep from showing too much.

"No 'maybe' bullshit. The way your eyes roamed over me, I knew you were liking what you saw."

"You looked me over too," she challenged.

"Fuck yeah, I did. I ain't denying it. Tried to tell myself if I shut that down, I'd get you outta my system."

"But it didn't work?"

"Made it worse. Why do you think I was so closed off when we had lunch in that Mexican restaurant? I was trying to protect you, but mostly me. You know the old saying about wanting what you can't have. Wanting what you know is bad for you? I was living that in spades when it came to you, 'cause a woman like you could be deadly."

"How am I bad for you?" She cocked her head thinking it should be the other way around. Wasn't he the bad boy corrupting the good girl? Sounded a bit clichéd, but totally true.

"Ohhh babe, you are, in so many ways bad for a man like me." He leaned against the counter like the revelation drained him.

"Explain."

"Me getting close to you is dangerous, but me caring

about you could be deadly—for both of us. The people I deal with don't care if people live or die especially when it comes to money. Some of them don't care if *they* live or die."

Suddenly, it all fit together. The ominous stranger at the carnival, Demon's mention of money Python owed, and then the thug tonight saying he should just pay up.

"How long have you had a problem with gambling?"

Virginia's out of the blue question threw him for a minute. She expected him to deny it, but she wasn't going to back down.

He huffed out a laugh. "Who the fuck knows?"

"That guy tonight said you owed money, and your friend at the carnival hardly looked friendly." She artfully left out Demon's visit and his threats. "Probably living in one of the biggest gambling cities in the world doesn't help either."

"Nah, it's not that. I probably had a problem with gambling the first time I placed a bet. I'm all in or nothing." He raked his hand through his hair. "Back in the bad old days I didn't do a bump of coke or a couple of pills. Nah, I hovered up lines of blow and swallowed handfuls of pills. Sometimes I didn't even know what day it was. Then I hooked up with Cobra, he got me straight, and we talked about starting the Serpents. Cobra got me interested in life again."

"So, that was a good thing."

"People I knew were amazed how I just quit hard drugs cold turkey, but all I did was trade one addiction for another. Sure I quit the dope, but I started gambling. Kinda the same but different. The act of gambling isn't going to physically kill me, but the money lost is the same. The high when you place the bet is the same. It doesn't matter if you win or lose. The ache, the need for the next bet, it's the same damn feeling, same sensation."

"Professionals say most addictions are a way to fill an emptiness." She paused when his eyes connected with hers.

"I'm about as empty as you can get."

"I know about feeling not good enough. My father is a very successful businessman in Los Angeles, and I know I've disappointed him by moving to Las Vegas and not joining him in the family business." It was a broad explanation, giving away just enough.

"What kinda business?"

"Communications." Another understatement. Century Media controlled three of the biggest cable channels in the country, and there was a good chance he'd recognize her father's name.

He continued to study her, then his blue eyes darkened and narrowed. "Great, so you got it all figured out. I'm a former drug addict and a deadbeat gambler and you disappointed your rich father. I don't have time for all this psychology bullshit." His voice cut through her sharp and meant to sting. "Asking me questions, acting concerned like you care. You got your walk on the wild side. You got to see how the other half lives and do a little slumming, yeah?"

"No, no." She wanted to say so much more, but his cutting words and the brutal way he delivered them stunned her.

"Was this all some kinda joke for you, or just all a bullshit way to get a juicy story. Hope your editor liked it, babe, 'cause story time is over. I don't want you anywhere near me or my club."

"You don't understand." She reached out to him, and he pushed her hand away.

"Nah, I don't want you feeling sorry for me. I don't want you feeling anything for me."

He stepped away from her, swiped at his phone, then mumbled into it and disconnected the call. "Rattler's coming to take you home."

A blank, hard expression covered his face before he turned his back to her like she wasn't there.

"You're just dismissing me?"

"I got nothing else to say to you."

"And that's it? After all we've——" She wouldn't use sex as a weapon because for her it had been more than sex. She'd experienced emotions and passion for the first time, but maybe that was her mistake. For her, they were firsts, but for him, it was just business as usual.

Ten minutes later his phone buzzed, he glanced down at it, then turned to her. "Rattler's here."

Her eyes burned, but she refused to cry or cause a scene. She refused to let him see what he was doing to her. He kept his back to her as she gathered what little pride she had left and walked out of his apartment, down the stairs, through the club, and out to Rattler waiting in the SUV.

———

When the door to his apartment slammed shut, he headed for the bar and poured himself a double shot of Jack, then stared at it and pushed it away. Why bother getting trashed and suffering with a goddamn hangover when it wouldn't work anyway.

He slumped onto the couch and Kobi trotted over. Python scratched him behind his ears, and the dog stared up at him and cocked his head. Even the ninety-pound beast knew he'd fucked up.

"Yeah, Kobi I just kicked the best thing that ever happened to me right outta my life."

The animal stared a few minutes longer, then rested his head on Python's thigh. No matter what stupid-ass thing he did, the dog still loved him. Python patted his head, remembering the sketchy days when he'd first found him. Virginia thought he saved Kobi, but it was the other way around. Back then, Python was at his lowest and he needed a lifeline.

He leaned in and hugged the big beast around the neck, and fuck if he didn't jump up on the couch next to him.

"It's just you and me, buddy, but at least for once I did the right thing." Kobi nuzzled his snout into his lap. "Crazy though, I miss her already."

CHAPTER FOURTEEN

Python let the dry desert air clear his brain and wash over his body. He'd already ridden an hour out on I-15 and he'd been alone on the road for the last half hour, pushing his Harley hard, throttling down and hitting it way, way over the speed limit. Oh yeah, this was what he needed.

It tore him the fuck up the way he turned Virginia out, the way the pain and sadness radiated through her whole body as if he'd gut punched her. It hadn't been easy on him either. He must've stared at the door a good twenty minutes after she'd left. His mind playing tricks with him, alternating between wanting to run after her, wanting her to come back, and being glad she'd left.

He hated the words he'd said to her, but it was the only way to make sure she never came back, make sure she hated him. He was good at being a first-class bastard. Too good. There wasn't enough liquor in the state of Nevada to squelch the way the center of his chest ached.

As the Serpents' sergeant-at-arms, he was responsible for carrying out deals and breaking heads when treaties were shit on. The other brothers depended on him and his abilities. He wouldn't back down and give in to the overwhelming pain surrounding him and weighing him down since he'd sent Virginia off. He wouldn't act like a pussy by letting a woman get under his skin. Serpents first and always.

He was meeting up with the Rats' prospect to work up a deal and get this job done for the club. After he eased off the highway, he rode another five miles in over the same dirt road toward Searchlight, where he and Rattler had torched the Rat's weed house. It was a perfect meeting place and halfway point out in the middle of fuckin' nowhere, fitting for a shady deal to be made to undermine a fucked-up MC like the Rats.

He eased closer to the burned-out house and saw the prospect leaning against his bike. Python cut his engine, removed his helmet, and the prospect straightened up and waited. Python rolled his shoulders and jerked his neck from side to side to relieve the tension from the high-speed, hour-long ride.

Their last meeting hadn't given Python much time for observation, but now he took in every detail. Python's intel said the prospect's name was Blade. He was definitely younger than Python, probably twenty-six ... twenty-seven, toned muscles, maybe six feet tall. Blade pushed off his bike, stepped to Python and squared his shoulders, but he was still a good five inches shorter than Python. They eyed each other and Python stayed silent.

"So, why am I meeting you out in the middle of the desert?" Blade asked, a hint of challenge in his voice.

"I don't know, why are you?" Python slouched against the side of his bike and crossed his arms over his chest while he stared the kid down. Answer a question with another question. Old trick, but it always worked.

Blade jerked his thumb toward the charred remnants of the house. "Shit got crazy last time we were out here, barely made it outta there alive."

"Yup, that's 'cause your psycho of a president doesn't follow the rules."

Blade kicked at a few loose stones with his boot. "Some of us ain't happy."

"I guess *that's* why you're meeting me in the middle of the desert."

"What are you offering?"

"A place to ride with a real club whose leaders aren't strung out and putting their members in jeopardy."

Blade grunted and shook his head. "Demon's getting crazier by the minute."

"So I heard."

"A lot of shit goin' down." Blade jerked his head over his shoulder, like somebody might hear him out in the middle of nowhere, then leaned into Python. "The other prospect, Hawk. The one you shot in the leg. Demon iced him."

Just like Python thought. His eyes burned a hole through Blade, and his deadly stare made the kid pull on the chain attached to his belt.

Blade inched closer to Python. "Demon took me with him to the hospital after Hawk had surgery on his leg. He was still out of it. Demon made me stand outside the door. I watched him put a pillow over Hawk's face. Then we walked outta there like nothing happened." Blade drew in a long, deep breath. "Me and Hawk were friends, decided to prospect together . . . and Demon offed him just like that."

Python shrugged. "I ain't interested in your sad stories. I wanna know if you think the others will turn."

"Definitely. Nobody's happy." Blade rolled his lips in. "Demon's got us in deep with some twisted shit. Underage illegals, drugging them, selling them off or forcing them to do porn. Half the time he don't even feed them regular. And the kinky shit he gets up to with some of them ..." Blade drew in a deep breath and blew it out. "It's fucked up."

"All right. You go back and you let your brothers know the deal I'm offering to come to Vegas, but—and this is a big fuckin' but—anything goes wrong and there's any more hits on our places and I'll know who spilled."

Blade threw up his palms. "No man, I wouldn't do that. I want outta this, and so do a lot of the other guys."

"You get the word out nice and quiet with everything on the DL, then you get back to me." Python narrowed his eyes. "You can either side with us or go down with him, but I promise you, either way that motherfucker Demon is over."

"I get it."

"And let anybody thinking about prospecting for the Serpents know we don't put up with no bullshit. No side deals and nothing shady. Everything goes through Cobra."

"I get it."

"And the women who hang around our clubhouse like to fuck. Some of them like kinky shit, some of them don't, but nothing goes down without their okay."

Blade nodded vigorously. Python's reputation with the Serpents preceded him, so Blade's eagerness to please wasn't a surprise, but Python didn't believe anything, even when it was standing right in front of him, and even then, sometimes he called bullshit.

"You got twenty-four hours. No more, no less. You use the burner number I gave you to solidify this deal."

Blade held his fist out. Python gave him a once over, cocked his head, then tapped Blade's knuckles.

Python turned toward his bike and unstrapped his helmet, but Blade stood in place staring at him. "You got something else?"

Blade mashed his lips together and swallowed hard. "How do I know, in the end, that you won't let us patch-in . . . that this"—he motioned between them—"isn't some kind of a setup?"

"You don't." Python threw his leg over his bike. The silence of the windless day surrounded them. "But what's the alternative?" Python flipped down his visor, throttled the bike, and angled it toward the dirt road.

When Python hit I-15 again, a smile crept across his lips. He had the prospect just where he wanted him. He'd dangled the carrot and Blade chomped on it. He had no doubt plenty of the Rats wanted out, but he was savvy enough to also know some would want to fight. Didn't matter though because the Serpents had the power and the support of other clubs. The Rats had burned way too many bridges with their greed and slimy dealings, screwing up any allies they might've had along the way.

———

When Python pulled up to Joker's motorcycle shop in Henderson, he patted his pockets until he came up with his smokes. He lit up and drew deep, wishing for the premium weed the Serpents grew. That would definitely take the edge off, but he'd have to wait till later when he could hit up the stash at his apartment.

He took a few more hits off the Marlboro, then ambled into the garage. In the last few months, Joker had set up a good business fixing motorcycles and tricking them out. He'd even hired a guy who did custom paint jobs. The Serpents had thrown a lot of business his way, but Joker's grade A work spoke for itself.

The place hummed with activity and the sweet sounds of the Stones. Joker loved old-school rock, and right now Mick was screaming about his lack of satisfaction. Python got that message loud and clear. Right now, satisfaction or anything close eluded him in a big fuckin' way. He ground his cigarette under his boot and sucked in the potent smell of exhaust and gasoline, a heady combination and just what he needed to calm the static.

As usual, Joker was elbow deep in the skeleton of a bike. In the past few months, he'd made a good life for Daisy, and his son, Derek. Python would have to use all his abilities of persuasion to sway him to the club. He joined Joker in the bay and watched him for a few seconds before Joker realized he wasn't alone.

"Hey, man." Joker wiped his hands on a greasy rag before straightening up and offering his fist.

Python returned the gesture, then Joker jerked his chin toward the inner office where the din of music and rumbling motors were muted. Joker closed the door behind them, then leaned down to a portable fridge and extracted two bottles of cold beer. They popped the caps and clinked the bottles together.

"Just what I needed." Python drank deep, clearing his throat of the desert dust. He nodded toward the interior of the garage. "You got a nice shop here."

"Everything I always wanted. Finally feel like I'm where I should be."

"How does your son like living in the desert?"

"Loves it. Only a freshman and he's playing varsity foot-ball. Kid's a natural."

Python didn't doubt it. He'd only met Derek once, but the kid was already six feet tall and built like a leaner version of Joker.

"And Daisy's good?"

Joker's dark eyes sussed him out. "Yeah, she is, but why don't we cut the bullshit small talk so you can enjoy that beer."

Python smiled at his directness. Joker was nobody's fool, he'd outsmarted his psycho president in New York and outran a vicious cartel in Miami. The man knew survival and how to stay alive. One of the main reasons Python stood in his garage today.

"The shit we were going through with the Rats a few months ago has gotten hotter. We gotta shut 'em down."

"So what does that have to do with me?' Joker took a pull off his beer.

"You gonna make me say it?" Python challenged.

"I already told Cobra, I'm not interested."

"And I don't buy it. You're one of the few who was actually brought up with the club mentality. Your Daddy was a president. You got this shit in your blood. Can't shake it off that easy."

"All true, but maybe that's the same reason why I don't want back in. I've seen what it does to families. The undercurrent, the secrets and lies, until it tears it wide open."

"Doesn't have to be that way."

"But that's what I know." Joker placed his beer on the scarred wooden desk and fished his smokes out of his pocket. He lit up and drew deep, like he needed the nicotine hit for the strength to continue. "I watched my father fuck random club whores till it drove my mother to the needle. Then I lost my first wife because of a club grudge. Not even anything important, just one motherfucker flexing and wanting to teach me a lesson took my son's mother away from him." He tipped the beer bottle to his lips and swallowed, then hit his cigarette. "A power struggle in that same club got my son shot. I won't take a chance with Daisy or put Derek at risk." He wiped his mouth with the back of his hand, his eyes hooded and somber. "I'm not willing to make that mistake again."

Python lit up his own smoke. "Cobra needs you, we need a man who knows the life and has the balls to live the life." Python paused, then went to a place he hadn't intended. "The Serpents had your back before we even knew you. We stood up for you because you were a brother from our charter club back East, but now you can't repay the favor?"

Sure, guilting him was a dick move, but Cobra said he wanted Joker in the club, and to use anything that worked, so . . . Python wasn't above screwing with Joker's head and piling on the guilt if it got results. Although Python loved throwing a fist, well-placed words could work just as good.

"Ahh, no, man. I came through for Cobra when he needed it. Or did you forget those bullets whizzing past our heads in the Valley View warehouse?"

"Nah, that's the problem. You're too good to lose." Python stubbed out his cigarette in the metal ashtray.

"Daisy's knocked up. She's having my kid."

"Congratu-fuckin-lations, man." Python slapped Joker on the back and they did the man-hug thing. "Great news."

"It's the happiest I've ever seen her, and I ain't putting that in jeopardy."

"And I ain't asking you to, but the Serpents need a VP, and we want you." Python nailed Joker with a look that sent most men running, but he wasn't surprised when Joker met him glare for glare. The man's insides were rock and steel with just enough heart and guts to make him the perfect VP.

"What do you need done?"

"Ahh, fuck yeah, I knew you wanted it." Python fist pumped, then slammed his hand on the desk. "We are gonna throw you the best fuckin' party, VP."

"Not what I said." Joker narrowed his dark eyes. "I asked what you needed, but I don't want any fuckin' titles."

"C'mon, you gonna tell me you'll ride with us, but you won't step up as VP?"

"I'm tellin' you I have your back with the Rats. Whatever you need. One time, one deal, no party, no title, no VP."

Now it was Python's turn to be silent and take it all in. Not what Cobra wanted, but it was better than nothing. And they did need all the manpower they could get to tear down the Rats, but why couldn't Joker just jump all in.

Joker finished off his beer, pitched the empty into the metal drum in the corner and turned back, his expression set. Negotiations over. Joker put his deal out there and it was up to Python to nay or yay it.

Python blew out a heavy breath. "All right. We'll do it your way, but I guarantee when this job is over, you're gonna catch the fever again and want back in."

Joker shook his head. "Don't count on it."

Python furrowed his brow, not fully able to figure this man out, but he wouldn't dwell on that now. Too much to do.

"I'll get back to you on the where and when. Probably another few days to put it all in motion," Python said.

"My word is my word." Joker leveled him with an even stare.

Python finished off his beer, the two men fist bumped and the deal was done.

———

The ride back to Vegas ended too fast and just going over the city line filled him with a faraway dread. A cloud hovered along the edges of his mind and grew darker and bleaker as his thoughts drifted to Virginia.

The negotiations with Blade and Joker this afternoon played as a great diversion and kept his mind away from the gnawing pain in his gut. He easily put the club first and loved the art of negotiation, but now his other anxieties came roaring back.

He sped down Flamingo, passing the Mexican restaurant where he and Virginia had lunch and remembered the clean, fresh smell of her hair and the shy, almost timid way she'd interviewed him that first day. He'd been smart in the beginning, holding back and keeping his distance, but then he got stupid and let his dick and his emotions do his thinking. A badass biker who broke heads for an outlaw motorcycle club letting down his guard and feeling stuff he hadn't felt since . . . Zelda. Emotions he hadn't acknowledged for ten years, emotions he had no right feeling. Fuckin' ridiculous.

He swerved into the Chick-Fil-A parking lot for two reasons: he hadn't eaten in two hours, and he was goddamn hungry. Riding and wrapping up a good deal always cranked up his appetite, and if he didn't eat at least every two hours, he got hangry. A real thing his brothers ragged him about all the time.

Plus, he had a soft spot for the hot brunette with the long legs, big tits, and puffy lips working behind the counter on Sunset. He sauntered into the fast food restaurant, and just his luck, there was Monica taking orders for waffle fries and chicken sandwiches.

What the hell a knockout like her was doing at this dump he'd never know. He'd offered her a job at Ecstasy more than once but she said it would go against her Mormon religion. Funny though, the Latter-day Saints gave her the okay for threesomes and some of the wildest sex he'd ever had right out back in the parking lot after closing.

Her eyes found him standing third in line, and as soon as they widened and darkened he knew what she was thinking. Just what he needed to rid himself of his demons. Crispy batter-fried chicken, crunchy waffle fries and hot sex—a winning combination.

One sure way to get over somebody, was to get under somebody.

A few minutes later he was belly up to the counter, and shit if her tongue didn't swipe over those plush lips followed by a huge smile. Python smiled back and waited, but nothing happened. His heart didn't race, his gut didn't tighten, but most frightening of all, his dick remained still and limp in his jeans. What the ever-loving-fuck? Just thinking about what him and Monica could get up to usually had him about to bust, and here she was in real-life, living color and nothing. Scary.

He realized she was talking to him while he lamented about the lack of activity in his jeans, and when she cocked her head and stared, he snapped back to real time.

"You all right, baby?" Even her voice was wet dream material.

"Yeah, yeah. Give me a spicy deluxe and two orders of waffles fries."

She grinned wide and leaned in. "Can't wait to taste your spicy deluxe."

Some kind of a weird grunt escaped his lips, and her brows knitted together.

"You sure you're all right?" she asked him again.

He wiped the sweat beading up on his forehead even though the AC was cranked and spitting out chilled air overhead.

"I get a break in fifteen minutes." She winked and went back to keying in his order. "Maybe I could give you a *hand* with your order."

Yup, she was offering a hand job, maybe even a blowjob. She kept staring at him and he waited for his body to react, but nothing. Fuckin' nothing. He slapped some money down, pushed away from the counter, and got the hell outta there. Monica called after him and the people behind him stared, but all he wanted to do was get on his bike and get gone.

Ten minutes later, he pulled up to the Gold Mine. A cold beer or three, shoot some pool and he'd be fine. Probably didn't get enough sleep last night with all the drama at Ecstasy and then ... Virginia. No, he wasn't gonna go there. They were over, done and that's the way it had to be, the way he wanted it to be. He'd made the move and thrown her out, so why all the weird feelings and second guessing?

He swung through the door of the Serpents' bar and the cool, dark surroundings slowed the erratic thumping of his heart. Python knocked on the bar top, and when he called out for a shot and a beer his breathing eased.

"Hey, how's it goin' brother?" Rattler placed the brew and the shot of Jack in front of him. "You look a little rough."

"Got a lot of shit rolling around in my brain." Two seconds later the Jack slid down Python's throat followed by a healthy gulp of the beer.

"Things go all right out in the desert?" Rattler shot him a wary eye.

"All good." Rattler knew he wouldn't discuss club business right out at the main bar, but wouldn't he be shocked to know Python's edginess had nothing to do with the deal he made with Blade or the threat of the Desert Rats.

No, his amped up nerves had to do with a five-foot-three platinum blonde who had his gut twisting and his heart . . . aching? But it wasn't just that. It was the fear of wanting more, and then the bone-crushing, mind-numbing reality of losing it all, or never having it in the first place.

"Your little blonde reporter looked pretty upset last night." Rattler kept eyes on him as he wiped down the bar. "Looks like you broke another heart."

Python smirked 'cause that's what Rattler expected. Let him think what he wanted. *Keep it simple, stupid* had been his motto since the bad old days. If you didn't have anything, you didn't have anything to lose.

Python rapped his knuckles on the wood bar, and Rattler set up another shot. Fuck, all this deep thinking would kill him.

CHAPTER FIFTEEN

Virginia tried to talk herself out of the depression surrounding her after Python literally threw her out by keeping in mind that they'd only known each other for two weeks. He'd never made any promises and wasn't a man to plan a future with, but when all logical thinking failed, she reverted to the remedy that always worked. Writing.

When the idea came to Virginia at two in the morning, she'd dismissed it as ridiculous, but the more she mulled it over, the more doable it sounded. Yesterday, when she proposed her idea to her editor, Mr. Larsen, he made it clear he wanted a story with "teeth and guts." A rather vivid analogy, but Virginia got the picture. She'd come up with an exposé with much more than a look into the workings of a gentlemen's club. She'd dig deeper and reveal the grittier side of Vegas, the side never seen by the tourist from Nebraska.

From the first night at Ecstasy, she envisioned a behind-the-scenes account about the dancers and what better and what better way to get the real story than to go undercover this Saturday night.

Her phone buzzed and for once seeing her mother's name encouraged her.

"Hi, Mom." Maybe this new relationship her mother wanted to forge would include listening and helping her with her problems.

"Hi, dear, just calling to confirm this weekend."

"Great. I thought I'd come on Sunday, and I took a personal day on Monday so we can spent two days together."

"Oh, I assumed you'd be coming on Saturday," her mother said.

"No, I have a work thing Saturday." She'd keep the undercover work at a seedy strip club for when she and her mother were on sturdier ground.

"Can you change it?"

"Not really."

"I see." Her mother sighed. "I really wish you had told me this."

"What's the difference?" It wasn't like her mother had a job or had to worry about timeframes. For her, every day was Saturday.

"You know Bonnie, my tennis partner, well, she sprained her ankle and won't be able to play in the Orange Grove tournament on Saturday, and I was hoping that—"

"You were hoping that I could play?" A heavy rock settled in Virginia's stomach.

"Yes, of course."

"And all that talk about the past and sailing was just—"

"Oh, Virginia, please, let's not get dramatic. You're an Open level player with a Division One ranking. With you as my partner, I'm sure to win and—"

A perverse thrill shot through Virginia's body, a liberating release to stop wishing for a relationship with her mother that would never happen. The need to yell at her mother's self-centeredness dissolved, leaving her unusually calm.

"Sorry, Mom, Saturday just doesn't work for me."

Her mother harrumphed. "I should've known you'd disappoint me."

"Goodbye, Mom." I should've known too.

———

"Are you sure this is going to work? Nicole asked for the third time.

No, she wasn't sure it would work. In the past week she wasn't sure of anything, least of all her feelings. The pit in her stomach Python left, and the emotional rollercoaster with her mother. Time to stop thinking about the past and move on.

"How about this?" Nicole's voice jogged her out of her musings. Her friend had come through for her this last week by bringing her brownies and her favorite chocolate chip ice cream from Baskin-Robbins. Nicole might've sat and listened to her bemoan her life, but the frayed uber-short denim skirt she held up was a definite no.

"You're missing the whole point." Virginia wrestled clothes out of her closet and laid them on her bed. "I'm going for the sexy librarian look not an all-out hoochie stripper."

After all, hadn't both Rattler and the bouncer at Ecstasy mistaken her for an exotic dancer. A woman alone going into a strip club had to be a stripper, right? Sadly, some stereotypes were still very much alive and well.

Nicole held up a gold lamé halter she'd brought over. "So, not this then?"

"Definitely not that."

With the help of the station's new database and the photo she'd taken at the carnival for the Forgotten Kids, Virginia found out the identity of Python's mysterious enemy. His alias's included "Harry Smith" or "Harry Jones," not very imaginative, but to the gamblers who owed him money, he was "Harry Houdini." He was a vicious bookie who used the Desert Rats MC as muscle and who thought nothing of breaking body parts and using threats and intimidation. The last tactic Virginia experienced firsthand from Demon.

"I have to admit, you do have a sexy vibe going on. I think guys would really go for it."

Virginia laughed. "I'm not performing, I just want to get into the club without standing out."

"At the station you'd definitely get looks, but at a strip club?" Nicole stepped back, appraising her with the critical eye of a runway designer. "Who would think one of your plain button-up shirts and black skirts had so many possibilities."

"Especially when you only button my blouse halfway, add a black bra that pushes my breasts up to Montana, and roll my skirt till it barely covers my ass."

"Yup, this might just work." Nicole dipped into the large tote she'd brought to Virginia's apartment. "But you have to wear these."

Virginia's eyes widened at the four, no, five-inch red stilettos. Nicole held one in each hand and offered them out to her like they were the answer to world peace.

"I don't know." Virginia's mind flashed to her clumsiness and then specifically to slamming her head into Python's doorjamb because of high heels. And those shoes were nowhere near the height of these instruments of torture Nicole displayed. Although, to be fair, her act of graceless bungling had more to do with Python's body splayed out like a Roman emperor.

"What were you planning on wearing?" Nicole jerked her thumb to the line of flats and sneakers lining Virginia's closet. "Those?" She made a condemning face and Virginia wanted to defend her shoes.

"You know—"

"No discussion, no argument. You're wearing these and that's final." She shoved the red objects designed for bodily harm into her hands. "Put them on."

Virginia huffed out a sigh, sat on the bed and did as she was told. "You know, you're very bossy."

"It's the Aries in me, I can't help it. Plus, I'm always right."

Just her luck that she and Nicole wore the same size seven, so she couldn't claim they didn't fit. Virginia slipped them on and carefully pushed herself off the bed. She reasoned if things went drastically wrong, the bed would cushion her fall.

"That's what I'm talking about." Nicole clapped her hands. "You look great and so freaking sexy."

Virginia cautiously made her way over the carpet to the full-length mirror hanging on the back of her closet door. Nicole was right, she did look good.

"Not too bad." Virginia turned sideways, checked out her butt which the shortness of her skirt totally flattered. "Although I have to admit it's a bit scary up here. I don't think I like being this far off the ground."

Nicole laughed as Virginia checked out how the black bra peeking out of her half-buttoned white shirt made her look busty. She'd bought the bra last month for a dress she never wore because her date stood her up. Yup, her dating life sucked. She'd shoved the never-worn bra into the back of her drawer, but she'd have to reassess that decision.

"We're not done yet." Nicole motioned to the chair in front of her small vanity table. "Sit down and let me get your hair and makeup to match that bangin' outfit.

A half hour later Virginia's hair was a bit poofy, but full and flowing, and she sported smokey eyes and pouty lips. The face reflecting back at her differed drastically from her usual look, but Virginia had to admit that she liked it, and unexplainably, it made her feel somewhat powerful.

"The last time I did all this you never left your apartment," Nicole groused.

True. The biker party that never happened because once she and Python laid eyes on each other neither could be responsible for their actions. She'd planned on breaking it off with him that night, but instead they fell into bed.

She'd been enraptured by multiple orgasms before she tried to figure out a man whose mysterious ways confounded her. Python was a paradox of someone who hurt people physically for his club, yet treated his dog with love and devotion and cared whether the homeless people who lived in the drainage tunnels had enough to eat. He was a man who helped people he barely knew, yet kept himself closed off emotionally to the point of alienation.

Nicole met her eyes in the mirror as she readjusted one of Virginia's curls. "I know you miss him, but you'll bounce back." She waved her hand over Virginia's outfit. "Who knows, tonight might be the beginning of a new career."

Virginia laughed, stood up a bit wobbly, and encircled Nicole in a bear hug. "You're such a good friend."

"Just please be careful," Nicole said.

Virginia walked toward the bedroom door. "They're really not that hard to walk in with the huge platform in the front."

"I wasn't talking about the shoes." Nicole hit her with the evil eye. "I wish you'd let me go with you."

"I'll be fine. And that would defeat the purpose. I'm trying to blend in so I can seek out some information."

"Are you saying I can't get my stripper on?" Nicole did a bump and grind against Virginia's dresser.

Virginia flicked her hand at Nicole's very voluptuous figure. "With your figure, you'd be in high demand."

"Be safe, call me if you need backup, and—"

"I'm going to a strip club, not into battle."

"That area can be sketchy and—"

Virginia silenced her with a look. "You're so cute when you go all mama bear."

———

The Serpents filed into the back room of the Gold Mine, eagerly awaiting Python's report and anxious to know how their enemy would fall. Python filled them in on his meeting with Blade, the Rats' prospect, and Joker's willingness to ride with them but not take the VP position. He ended with Crystal's overdose, then waited for Cobra to react.

"Just as I suspected." Cobra leaned into the table. "Demon doesn't have the loyalty of his patched members or his prospects, but pushing junk in the club goes way over the line."

"According to this guy, Blade, he's doin' some fucked up shit," Python added. "I gave him twenty-four hours to organize his guys, then we move."

"I say we drive our point home," Cobra said. "Forget their clubhouse and start at the Shangri-La. Get up in there and do some damage. Let them know it wasn't a good idea to move in on us in the desert."

"We'd be doin' the community a favor," Rattler said.

"I say we move quick," Boa added. "Don't give those fuckers a chance to catch their breath."

"Fuck, yeah. Hit 'em hard, hit 'em fast." Rattler and Boa tapped fists.

"A few of the Rats' prospects and even a patched member already contacted me," Python said. "We're keeping everything quiet for now, but won't that be a pretty sight when we hit Demon with his own guys?"

"Just what he deserves after torching our weed house and trying to push drugs at Ecstasy," Cobra said.

Boa slammed his palm on the scarred wooden table. "Fuckin' guy will lose his shit."

"What do you say, brother?" Cobra turned to Python.

"We'll wait to see if we hear from more of the Rats jumping ship, then we move in."

Grunts and nods filled the room, then Cobra slammed down the gavel. Rattler, Boa, and the others patted Python on the back or tapped fists as they left, signifying a job well done.

Cobra jerked his chin at him and Python stayed back. Then his president slowly extracted a Marlboro from his hard pack, stuck it between his lips and lit up. He leaned his hip against the table and blew smoke toward the ceiling. Fucker sure knew how to build suspense.

"I'm disappointed Joker won't be coming on as VP." Cobra sucked in another drag.

Python shrugged his answer. He'd just explained all that about five minutes ago, so why the drama now. "I guess Daisy being knocked up has him a little rattled, but he'll come through. He's true to his word."

"Fact. He's a tough fucker and it's hard when you got other people to think about."

Anybody else listening in would've thought Cobra was talking about his ol' lady, Sheena, but Python heard the subtle lilt in his voice. They'd gone through too much together for him to miss the signs. Cobra was fishing, but he didn't have the right bait, 'cause Python wasn't biting.

The two men held each other's gaze, but Python stayed quiet.

"You seemed distracted tonight." Cobra tried another tact.

"No more than usual."

"Glad it all worked out with Crystal the other night." Cobra ashed his cigarette.

"I told her I'd help her, but until she gets clean, she's out."

Cobra nodded but kept staring. "You missed a good party at the Gold Mine the other night."

Geez, fuck, was Cobra dragging this out just to torture him? "Why don't you cut the bullshit and just ask me what you wanna ask me."

Cobra laughed right in his face. "All right, what's going on with you and the reporter?"

"Nothing."

"Bullshit," Cobra fired back. "Rattler saw you leave with her after the carnival. He said you didn't go back to your apartment, and then when I called, it sounded like you'd been fuckin' your brains out all night."

"Since when does Rattler tag my ass, and when you called me, it was four in the morning, so yeah, I was a little beat."

"Nah, nah, I've seen you up for over twenty-four hours straight. There's a big difference between tired and fuckin' tired." Cobra, the pain in the ass, smirked at him like he knew all the answers. "So why don't you just come clean and admit it so I can tell you what a mistake you're making and how she's all wrong for you."

"Sorry, beat you to it. As of last night, we're done—over." Saying the words was like driving a hot poker through his gut. "Rattler must've left out the part where he took her home after I threw her out."

"It's for the best. She don't know what you're about. She lives a straight life." Cobra slapped him on the back. "Let's have a beer."

"Can't." Python turned and left the backroom before the nosy fucker had a chance to ask any more questions 'cause where he was going and what he was doin' was his own damn business.

CHAPTER SIXTEEN

All Virginia's tough talk and independent attitude wavered a bit as she pulled into the parking lot littered with potholes next to the Shangri-La. She silenced her phone so there would be no interruptions, then exited her car and double chirped her locks just to make sure. Last time she'd had Brian from the station with her, but going it alone was a whole different thing. Virginia chose the back entrance, assuming all strip clubs had the same policy about dancers entering the rear door. She maneuvered her way over broken bottles that apparently missed the dumpster and discarded—condoms. The pungent stink of rotten food, garbage, and urine stung the back of her throat.

She passed a shadowy couple, but kept her eyes straight ahead. She didn't need to see or imagine what they were doing, but it didn't stop the vision of her and Python inside the ladies room of this very club and what they almost got up to.

She drew herself up to her frightening new height and approached the rear door with manufactured confidence. She would go in and get the information she needed to complete her story and make it newsworthy. Squeezing her eyes shut, she repeated her mantra, "You can do this."

The four words gave her a slight boost but did absolutely nothing for the hammering in her chest. To her surprise, there was no one manning the door. She entered and the pounding beat of heavy metal music joined the thudding of her heart, producing a conga line in her chest.

A few feet down the dim, narrow hallway, she encountered a huge bear of a man whom she would've expected to see outside the door.

He blatantly eyed her, then grunted. "You the new one?"

"Yes." Apparently, strip clubs and exotic dancers used the revolving door theory of employment.

He grunted again, then jerked his head toward the door to his side.

She entered a small, overly crowded, dank, depressing room with exposed pipes on the ceiling, a stained and cracked concrete floor, and an overpowering combination of every sickly, sweet perfume on the market.

Much, much different than the dressing room at Ecstasy. Most of these women were young, almost too young to be of legal age. Many of them also spoke in their native tongue and seemed to congregate together.

Her reporter's mind put her in such deep observation that she startled when someone tapped her on the shoulder.

"You new?" A rail thin brunette asked, then motioned to the end of a long, narrow dressing table running along one wall. "There's room at the end."

"Thank you."

The girl teetered off in shoes even higher than hers, and Virginia made her way through the bustling room. She settled into a wooden chair missing its back slats, and busied herself with her hair. She'd get a feel for the room and then try to insinuate herself into a conversation.

Virginia silently berated herself for not taking her language classes more seriously because she noticed quite a few of the women were speaking Spanish. The closeness of their space made it impossible not to notice each other. She smiled into the mirror at the girl to her right and was met with a scowl.

Okay, maybe fitting in would be harder than she thought. On the upside, the club was open until four in the morning and it was only midnight. On the downside, someone might *out* her as an impostor, and she'd be forced to prove herself by going on stage—*not!*

On Nicole's insistence, Virginia brought a large tote bag with makeup, hair brushes, and a curling iron. Virginia had no intention of using them, since Nicole had done such a great job, but it was more to blend in.

While she faked fixing her hair, the reflection of a naked abdomen appeared behind her. She swiveled in her chair and gazed up at a ridiculously tall woman with familiar tits. Yup, it was Miss Tits from her brief encounter on the wild side with Python in the bathroom of this exclusive establishment. Perfect. Although, her glaring sneer was not encouraging.

"Are you new?" Her hands on her bare hips radiated intimidation. And those tits were still unbelievable.

"Yes." Maybe this could work in her favor. And yes, once again, Virginia was face to tit with this woman.

"What the hell kinda outfit is that?" A tinge of ridicule laced her voice. An amazing feat for someone in only a g-string.

"A seductive librarian. You know, subtle and all buttoned up during the day, and a wildcat at night." Pretty much described her with Python.

She jerked her thumb toward the door. "These assholes

aren't into subtle. They like it all out front and in their face."
For emphasis, she lifted her breasts and squeezed them
together. Quite impressive.

"I'm going for a different look." Virginia ventured. Deep
down she wished she had the confidence to strut around half
naked like this woman.

"You'll never make any money, and don't think for one
minute you're taking any of my regulars."

"Wouldn't think of it. I obviously don't have your—
assets." Virginia lowered her eyes playing the sympathy card.

"You look familiar." Miss Tits shifted her hips yet
remained steady on the stilettos. Admirable.

"I was here last week." Okay, now she'd gamble a bit.
"With a friend of yours, Python?"

She twisted her lips into a sneer. Then pointed her hot
pink talons at Virginia. "Right, you two were getting it on in
the john."

"Not exactly, I don't even know him that well."

Miss Tits furrowed her dramatically drawn eyebrows.
"Yeah, right." She narrowed her eyes again. "Then why were
you here?"

"I came to interview for the job." That sounded logical.

"Interview?" Miss Tits scoffed. "You mean you sucked
Demon's dick. That's the only job requirement in this
dump."

Virginia's jaw tightened at the thought of putting anything
of Demon's in her mouth. *Stay on track.*

"I don't know what your game is"—she leaned in, her bare
breasts swayed at the sudden movement—"but don't think
you're gonna take any business away from me." She spun
around, cocked her hip, and strutted away.

"Python was in the ladies room looking for you that
night." Virginia shouted over the din in the dressing room.
"From the way he was looking at you, I'll bet you two ended

up together." Virginia really didn't want the answer, but if it worked—

———

Python pulled up to the two-story building surrounded by green grass, shrubbery, and trees. A weird sight out in the middle of the Nevada desert. He parked in his usual spot, then walked past an olympic-sized pool surrounded by palm trees and more tropical gardens.

Inside, he nodded to a few of the girls lounging on over-stuffed couches and chairs that lined the bar and reception area. He traveled over the plush carpeted hallway and pushed through the door that read: Male Employees. Inside was a large bathroom area with showers on one side and a row of lockers on the other. Python punched in his code, opened the locker, and hung his cut on the hanger; then he stripped off his t-shirt and put on the clean shirt folded in the bottom of the locker that read: Security. He returned to the main room, smirked at some of the guys eyeballing the women working tonight, then climbed the single flight of stairs. He took his post halfway down the hall where he could see the entire second floor.

"How're you doin' tonight, sweetie?" Honey said, as she swayed her bangin' body in her stripper heels past him.

Python chuckled to himself. The short, skinny guy trailing behind her flashed him a nervous smile as if he were going to his execution rather than having sex for money.

Running security at Cotton Candy's Brothel and Spa wasn't the best gig in the world, but it sure did give him a laugh on a regular basis. Thanks to a former dancer at Ecstasy, he raked in five thousand a week for two nights' work. In another week he'd have half what he owed Harry, which should get the bastard off his back for a while.

Candy came out of one of the other rooms and strolled over to him. "Hey sugar, we'll need you in the basement in about an hour." Then she hit him with a killer smile and surveyed the first floor for a minute before taking the stairs.

No need to say anything else, Python knew why he was hired. Just like the old days—muscle. The one thing he could always count on. Candy and her brother owned Cotton Candy, and aside from premium sex, happy-ending massages, and erotic spa treatments, they dealt in guns coming up through Arizona from Mexico. They were close enough to the border to make their basement one hell of a storage and drop-off point before the assortment of artillery made their way to other parts of the country.

Python oversaw the deliveries and the exchanges, making sure nobody got greedy. Most of the guns were delivered by low-level gang members out of SoCal, and since Python never wore his colors, there was no tie-in to the Serpents.

Going on his third week and so far all went smooth. The hardest part was sneaking away from the Serpents, namely Cobra. He could be a nosy son of a bitch, plus he'd hate what Python was doing, but there was no way he'd take money from the club to pay off his debt or let Cobra bail him out again. He might be a sinful biker and a shit-poor gambler, but he wasn't a moocher.

———

Miss Tits spun around. "Hmmm ... I wish Python was looking for me. He was in some tight meeting with that asshole, Demon."

"You know these guys, the club always comes first." Thank God for research. "Fucking annoying." And Virginia's short stint in college theater.

The top-heavy bombshell closed the distance between

them and slid over a rickety stool. "Newbies sit here. You gotta work your way up for a seat at the mirror."

Virginia quickly shuffled onto the stool, letting the other woman feel superior. Amazing, even strip clubs had a hierarchy.

"I'm Virginia," she offered.

"'Virgin Virginia,' could be your stage name, especially with that look."

Great, now she had a stripper name. Her mind wandered to those weird Facebook tests that found your inner stripper.

"I go by 'Kitti Kat.' Kitti with an *i*." She motioned to her cheetah g-string. "Fuckin' cheesy I know, but these assholes dig it."

Virginia couldn't help the smile when Kitti referred to the customers as assholes again. This woman's experiences were probably a story in itself.

"My real name is Madeline." Her voice softened a bit.

"Hi, Madeline." Virginia offered her hand and a beat later they shook.

Madeline reached out and touched Virginia's hair. "Nice. Are those extensions."

"No, it's my hair." Virginia's non-existent beauty routine barely squeaked in at the low-maintenance level.

Madeline's eyes widened. "Amazing."

Virginia took it as a compliment.

"You oughta think about getting your boobs done, though." Madeline shoved hers up again. "Best investment I ever made. These guys say they like ass, but the boobs are the moneymakers." She flailed out her arm around the room. "You ask any of these bitches and they'll tell you," she shouted, "it's the boobs that get you to the bank, right, ladies?"

The other women hooted and hollered and fist bumped and hip checked one another while shaking their own assets.

Madeline picked up a pack of cigarettes off the dressing table, lit up and then offered one to Virginia.

"No, thanks."

Madeline dragged deep, surveying her through the smoke. "Something about you don't fit with this dump." She dragged in more smoke. "You're not a cop or something?"

"Oh, no," Virginia assured her. "Just trying to supplement my income."

"Aren't we all. But why here?"

"I guess I could ask you the same question. You obviously know the ropes, and have a following, so why wouldn't you work at some of the bigger, glitzier clubs like Hustler or ... Ecstasy?"

Virginia tried to make throwing in Ecstasy sound random.

"Funny you picked Ecstasy. Owned by the Serpents, run by Python."

"I just know it's one of the top clubs, and with your experience, I thought—"

"Too many fuckin' rules." Madeline leaned in. "I'm not a druggie, but I like a bump sometimes or a hit off the pipe. Who doesn't, right? But at Ecstasy, it's a ticket to the unemployment line. Plus, they take a higher percentage off the top. They gotta pay for the fancy shit in the club and all that security. In this place, they don't care what you do as long as the place is packed and you're sober enough to shake your ass on stage."

"Interesting." Virginia forced herself to hold back the barrage questions flooding her brain.

"And there's a lot of other ways to make money in the private rooms here, but Ecstasy is against that too. My body, my choice. I mean, if I wanna fuck some guy for money, I should be able to call the shots, right?"

"Absolutely." Wow. No matter what her relationship with

Python, she had to admire him and the Serpents for running a legitimate club.

"But you gotta be careful. Just last week, there was a shooting in the parking lot out back. Crazy fuckers with gang shit arguing over some bitch. Fuckin' and money, that's all these assholes care about."

"I appreciate you telling me all this." Virginia had no problem playing the lost lamb, especially since Madeline seemed to enjoy playing big sister.

A curvy woman with waist-length curly red hair grabbed for the pack of cigarettes on the table, and Madeline threw up her arm. "Buy your own damn smokes."

The redhead glared at Madeline and huffed. "Stingy bitch."

Madeline laughed. "You got that right. I work hard for my money, baby."

The redhead turned her kohl-lined eyes to Virginia, then jerked her thumb at Madeline. "She might be a tight-assed ho, but she likes to take the new girls under her wing. She's a real mother."

An olive-skinned girl with huge brown eyes leaned back in her chair. "A real motherfucker."

"Talk all the shit you want," Madeline lifted out of the seat and wiggled her butt. "You know you love my sweet ass."

"We sure do, baby. Now give me a damn cigarette." The redhead nabbed the pack, plucked one out, and lit up. "We like to rag on this slut, but we love her."

Madeline waved them away, laughing. "Go back to your sorry-ass lives and let me school this poor girl."

She turned back to Virginia. "They're just playing. There's a few of these bitches you gotta watch out for, but those girls are cool."

"Thanks for helping me out."

"Life sucks most of the time." She took one last drag and

crushed the cigarette in the plastic ashtray. "I'm here for the money. I got three mouths to feed and their deadbeat daddies ain't nowhere to be found."

It always amazed Virginia the things people would tell her if she just stayed quiet and listened. In her short time as a reporter, she'd had people reveal their darkest, deepest secrets with little provocation. Sadly, most people just wanted a sounding board and someone to listen.

"That's tough." Virginia sincerely meant that, but she had to ask. "So, the father's don't help you out at all."

"Hell, no. Two of my baby daddies are up in Ely State Pen, and the other one split the minute I told him I was knocked up. Assholes, all of them."

This shed new light on why Madeline frequently referred to men as assholes.

"That's why I got a soft spot for Python. He looks rough and all, but he's really a good guy. He helped a friend of mine a couple of months ago. She had this asshole boyfriend who was always taking her cash and beating the shit outta her. Python stepped in." She smirked. "Haven't seen that fucker since."

That revelation was both enlightening and frightening, but the underlying subject rang true. Although he tried to deny it, Python had a big heart and a sense of justice. Street justice.

"I've tried to get with him a few times. That snake tattoo and that tongue piercing." She fanned herself. "I get wet just thinking about it."

Yup, Python's snake tattoo was epic, and Virginia vividly remembered his talented tongue, but thinking about that now caused a deep, painful ache.

Madeline shrugged. "But, so far no luck."

Madeline turned out completely different than Virginia originally had thought. She might've been rough around the edges and made some bad choices, but she was trying to support three children the best way she knew.

"I suppose you know why they call him Python." Madeline grinned.

"He's a member of the Las Vegas Serpents."

"Let me tell you, that's not why. I've heard his dick is huge —like off the charts. There was this one girl who used to work here, and she said she couldn't even suck him off he was so big, and let me tell you, this bitch is queen of the blowjobs. I mean, she could suck a drainpipe, and yet he was too much for her."

"Hmmm." Madeline's graphic description sent a fire through Virginia's veins. She vividly remembered every inch of Python and, yes, giving him a blowjob was a challenge she'd met head on. *Really* head-on. When would her brain take a vacation?

"He's been with a lot of girls I know."

No surprise there. The first night Virginia met him, he had two women in his bed, but she had to let Madeline talk and try not to be too inquisitive. This woman was way too street smart to be fooled by obvious questions.

"But he's never an asshole. He's not into settling down, but he don't make any promises either."

Virginia couldn't decipher that information; she had to stay on track.

"I understand a guy named Harry owns this place." Virginia held her breath, waiting to see what Madeline's reaction would be.

"Demon and the Desert Rats own it." Her face flattened out and closed off. "I don't know any Harry."

"Oh, good"—all right, she'd go a different way—"because I knew someone once who owed him some money, and it didn't end well."

"A lot of bullshit goes around."

"Just as well, must be hard enough having to deal with Demon."

Madeline mashed her pouty lips together. "It's not gossip." She cut a look over her shoulder and then leaned into Virginia. "Harry's a *first-class* asshole."

CHAPTER SEVENTEEN

An hour later, Python left his post on the second floor and headed for the basement, more like warehouse for every firearm known to man. The space spanned the entire length of the upper floor and was set up with boxes on pallets, each aisle labeled.

Just before he got to the loading dock, his phone buzzed. He didn't have the luxury of ignoring phone calls, so he fished the cell out of his pocket and frowned at the unknown number.

"Yeah." Python leaned against one of the pallets.

"Just calling to see how close you are to settling your debt."

Python's back stiffened at the sound of Demon's voice, then a dull ache radiated through his skull. "I deal with Harry, not you."

"Right, but here's the thing, Harry don't wanna deal with you anymore. He's getting impatient, and he's afraid he might lose his temper. That's why he's putting me on it, 'cause I don't give a fuck. I like losing my shit."

The sick bastard kept his voice conversational as if they were discussing the point spread on next week's game.

"I'll have half the money by the beginning of next week."

"Not good enough." Demon blew out a long, dramatic sigh. "If you weren't such a stubborn motherfucker, this could all be settled."

Python's jaw clenched and he ground his teeth, wishing the prick was in front of him so he could shove his fist in his face.

"You say you got half," Demon continued, "so, let the Rats settle the other half, and you get the Serpents to let us come into Nevada and run our business."

Business. Doped up underage girls forced into prostitution when they weren't cooking meth out in the desert.

"Go fuck yourself. The Serpents aren't letting that fly in our territory."

"Why you gotta make things so fuckin' hard?" Another pause. "You know how easy it is to get these girls to do what we want? Give them a taste of the good stuff and soon they're begging for it, willing to do whatever we say."

"I know how it works," Python ground out. Half of them never made it out alive. He'd done some shitty things in his life, but he'd never hurt a woman.

"Right, so I'm guessing you wouldn't wanna see that sweet reporter of yours all strung out and sucking off every Rat in the club just to get some juice."

Python's breath caught and he cursed himself for the tell. "What the fuck are you talking about?"

"That little blonde bitch would look so sweet on her knees, her arms locked around my thighs as she sucks my dick. I could split her in two."

"You leave her outta this, you cocksucker."

"Too late. Already paid her a visit."

Python's heart jackhammered against his ribcage. "What?"

"Went right to her apartment, and guess what, she let me in."

Python tried to school his reaction, but a cold prickle of sweat bathed his neck.

"Told her if things didn't go right with you, I'd come back. Hmmm, sure am looking forward to that."

"You leave her the fuck alone or I'll—"

"You'll what?" Demon challenged. "You don't have the money you owe, and you won't let the Rats do business. You got nothing." He barked out a laugh. "I'll bet her snatch is tight too."

"Hey, Python," Joe called out from the loading dock. "Shipments here."

Python growled into the phone. "I swear to fuck, you put hands on her and I'll make you wish you were dead."

"You gotta catch me first."

"I'll get you the money by tomorrow, just keep her outta this."

"Tick tock, motherfucker."

The dead air of the disconnected phone filled Python's ear until Joe yelled for him again.

"I'm coming." Python stalked between the boxes as he swiped at Virginia's number. When it went straight to voicemail, his thumbs flew over the screen as he sent her a text.

Virginia: Call me now.

This was bad. Demon went to see Virginia, but she never said anything. Maybe he was just bullshitting, trying to get at him. Fuck, he didn't know what to think.

He hit the loading dock just as three Escalades pulled up. One of the gangbangers walked up the ramp with a backpack dangling from his fingertips while his underlings unloaded the SUVs. He hoisted the bag onto a nearby table, and Python unzipped it and examined the contents: neatly wrapped packs of hundreds, equaling one-hundred thousand dollars.

Storing a shitload of guns out of sight and off the grid wasn't cheap. Python slowly fanned through each stack because his first night on the job they tried to do the old switch. Hundreds on the outside with tens stuffed in the middle. He'd gotten some exercise that night. Candy and her brother were impressed, and those sorry fuckers never tried that again.

When Python was satisfied, he zipped up the bag. The others were just about done unloading, so the leader flipped him a two-finger salute and hopped back into one of the Escalades.

Joe pushed a button on the wall panel, and the heavy door slid back down. His job was to guard the merchandise, nothing more. Python slung the bag over his shoulder, whipped out his phone, and swiped Virginia's number.

"Fuck," he mumbled when it went to voicemail again. Where the hell was she, and why wasn't she picking up her damn phone? He checked his texts and nothing there either.

He stomped up the stairs, turned away from the main rooms and headed down the side hallway to the office. He swiped the keycard they'd given him, releasing the lock and letting him into a small room with a chrome and glass desk, leather chair, more plush carpet, and a safe against the back wall.

He punched in the combination, unzipped the bag, then stared at those neatly wrapped stacks. Just three of them would get Python outta the shithole he'd dug for himself and keep Virginia safe. He could just stuff them in his shirt and walk right out. His fingers twitched to feel that cold, hard cash. So fuckin' easy. What was the big deal? He'd done worse.

Virginia concentrated on keeping her face impassive. "So you've heard of Harry?"

"You're not involved with him, are you?"

"No, no. Just some things I've overheard."

Madeline wrapped a silk robe around herself, then turned her chair with her back to the rest of the room. "Last week, I was in Demon's office . . . taking care of some business." She rolled her eyes. "Anyway, he was on the phone with Harry, and Python's name came up. That asshole, Demon, talks in front of me like I'm a piece of furniture, but sometimes it pays off. Something about bad shit happens to people who owe him money. When I tried to get Python alone the other night to warn him, he blew me off and then left before my set was over."

"Do you think he's in real danger?" Virginia's heart picked up speed.

"Python's one of the good guys. I mean, he's a *bad guy outlaw*, but he's not like Demon. I've heard some fucked up stories about the shit Harry has Demon do to people who don't pay up. I'd just hate to see something happen to Python, you know?"

Yes, Virginia did know and that's what made trying to forget about him so hard. Impossible and heart wrenching.

When Madeline left the dressing room to do her set, Virginia contemplated trying to chat up some of the other girls, but Madeline's revelation about Python's situation gnawed at her.

Yes, he'd basically thrown her out without explanation, and yes, he was a giant of an outlaw who was no stranger to violence or taking care of himself, but if something happened and she hadn't at least warned him, she'd never get over the guilt.

She hauled her large tote bag over her shoulder and headed out to her car. She'd call him from there and at least warn him. Leaving the Shangri-La was just as uneventful as arriving. A loose set of rules applied to the entire club, and apparently, the dancers could come and go as they pleased.

A loose set of rules also applied to the upkeep and outside area, and again, Virginia stepped cautiously over the cracked pavement and random garbage strewn over the area.

Car keys in hand, she chirped the locks, then flinched at a noise behind her. She whipped around but the dim lighting cast yellow shadows over the overflowing dumpsters. Virginia picked up her pace as she rounded the building, her eye on her car in the lot. The sensation of another presence or being followed clawed at her. She walked a few more steps, then spun around again. Something jumped out of the shadows, and she squeaked out a yelp as a scrawny alley cat jumped from the top of the dumpster.

The debilitating adrenaline jogging through her veins sapped her strength. Her core sagged and she chastised herself for her cowardly ridiculousness.

She drew in a cleansing breath and walked across the lot to her car. After settling into the driver's seat, she locked the doors, and her eye caught a post-it note stuck to the dashboard. She peeled it off and gasped.

Tick, tock, pretty lady. Time for another visit.

Virginia swiveled her head in all directions, then realized whoever left this was long gone. She shoved the key into the ignition, gripped the gear shift to quell her trembling fingers and slammed the car into reverse, then backed out and sped away from the Shangri-La. Her eyes darted from the road in front of her to the rearview mirror, convinced someone would be following her. By the second traffic light she willed herself to calm down.

Virginia dug her hand into her purse for her phone. She'd

forgotten she silenced it before entering the Shangri-La, and as soon as she turned it on, it dinged and chimed with missed calls and texts—all from Python.

————

Python stared at those neat stacks of hundreds, then yanked the zipper up and threw the bag into the safe, slamming the door before he made another shit poor decision.

One of the reasons Candy paid him so well was because he was an outlaw, knew how to handle himself, and could be trusted. The last thing he needed was Candy on his ass. She was all down-home charm, slopping sweetness all over, but he'd seen the southern belle lose her shit a few times. She was the type who'd blow your brains out and wrap your body in a lace tablecloth. Fuckin' scary.

Out in the hallway, he checked his phone again and called Rattler to fill him in on his conversation with Demon, then told him to go over to Virginia's apartment and stay with her till he got there. It made him feel a little better, but not much, because if something happened to Virginia he'd … Ahh, fuck, he was screwed.

An agonizing hour later, after subduing a fight between two guys, one who didn't know his boyfriend was also into girls, Python's shift finally ended.

Rattler got back to him earlier saying Virginia wasn't at her apartment, which only amped Python up more. On his way out to his bike, he tried her again.

"Python?" Shit, she sounded breathless and scared.

"Are you all right? I've been calling and texting you all night."

"I'm fine, but—"

"Are you home?" Python straddled his bike.

"No, I went to the Shangri-La and—"

"What the fuck are you doing there?" He yelled into the phone.

"I wanted to get an interview with the girls, and then when I left in my car ..." Her voice shook and shattered. Damn, he shouldn't have yelled, but hell, he'd never been this scared in his life.

"Get outta there now. Go to Ecstasy. Cobra and Rattler will meet you in the lot. Don't get outta your car until you see them, understand?"

"Where are you?" Her whispery voice sounded so small and scared.

"I'm on my way." He revved the throttle. "Just do as I say and go to Ecstasy."

He made a quick call to Cobra, then peeled out of the parking lot and pushed the Harley past all limits.

CHAPTER EIGHTEEN

Python carved the forty-minute ride back to Vegas down to twenty-five, but it still seemed to take forever. At exactly four a.m., he zoomed into the empty parking lot, backed into his space and practically jumped off the bike.

He barged through the back door, and the cavernous room echoed with the sound of ice hitting a glass. Python scanned the empty room till his eyes rested on Virginia sitting at the main bar with Cobra alongside her and Rattler bartending. He released a long-held breath, then slowed his pace and joined them.

Rattler reached over the bar, shoving a whiskey glass with two fingers of Jack into his hand. Python finished it in one, then focused on Virginia.

"Are you all right?" Dumb question. Her pale face told him the answer. He wanted to drag her into his arms and never let go.

Her head jerked several times, and then she swallowed hard.

"I made her one of my specialities." Rattler held up a

shaker and Python zoomed in on the Patrón, Cointreaú, and lime juice.

Python shot a look between the two men, then jerked his head to the back of the room.

They formed a tight circle as Cobra rubbed at the scruff on his jaw. "Something's got her shook but she wouldn't tell us what it is."

"Demon called me tonight. He's been threatening her." He flashed a look at Virginia. "Trying to get at me through her."

"Fuck!" Rattler slammed his hand against the wall.

Cobra growled. "Tomorrow night we end him and that shithole strip joint."

Cobra cocked his head. "Where were you tonight?"

When Python didn't answer, Rattler chimed in. "Where you bangin' that chick who lives out in the desert?"

"Fuck, no. I was at Candy's."

Both men furrow their brow, then Cobra said, "What the hell are you dragging your ass out there when we got free pussy at the Gold Mine?"

"I wasn't fucking, I was working. Security."

Cobra and Rattler exchanged a look. "Give us a minute," Cobra said to Rattler.

"I'm gonna head out." Rattler slapped Python on the back. "Stay cool, man."

"You know they run guns outta the basement of that place," Cobra said after Rattler left.

"Why do you think Candy and her brother hired me? Tiffany hooked me up with the job. They've had some trouble with money and guns disappearing, so they pay me five grand a week for two nights' work. I check in the shipments, make sure the payoff is right, glare at them with my mean mug, and keep my mouth shut."

"I told you I could help you out with the money."

"And I told you I wasn't gonna take club money for my screw up."

"Right, and now you got Demon up your ass." Cobra lifted his chin in Virginia's direction. "What's goin' on between you two?"

"Nothing."

Cobra pulled a look calling bullshit on him.

"I tried to do the right thing, I sent her off last week, but—"

"I saw the look on your face when you came in here tonight. You fuckin' care about her."

"What if I do?" Python tightened his fists at his side. He had no intentions of hitting Cobra, but he sure wanted to slam into something.

"Aside from the fact she's all wrong for you, not one of us, and being threatened because of you. Absolutely nothing."

"I get it. I fucked up. Again."

Cobra glanced over his shoulder at Virginia and then back to him. "She's shook pretty bad. Go take care of her, then tomorrow night we take care of the Rats." The two men tapped fists.

Virginia's eyes never left his as Python closed the distance between them. He jerked his head toward the back stairs. "C'mon."

———

Python waited until she slid off the barstool, then he placed a firm hand on the small of her back. The clenching in her stomach subsided as soon as Cobra and Rattler zoomed into the parking lot of Ecstasy a few minutes after her. These big tatted men threw off a powerful vibe laced with confidence, and Virginia found it comforting. They escorted her into the empty strip club without too many words and settled her at the bar. They'd come for her because of Python, and again, she marveled at the bond and trust these men shared. If one needed the other, they were there—no questions asked. That kind of loyalty was rare. She'd never even experienced that connection with her own family.

Python silently followed behind Virginia as they climbed up the cement stairs that lead to the second floor. His boots scuffed and echoed against the cinderblock walls of the stairwell. He yanked open the heavy fire door, and after they entered the short hall to his apartment, he unlocked the door and guided her through it, then nodded to the couch.

Python pulled over a chair as Kobi trotted into the living room. He reached down, patted his back, and the dog settled beside him on the floor.

Virginia realized they'd sat this exact way the first night she'd barged in on his threesome. So much had happened since that night—so many highs and lows—denying her feelings for this dangerous and generous hulk-of-a-man, then giving in to them, only to have him break it off in a way she still didn't fully understand.

The tats on his forearms shifted as he leaned forward into her space. She licked her lips and waited, having absolutely no idea what his next words would be. His gaze skated over her outfit, then his brows knitted together.

"I wanna know why you were at the Shangri-La tonight, and why the hell you're dressed like a librarian in an X-rated bookstore? Then I wanna know what got you so shook up."

Python didn't believe in skirting around a subject. She guessed this was a key attribute when interrogating rivals, but he was going to hate her answers.

"I went there to interview the dancers. It was the last part of my report. Kind of a behind-the-scenes story, and I thought it would be better to blend in and make them think I was one of them."

"Damn stupid idea going there alone," he ground out. Then he was silent as his lips flattened out. "That outfit is hot as hell, but please tell me you didn't get up on stage."

Virginia laughed out loud, half from what he'd said, half as a release from long held stress. "No, I didn't get any further than the dressing room."

"Thank fuck for that." He arched his bow. "What had you so shook on the phone? Did some asshole put hands on you?"

"When I got out to my car there was a note." She dug into her tote bag, angling her hand past her makeup case and curling iron, and finally pulled out the paper with the scribbled threat.

She handed it over to him, and his eyes widened two seconds before he slammed his palm onto the coffee table so hard that the TV remote jumped to the floor.

"Fuckin' bastard," he gritted out. "You said this was on your car?"

"Inside, on the dashboard."

"So he broke into your car."

"Nothing was damaged. I didn't even know until I saw the note on the dashboard."

"That's cause he's a pro. Did it to spook you." He crumbled the note in his balled up his fist. "And why didn't you tell me Demon came to your apartment?"

"Because of this. Because I knew you'd get upset." Now she feared telling him about the conversation Madeline overheard between Demon and Harry. It would only enrage him more.

"Damn right, that bastard is over."

"I won't be responsible for you murdering a man."

"No murder."

Oh, thank God, he must've meant a beating. She didn't approve of violence, but for Demon, she could make an exception.

"Justice, retaliation, ending him and giving him what he deserves. Biker code: You fuck with me, I fuck with you worse."

"I can't allow you to do that."

"There's no allowing, babe. It's the way it is. He knows the rules and he knows he went over the line when he threatened you. His end is on him, not me."

"But maybe—"

"He's been pushing me and the Serpents for months. If we back down and don't even the score, they'll just keep pushing."

"I won't be a catalyst for this kind of violence."

"It has nothing to do with you."

"The only reason this came to a head is because of me. You can't deny that."

"He moved into Serpents' territory, then he messed with what's mine. That's all the incentive I need."

His phraseology set her on edge. Virginia wasn't his possession, yet she knew the territorial mentality of bikers from her research.

"But I'm not yours. You sent me away." She had to clarify the truth.

"I tried, Virginia. I tried to deny what I felt for you. Tried to do the right thing, but I think about you all the damn time. Thought once I fucked you, I 'd get you outta my system, but it only made me want more of you."

She hadn't expected flowery sonnets from this tough tatted man, but the anguish in his voice transformed his blunt words into a touching and soulful declaration.

"I shouldn't be with you." He scrubbed his hands over his face. "But I can't let you go either."

"This last week has been hell for me too. I've worried about you and wanted to be with you." She leaned in and rested her hands on his shoulders, getting right in his face. "I died a little when you pushed me away." Virginia's words rushed together and her throat tightened. She tried to control her shaky voice, but the stress of the night crashed over her. When he drew her to him what little restraint she had fell away, and she collapsed against him as silent tears seeped from her eyes.

He gathered her onto his lap in the oversized chair and she reveled in his scent, setting him apart from any other man. She burrowed in deeper, never wanting him to let go. His lips found hers, then his tongue pushed past the seam of hers.

"I want you." Twisting in his arms, she faced him and straddled his lap, her tight black skirt riding higher on her thighs. "And worse, I need you."

Python's broad palms pushed the skirt to her waist. "I can't believe you went to that shitty strip joint dressed like this." His gaze level with her black push-up bra. "You're pretty gutsy." His grin told her he was loving her wild child attitude.

She wiggled her ass under his firm grip. "So you like the naughty reporter outfit?"

"Hell, yeah. I mean, I thought you were sexy that first night in my bedroom, rocking that innocent, uptight look."

"Uptight?"

"Uptight on the outside, but dirty as fuck on the inside. I knew you'd be a firecracker in bed, and I was right." He unbuttoned her straining blouse, licked his lips, then nuzzled his face between her breasts.

Holding his head tight to her, she moaned and shivered when his short beard tickled her sensitive flesh. He eased away the lace of her bra and teased her nipple with his tongue.

Her thighs clenched, and when she ground down over

him, he squeezed her bare ass until she yelped. "You like my hands on you."

A statement, not a question. This man knew what she wanted, knew what she liked and was able to deliver. He squeezed again, then slapped the tender spot. A sound she'd never heard bubbled up in her throat, along with tingling in her toes.

"My woman wants it a little rough."

"Mmmm," she purred. Yup, it was a purr. Python knew how to light her up and set her on fire.

She fumbled with the heavy metal of his belt buckle, undid the leather, and popped the button on his jeans. His honest emotions broke down all her barriers. No games, no fake words, just real and raw, putting it all out there in a way she'd certainly never experienced in any relationship.

Her own parents were guarded and fake, and her infrequent relationships with men barely lasted more than a few weeks. Truth, she'd only known Python for a little over two weeks, but the strength of their bond superseded good sense. Demon's threats alone proved danger surrounded Python, but the minute he walked into Ecstasy tonight, all her anxiety fell away. Just his firm hand on her back made her feel protected and whole.

"You're doin' way too much thinking." His low, gravely whisper shot heat down her spine and straight to her core.

Was he the best decision she'd ever made? Absolutely not, but he was definitely the best decision for her right now, right here.

———

Watching her undo his jeans made his head spin, and when she slipped in her delicate hand and wrapped her fingers around him, he groaned deep in his throat. Even Kobi lifted his head for a better look at what was undoing his master. Then, damned if the big beast didn't stick his tongue out and pant.

Python reached down and stilled her hand. "You keep that up and I'm a goner." He placed her hands on his shoulders, then gathered her in his arms. "Want you all sprawled out on my bed where I can give you what you deserve."

She wrapped her arms around his neck and he stood up. Python staggered into the bedroom, laid her out on the bed, and toed off his boots; then he pushed away his jeans and hovered over her.

The paleness of Virginia's unmarked skin drastically contrasted with his tatted, tanned torso. Another reminder of their differences and how he was wrong for her, but what the hell could he do? The minute Python walked into Ecstasy tonight, he knew what he wanted. Fuck, he knew what he wanted the first night she barged into his bedroom.

He wasn't a stupid man. His wits and acute senses kept him alive for thirty-five years, but now it all didn't mean shit. All that mattered was Virginia, protecting her, being with her, and making her happy in any way he could.

Over the last week without her, he'd been surrounded by exotic dancers, the girls who worked at Candy's, and the unlimited supply of women who hung around the Gold Mine. Yet Virginia, the delicate five-foot-three reporter with the silky blonde hair invaded every minute of his day.

Python had only known her sixteen days; yeah, like a lovesick teenager, he'd counted them, and she'd weaved her way into his—heart? The one organ he'd never had much luck with, the one he assumed died long ago, until Virginia.

"What was it that you said to me before about thinking too much." Her soft voice jogged him back to the here and now.

"Just wondering how a thug like me got so lucky." He kissed her shoulder and the gentle act surprised him.

"Funny, I was thinking how lucky I am." She smiled up at him. "I've never felt this in sync with anyone, and I know it's only been—"

"Sixteen days." He interrupted her and grinned. "Yeah, the outlaw biker who can have any pussy he wants has been counting the days we've known each other."

"There's that wonderful honesty of yours again." She rolled her eyes.

"You want honesty. There's this girl at Chick-Fil-A who I used to roll with. Real hot piece, and guess what? When I went to see her, all I could think about was you. Ran outta there like the place was on fire."

"I know somewhere in that sentence you're trying to tell me something." She laughed, then ran her palms over his chest resting them just below his shoulders. "Never been a fan of snakes, but I have to say, your python tat gets me going."

He slid his hand under the stretchy skirt, then over her hips and down her thighs. He growled at the sight of her black lace thong. "Did you buy this sexy shit just for this make-believe stripper outfit or ..." Maybe he really didn't want to hear this story.

"The bra and thong are a set I've had but never worn before. You're the first to see it."

"All right." The cocky, arrogant biker in him liked the shit outta that. "You just made my night, babe." He hooked his thumbs in the thin elastic of the thong and slowly slid it over her hips and down her thighs. He held them up in the crook of his finger. "Don't think you're getting these back. They're mine now."

She wiggled her hips against the mattress. "I know you're

supposed to be the bad boy, but I love how you make me feel naughty too."

"I'mma make you feel way more than naughty." He flinched when her hand slipped between them and squeezed. He reached for the drawer in his nightstand and pulled out a strip of condoms.

"You weren't kidding about always being prepared." She joked.

"I'm like a regular Boy Scout." He twisted his face into a goofy smirk.

"Right, a tatted, ripped, edgy Boy Scout with multiple piercings." She leaned up on her elbows and sucked his nipple ring between her lips.

"Fuck, babe, you wanna make me blow before we even get started?"

She smiled around the metal bar, and he gave her ass a firm slap. "I'll play all you want, but right now I gotta get in you."

He spread her legs wide, sheathed himself and nudged in the tip. She angled her hips giving it all to him. He'd never done anything good in his miserable life to deserve her, but this, right now, was the best thing he'd ever had.

He thrust slowly at first, knowing he was big, to give her a chance to adjust. Her lips parted and he leaned in, capturing them in a deep, soulful kiss, branding her. His hips drove deeper, grinding against her spot. "Gotta make you mine."

She broke the kiss, their faces only inches apart. "Are you mine?"

Her brown eyes darkened and pinned him, daring him with the question, daring him to express unknown, never experienced emotions.

"Only you—only me."

She rose up to meet him and their bodies moved together, painfully perfect, incredibly disastrous. Her rights and his wrongs wiped clean and melded together. Virginia stiffened, yelled out and her body tightened around him not once, not twice, but three fuckin' times. Then her beautiful lips purred out his name and he lost it, hammering hard, gripping her hips, and sweat dripping down his back.

"Fuck, yeah," he yelled out as he blew apart. This was where he belonged.

Python fell to her side and draped his arm around her waist, the scent of their sex heavy in the air.

"Having you here, giving it all up to me makes all the bullshit disappear."

Virginia crossed her arms over his chest and rested her head on her forearms. "I want you to promise no matter what happens, you'll never turn me away again."

He drew in a deep breath. "I can't make that promise if something is gonna put you in danger."

"Then we will talk about it and make the decision together. No more of you making decisions for the both of us. Deal?"

He wound his hand through her hair. "Deal." He hated lying to her, but he couldn't promise that either, now that they planned on taking down the Rats. His eyes burned from lack of sleep and he knew he wasn't thinking straight, but somehow he'd figure this out and keep Virginia safe at the same time.

Kobi picked that moment to jump up on the bed. His size made the bed dip, and after some rearranging of the blankets, he curled up at the foot of the bed.

Virginia laughed at his antics, then reached down and stroked his fur, and damn if the animal didn't look at her like he was smiling.

"That's a first," Python said.

"He doesn't usually sleep on the bed?"

Python laughed. "Usually the jealous fucker growls at the women in my bed."

"That's because you never had the right one here before." She snuggled into him and he couldn't deny her words.

He glanced at the bedside clock. "It's five a.m. Let's get some sleep."

Her head nestled into his shoulder and he heard her deep breathing before his eyes shut. His exhausted brain skittered from Virginia's soft body to flashes of Demon and Harry in a twisted, dream-like restless sleep.

CHAPTER NINETEEN

Shards of sunlight, heavy breathing, and something wet on his arm had Python struggling to surface from the depths of sleep as he rubbed at his eyes and tried to focus. Virginia's soft hair fanned out over his chest, daylight streamed through the half-closed drapes, and Kobi stood on the bed panting with his big tongue hanging out.

A quick glance at the clock said the poor dog was way overdue for a run and some food. Like Python, Kobi ate at regular intervals, and if a feeding was delayed, he made sure Python knew about it. The dog also had hangry issues.

Python tried to slide Virginia off him without waking her, but Kobi wasn't giving him much room to work with. The animal seemed to be grinning at him.

He swung his legs over the bed and the dog jumped onto the floor and did his crazy, hopping I-can't-wait-to-go-outside dance.

"All right, all right. I know. You've been patient." Python snagged a pair of sweatpants off the floor, shoved his feet into his unlaced workout sneakers, and swiped his cigarettes and lighter off the dresser. He shot a look over his shoulder for one more glimpse of Virginia and smiled. Sweetest person he'd ever known.

Kobi beat him to the door and pushed at it until he threw the locks. Then he waited until Python yanked the stairwell door open before he took off down the stairs. The minute Python punched in the alarm code and released the back door, Kobi was off. No chance of cars this early in the day, and Kobi took full advantage to run around from the blacktop to the grassy lot behind it.

Python squinted at the blaring, afternoon, Vegas sun, but he loved the heat. Coming from Arizona, and then settling in Vegas, he never understood how people dealt with the cold, snow, and ice of other parts of the country.

He smiled as he watched Kobi chase some lizards. He rarely caught them and when he did, he always seemed disappointed when his heavy paw ended their playtime.

Python leaned against the brick wall of the club and lit up a smoke just as Virginia came through the back door. He dragged deep and blew the smoke overhead while he savored her tan, bare legs sticking out from under a t-shirt of his that fit her like a dress. Sexy as hell.

Virginia also squinted at the glaring sun, then cupped her hand over her eyes. "Way too much sun this early in the morning."

"I hate to break it to you, babe, but it's one in the afternoon."

"Wow, how long did we sleep?"

"Considering we didn't go to sleep till five, we managed eight hours."

An SUV entering the parking lot from the other side drew Python's attention. Three days a week, the club opened for lunch, but today wasn't one of those days. Python kept eyes on the wandering vehicle.

Seeing, Virginia, Kobi ran through the lot and tried to

jump up on her. Python stuck the cigarette between his lips, squinted through the smoke, and grabbed Kobi's collar.

"That's all right." Virginia tousled his fur.

Python laughed. "Probably knock you off your feet."

The SUV paced around the perimeter of the lot, and Python pulled Virginia into his side. "Doesn't this joker notice there're no other cars and the place is closed?"

Python's back stiffened two seconds before the SUV's tires squealed, and skidded into a 360 degree turn heading straight for them. Python pushed Virginia toward the door seconds before he saw the barrel of a Beretta pointing out of the rear window of the truck.

Gunshots exploded around them as Python shielded Virginia with his body. The barrage of bullets pitted the brick wall, sending pieces of cement through the air, as the SUV peeled out of the parking lot on two wheels.

Python turned Virginia in his arms, not sure what he would see. Her eyes were wide and wild, but she seemed unharmed. He held her at arm's length and examined every inch of her body. When he finished, she clung to him.

"Are you all right?" she mumbled into his shoulder.

"I think so."

They separated, and again looked each other over to make sure. Virginia gazed past him, then clamped her hand over her mouth in a muffled scream. He turned around and froze.

Kobi was splayed out in the parking lot, blood seeping over the blacktop.

———

They ran to the wounded animal and Python crouched down beside him. He cradled his head and Kobi stared at him panting hard against the obvious pain. Kobi's pleading, confused expression tore at Virginia's heart.

"We have to get him help," she ordered. "Where's your vet?"

"Decatur Animal Hospital." Python stroked Kobi's head, his voice flat and emotionless.

"I'll run upstairs and get my keys, we can take my car." Her feet flew under her as she raced up the stairs, slammed into his apartment, grabbed her purse, and a blanket off the bed to wrap up Kobi. A thought of finding her thong flashed through her brain, but the tangle of sheets told her she'd be wasting precious time.

She found Python in the same place she'd left him. His blank expression chilled her, and she longed for the swaggering, take charge tough guy. She leaned in and covered the dog in the cotton blanket, then got in Python's face. "Pick him up and get him in the car." The tough love tone in her voice belied the pain in her heart, but it worked.

Kobi's heavy panting filled the silent car. A few times Virginia tried to reassure Python, but he only stared through the front windshield, stroking Kobi's head. Virginia swallowed hard a few times to hold back the tears, both for the dog and for this giant of a man shaken beyond repair. She sent up a silent prayer, begging somehow, someway this beautiful animal would beat the odds and survive a gunshot wound.

Ten minutes later, the packed waiting room of the Decatur Animal Hospital stilled when Python and Virginia stormed in.

"We have an emergency here," Virginia called out. People stared as a nurse came around the reception counter.

"What's the problem?" she asked.

"He was shot," Virginia said. "He needs help right away."

"How did this happen?" she asked.

"Are you going to ask dumb questions, or are you going to help this poor dog?" Virginia glared at the nurse.

"I need information before we can examine him." She waved her hand around the crowded room. "And as you can see there are other people ahead of you."

Python grimaced when Virginia eased back the blanket half-soaked with Kobi's blood. "This dog could be dying and you're wasting time. Get the vet, now."

The other people in the room chimed in saying they'd gladly let Kobi go before them, and the nurse backed down. "Fine, follow me."

An hour later, Python and Virginia sat in the waiting area of the animal hospital. She squeezed his hand and murmured reassuring words to him, but Python had barely reacted.

The quizzical looks they received were annoying, but totally understandable. A shirtless, tattooed guy sat clutching a bloody blanket next to a woman in an oversized t-shirt and bare feet. In her haste to gather her car keys earlier, she'd forgotten about shoes until the cold tiles of the hospital floor reminded her she was barefooted.

Virginia couldn't shake the nagging guilt of not telling Python about the threat Madeline overheard. How could she ever tell Python she might be partly responsible for this tragedy, or at least might've been able to prevent it.

Finally, the doctor emerged and told them Kobi survived the surgery. They removed the bullet, but it chipped a bone in his shoulder and he lost a considerable amount of blood.

"But he'll be all right?" Virginia ventured.

"He should be, but I'd like to keep him here for observation. Just to make sure."

The fifteen-minute ride to Ecstasy seemed to take forever. Virginia stayed upbeat and encouraging, but Python only mumbled his responses. She even tried to make a weak joke about their appearance, but nothing.

Obviously, the bond he had with Kobi outweighed his connection with most humans, but she didn't want to make the mistake of spouting empty words or making a bad situation worse.

She pulled into the back of the club, and thankfully, at four o'clock in the afternoon, it was still too early to be crowded. As they approached the back door, she observed the holes in the brick from the spray of bullets. She drew in a shaky breath, her mind reliving the horrific scene and just how close they came to severe injury or—death. Rattler was coming out of the office when they entered.

"Where the hell you been all day?" Rattler asked, but then his gaze skated between them, taking in their inappropriate clothing and the bloody blanket.

Python yanked open the stairwell door and let it slam behind him, leaving Virginia to deal with Rattler.

"What the hell is going on?" Rattler asked.

There was no good way to say it, so Virginia just blurted it out. "Kobi got shot this afternoon."

"What the hell? Is he all right?"

"He had surgery, and they think he's going to make it."

"How?"

"We were out in the lot earlier. Kobi was running around and an SUV pulled up and started shooting." The last word choked her.

"Shit, a drive-by?"

"Yes." Python mumbled the same word when they were driving to the hospital.

"Sons of bitches." Rattler reached for the stairway door.

Virginia gripped his forearm. "He's pretty upset. Could you give me some time with him first?" She cocked her head, her eyes pleading with him.

"All right. Me and Cobra will figure this out."

"Thank you. And could you have somebody bring him up something from the kitchen?"

"Sure." Then he turned back to her. "That dog means everything to him."

"I know." She trudged up the stairs, mentally preparing herself for the best way to reach him.

She found Python sprawled out on the couch, fisting a bottle of Jack Daniels. He flicked a gaze in her direction, then concentrated on refilling his glass.

She lifted a glass off the granite bar and joined him on the couch. "Are you sharing that?" She held out her glass, and he paused for a second, then splashed the golden liquor into the glass.

"I figured you'd be telling me not to drink, that it doesn't solve anything, and it only makes things worse." His voice hoarse and challenging.

It was the first full sentence he'd uttered in about four hours, so the raspiness of his voice didn't surprise her, although the accusation in his tone did set her back a bit. Virginia's natural ability to suss people out told her agreeing would work best.

"Right here, right now, I think liquor is about the only answer."

She could see his brain calculating her comment. A savvy man like him would know when he was being played, but when she didn't add anything else, he downed the Jack and set the glass on the table.

She kept her distance on the couch, sensing he needed his space, but the uneasy, tortured silence lasted a few minutes longer. There were so many emotions and words she wanted to say to him, but his body language told her he wasn't ready. He'd erected a thick shell around himself. She'd suspected he'd learned this behavior at a young age, probably explained his reluctance and lack of disclosure regarding his past.

He poured another shot but didn't pick up the glass. "I fucked up again."

She waited, thinking and hoping he might say more, but he didn't.

"Please don't blame yourself for this," she ventured.

His harsh laugh bubbled up between them, but he kept his eyes on the glass. "Okay, so who should I blame?"

"Whoever shot at us would be a start."

He spun around so quickly, it startled her. "Are you fuckin' kidding me? I know who it was." Then under his breath, he added, "And I know exactly what I'm gonna do about it." He reached for his phone on the coffee table, and she covered his hand with hers.

"Please talk to me. Please tell me what you're feeling so I can try to help you."

"There's nothing to say, and there's sure nothing you can do."

"Lashing out isn't the answer."

He snatched his hand out of her grasp. "You get it could've easily been you in some hospital bed, or dead, right?"

"Or you."

"Too bad they're such lousy shots." His lips twisted into a sneer. "Could've done everybody a favor."

"Don't say that."

She had her own theory about the shooting but kept it to herself for now.

He stared at her for a long few minutes, and she waited him out. "The Rats were targeting me. I owe money, a lot of money, to this guy—"

"Harry?"

He slammed the whiskey glass onto the coffee table. "What the hell do you know about Harry?"

"The database at the station is a valuable resource. After your conversation with him at the carnival, I did some research. It was one of the reasons I was at Ecstasy last night." She inched closer to him on the couch, dreading the rest of the story. "Madeline, the girl who caught us in the bathroom at the Shangri-La, overheard Demon and Harry threatening you. I was on my way here to warn you when you called."

"Why didn't you tell me this last night?"

"You were so upset when you found out he came to my apartment and about the note in my car, so I thought something else would only make the situation worse."

"You should've told me."

"I know, but I have a theory about the shooting." He shot her a disbelieving look, but she forged on. "You're a big target to miss, especially for people who know how to handle guns. I think they intentionally shot Kobi."

He cocked a brow and she continued, "Remember what you told me about going after something you love. Shooting Kobi was their horrible way of getting at you."

"You're right, they're pros. They don't make mistakes."

"I should've told you about the threat, but I was afraid for you and now ..." Her throat closed at the thought of Kobi's limp body in the parking lot.

He stared at his empty whiskey glass, and she sat perfectly still, trying to gauge his next reaction. Anger, rage, fury, frustration, his complex range of emotions could be on a collision course.

He opened his arms to her. "C'mere." She hesitated for a second, then leaned into his embrace, and he blew out a deep sigh. "What happened today is on me. I told you I had a problem with gambling, but I didn't tell you how bad."

She cocked her head to see his face. "How bad?"

"Fifty grand bad."

Her eyes widened. "You owe them fifty-thousand dollars?"

"Yup, and because of that, you were put in danger and Kobi got shot."

All the pieces of the puzzle had finally fit together—

Harry's ominous reputation and the threatening visit from Demon. These were deadly people who played for real and certainly weren't about to let fifty-thousand dollars slip away.

"I've been bringing in some extra money, but I still don't have it all." The despondency in his voice tore her apart. The virile warrior, broken down before her eyes. Her chest ached —for his anguish, for his pain.

"You asked me the other night why I gamble, and I gave you a bullshit answer, but the real question is—why do I blow my life apart? Why do I like taking risks even when I know damn well it'll end bad?"

Hard questions with even harder answers. She arched her back so she could see his face. "I know you're private about your past, and I respect that, but it probably has to do with something from long ago. And I know it sounds cliché, but it's usually true."

He bit his lower lip, and she prepared for him to blow her off with a flip comment, but when he stayed silent she knew what she had to do.

"I wasn't totally honest about my background either," she blurted out.

"I don't believe you've got any deep, dark secrets, babe."

"Maybe not dark, but I can definitely help you."

"Help me how?"

"You remember I told you my father was in communications in California?" She sucked in a deep breath. Ripping the lid off this box came with consequences.

"The communications company he owns is Century Media, and my father is the founder, Chet Curtis." She watched his brain decipher this information, then waited for the inevitable questions that usually followed.

"Huh, Chet Curtis. That's crazy." He paused. "I get why you kept it a secret. You didn't want to deal with the bullshit attitudes and stupid questions people probably ask you."

She gripped his massive forearms. Hard. "Yes, exactly right."

He cocked his head. "You changed your name."

"My first name is really Virginia, but Swanson is my mother's maiden name."

"Safer to keep shit to yourself."

"Safer, but not right, especially in this case when I can help you." Even if helping him would break her. "As you can imagine, I have a very nice trust fund, and removing fifty-thousand dollars from it would be relatively easy."

"Oh, fuck no, I'm not—"

"For once, just listen. When Kobi got shot you told me there was nothing I could do, but now there is a solution. Me giving you fifty-thousand dollars is like you giving someone five hundred dollars."

"I'm not gonna let you—"

"Gina told me how you'd paid for some of the girls to go to rehab and other stuff, so this is my way of paying it forward to you."

She painfully left out the part of giving in to her father, moving back to California, and never seeing him again.

"Nah, I won't let you do it. It's too much."

True, she'd be giving up way too much, but to save his life, yes. "We'll talk about it more in the morning."

He kissed the top of her head, probably thinking he'd won. She bit her lower lip, knowing there would be no going back from the deal she'd make with her media-mogul father. He'd probably have her sign a damn contract. Either way, all ties would have to be cut with Python, but if it meant saving his life ... Ironic, the very man she saved, she could never see again, and because of that she had to ask one more question.

———

"Now that you know my real name, you have to tell me yours," Virginia said.

"Don't laugh." He paused, and then. "Dwayne Jones."

"I like it. Almost sounds like a movie star name."

"Apparently, the nurse at the hospital where I was abandoned had a crush on Dwayne Johnson, "The Rock." Jones was a placeholder name, but since I never got—"

"Shhh, I get it." She drew him to her, and some of the pain eased, but it wasn't enough. She deserved the truth, too.

"I grew up in the system. A lot of people say that, and what they usually mean is they were in and out. Some kids go back to their real home when their parents get it together, but I ... don't even know anything about my parents. Just that I was left."

Virginia reached out to him, but he kept some distance between them fearing physical contact would weaken him.

"Some kids get adopted, but I wasn't that kid. And then there's the foster homes. Most are hell. A lot of people just take kids in for the money."

"And nobody does anything for them?"

"There's just too many unwanted kids." He drew in a deep breath. "I spent most of my early years in group homes, never having anything to call my own. The fact I was about five feet seven at eleven years old hardly made me the cute kid people were looking to adopt. By the time I was a teenager, I was bigger than most of the prospective dads."

"I can't imagine that kind of pain."

"As soon as I was old enough I joined the Army, but that wasn't the answer. Sure, I finally had some things I could call my own, but I was way too wild. I didn't know how to follow orders. I spent more time with extra duty and cancelled leaves. My pay had been cut so many times I was practically paying them. Surprisingly, I was honorably discharged, but I was still too young and stupid to know what I wanted."

"But you've risen so far above all that pain."

"Deep down it's still there. I'm an empty, selfish prick who goes from one mess to another. It's the way I was born, and it's the way I'll die."

"That's so untrue. The way you helped Crystal the other night, and then Gina told me how you loaned her money for her car ... even though you had a price on your head, you still reached out to others. That's not the act of a selfish person."

"Maybe the reason I gotta fix people is 'cause it makes me feel better. I don't know. Probably some fucked-up reason."

"I think it's because you have a big heart and you genuinely like helping."

Or, he hoped it would relieve the guilt of the one person he couldn't fix.

"There's something else I want you to know about my past." He'd never told anyone about Zelda, not even Cobra. "After I got out of the the Army, I did some time up at Ely State Pen. When I got sprung, I'd told you I hung out with the Desert Devils MC. As if that wasn't stupid enough, I started hooking up with the president's old lady, Zelda. She was wild and fearless, sometimes I think she wanted to get caught."

Virginia opened her mouth, but he put up his hand. He had to get this out. No more secrets.

"Anyway, he found out and beat her into a coma." Python spit the words out fast, but it didn't help the regret. "I was at the hospital when their clubhouse got raided. She died three days later. Her death tore me up and then blew me apart when the doctor told me she was pregnant."

"Oh, my God, was it your child?" Virginia clutched his hand.

"I don't know." The familiar burning behind his eyes had him blinking furiously. "After that, I just lived from day to day, roaming from one shithole to another. The first night I met

Cobra, I was dead drunk and started a fight with him in a bar. He knocked the shit outta me. The next day we sobered up, called each other assholes, and formed the Serpents. He was looking for something, too, and it turned out to be the closest thing I've got to family."

Virginia leaned in and hugged him. The warmth of her body calmed his demons. "You are so much more than you give yourself credit for." She hugged him tighter and when they separated her eyes were wet with tears.

"Don't cry for me, baby. After tomorrow night, we can start all over. Do it right."

She hugged him to her again, but she cried harder. Women and their emotions.

CHAPTER TWENTY

The Serpents rolled into the parking lot of the Shangri-La at four a.m. the next morning—the perfect time. All things crazy happened in the early morning hours. The place was closed, the strippers and bartenders were gone, and they could take care of business without interference.

Cobra threw his leg over his bike and turned to Python. "You ready to do this?"

"Past ready." Python was pumped and set to go—eager to get this done and get back to Virginia. "Everything's where it should be."

And that was true all around. The Rats' patched members and prospects all stepped up to denounce Demon. Last night he and Virginia unraveled their secrets, and telling Virginia about Zelda relieved a burden he hadn't realized he was carrying. Not only did he have a good woman by his side, but a woman who accepted his shady past and all his baggage.

He'd left her all snug and warm in his bed, and if all went as planned, he'd be back to her by daybreak and ready to move forward. Thirty-five years old and he was getting a fresh start.

Rattler, Joker, and Boa met the SUV with two of the Serpents' prospects as well as Blade, the Rats' prospect from Python's desert meeting.

Joker had a few words with them, then joined Cobra and Python. A baseball bat dangled from his fingertips. "According to Blade, everything's laid out with no blowback from the Rats."

Python never took anything for granted. Sure, the Rats' patched members told him there'd be no trouble, but he knew how fast things could turn to shit. "Never let your guard down" was a motto that had kept him alive.

"Fucker acts just like a VP to me, Prez." Python's shoulder butted Joker.

"Just what I was thinking," Cobra agreed with a sly grin.

Joker smirked then held out his fist. "Let's tear this motherfucker down." They all tapped, then headed for the tumbledown building.

Pushing through the dented metal door, the same stink of sweat, beer, and piss filled Python's head.

Cobra's steely glare observed the entire room in one glance, from the peeling linoleum floor to the broken-down tables and scuzzy bar. "Looks like we're doin' the community a favor."

"Stopping sleazy strip joints one baseball bat at a time." Joker flipped the bat in his hand and laughed.

Yup, Joker was back in whether his stubborn ass wanted to admit it or not. Maybe when they had his big swearing in party, Python would announce taking Virginia as his ol' lady. The thought came to him last night and he couldn't shake it, especially since she was cuddled up against him when it did, not balls deep in her fabulous body.

All right, fucker, put those thoughts away. It's time to take care of business.

Rattler and Boa stayed in the main room while Joker

supervised the prospects. A few of the Rats' patched members got up from a table and joined them. Game on.

Blade nodded his head to the back hall where Demon's office was located. Once Python and Cobra stormed the office, the real fun would begin. Smashing, trashing, and basically fucking this shithole up.

Cobra stopped halfway down the back hallway. "You ready to do this?"

––––––––

Virginia stepped out into the cool early morning air. It still surprised her how cold the air could get at night even when the days hit ninety degrees. She headed toward her car, passing the spot where Kobi was shot. The stain from his blood was still visible even though Rattler had sprayed it down. Poor Kobi. She'd silently prayed he'd recover, hating the thought of Python alone.

The minute Python left she'd made a beeline out of his apartment. Now, a half hour later, she threw two suitcases into the back of her Toyota, only taking her clothes and some personal belongings. Then she woke up her father, making the call he'd been dying to hear; however, her deal came with a fifty-thousand-dollar stipulation, to which he finally agreed. It seemed she learned something about the art of negotiating from him.

––––––––

Python and Cobra exchanged a look and did a silent count down. One, they drew their guns; two, they cocked their elbows; three, Python booted the door, slamming it open and banging it against the wall.

A bleary-eyed Demon raised his head from the line of

coke decorating the ass of a stripper bent over his desk. "What the fuck?" Demon bellowed.

He was wired tighter than usual. Not good. Not good at all.

When the girl raised her head, Python realized it was the same one who caught Virginia and him in the bathroom. The one Virginia interviewed, named Madeline.

Demon's beady eyes twitched toward the gun on the corner of his desk. A second later, he snatched it up with one hand and gripped Madeline around the waist with the other, using her as a human shield. Ten seconds was all it took for this whole plan to fall to shit, ten seconds for Python to realize for once in his life he cared if he lived or died.

———

Virginia chased the darkness as she crossed over the California border with the orangey glow of the rising sun behind her.

Leaving her apartment was bittersweet. The basic space gave her the independence she craved, and while it wasn't luxurious, it was hers. After six months, she hadn't accumulated much. Whoever occupied it after her would have new locks, thanks to Python, and later today she'd call Nicole and offer her the furniture and the brand new bed, also thanks to Python.

Whatever Nicole didn't want she could sell. Virginia wanted no reminders of what she left behind. In six months' time, she'd found one of the only true girlfriends she'd ever had and a man. Python. A man whom she'd never forget. Who bared his soul to her last night in an honest, heart-wrenching way. A man who . . . No, she had at least two more hours of driving, and sobbing uncontrollably would definitely not work.

———

Madeline gasped. Not bad considering she was only wearing a g-string with the barrel of a gun pressed to her temple.

"Don't be a punk. Let the girl go." Cobra moved away from Python to widen the space, making Demon have to look between them. "'Cause this shithole is going down, and guess what, your brothers are helping us do it."

"Bullshit! My brothers would never go against me."

Cobra barked out a harsh laugh. "Your *brothers* sold you out the first chance they got."

"Hiding behind a woman." Python stepped up. Sure, Cobra was president, but Python wanted this one for himself. "Typical Rat bullshit."

Demon huffed out a grunt. "Only reason I didn't blast that sweet piece along with that mangy dog was because I figure I can hit her up after Harry smokes your ass."

Python's jaw stiffened at the mention of Virginia and Kobi.

"Do you believe this guy?" Cobra shook his head. "Still talking shit on the last day of his life."

Demon sniffed at the smoke seeping under the door. "What the fuck is going on out there?"

"We already told you, we're burning this dump down," Cobra said.

Demon's eyes darted around the room while he squeezed Madeline tighter, pressing her head to the side with the gun. "I'll shoot this bitch if you don't get outta here."

While Cobra ragged on Demon, Python locked eyes with Madeline, then glanced to her six-inch stilettos. Madeline's eyes widened slightly, and Python hoped she got the message.

Python stepped to the edge of Demon's desk. "And you think by holding a gun to this bitch's head we're gonna back down." He shot a look over his shoulder to Cobra. "Like we care if this whore lives or dies." Python's hand hovered near the mound of coke. "Fuckin' sluts only good for suckin' dick."

"Fuck you," Madeline yelled, then lifted her heel and stabbed the spiky shoe into Demon's foot at the same time Python scooped up the coke and threw it in his face.

Demon sputtered and blinked hard to clear the dusting of coke in his eyes, enough of a distraction for Python to yank Madeline out of Demon's grasp and shove her behind him to Cobra. Madeline stumbled in her stilettos and Demon used that opportunity to lunge forward with his gun raised. He fired wildly, the sound deafening in the small room. Python leveled his gun at Demon's chest and squeezed the trigger —twice.

He clutched his gut and crumbled forward onto the cracked concrete floor, dropping the gun at his side. Python kicked it out of his reach and glared down at him. "That's for Kobi, and for scaring Virginia, you miserable piece of shit."

Cobra nodded toward the door. "C'mon, brother, we're done here."

Python tore his eyes away from Demon's body. The sound of breaking glass and destruction filled him with satisfaction.

———

At exactly 8:35 a.m., Virginia stopped on the circular driveway surrounding a fountain, bordered by palm trees. She sat for a few minutes, staring up at the European-style villa filled with hand-painted murals and two people as cold as the Italian stone floors and gold banisters. She remembered the elation she'd felt after leaving the towering monstrosity; and now she was back.

———

Rattler set up shots and beers along the bar of the Gold Mine as everyone filed into the empty space.

"Fuckin' unbelievable." Joker swung the baseball bat like a major leaguer. "Most fun I've had in a long damn time."

Cobra held up his beer bottle. "What's that you say, VP?"

Python lifted his shot glass. "Fucker, you miss the life, admit it."

"I admit it." Joker finished off his beer. "But instead of all this bullshit talking, hand me another beer."

It was only eight-thirty in the morning, but after a gunfight and then tossing and torching that shithole of a strip club, they were ready to let loose.

Cobra hoisted a backpack they'd found in Demon's office onto his shoulder, then headed to the back room. Joker and Python followed, knowing their president would want to do a recap before everybody got too wasted.

Cobra jerked his chin to the chair on his right and Joker sat down with Python taking his usual seat on Cobra's left.

"Good to finally have you with us, brother." Cobra and Joker tapped beer bottles.

"Took you damn long enough." Python joined them.

Python checked his phone. "One of our guys at Metro checked in. Looks like they're calling the fire arson. Blaming it on the Desert Rats' criminal connections." Python smirked. "Who knew?"

"Metro don't give a shit if we all get blasted as long as we keep it to ourselves and don't involve civilians," Cobra said.

"Same with the cops when Daisy and I were down in Miami. Keep your business clean and they just write it off."

Cobra dropped the backpack onto the table and unzipped it. "Can you believe this arrogant asshole?" Cobra held up a few packs of hundred-dollar bills. "Almost a hundred grand stuck under his desk."

"Good thing Madeline gave you a heads up or all this

scratch would've gone up in smoke." Python twisted his lips in disgust. "Fucked up she caught a bullet."

"Rattler dropped her at the hospital. Said it just grazed her."

Cobra pushed the pack in front of Python. "Found money." He jerked his chin at Joker. "We both agree you should take it."

Python put up his palms. "Ahh, no, man, it should be banked for the club."

"You goin' against the wishes of your prez and VP?" Cobra glared at him with those icy blue eyes.

Python drew in a deep breath. It sure would solve a lot of problems.

"But if you don't put the brakes on this gambling shit"— Cobra pointed his beer bottle at him—"the next time, I'll personally deliver you to Harry and tell him to cut off your balls as payment."

One thing about Cobra, he didn't beat around the bush. He'd put it right out there in anyone's face.

"There won't be a next time. I'm done with all that." Python meant every word. He'd already signed up for a Gambler's Anonymous meeting he found on his phone. Putting his club in danger was bad enough, but his relationship with Virginia would never work unless he got help. Python scooped up some of the banded hundreds, and his throat tightened at his club brothers throwing him this lifeline.

Python raised his head to say something, and Joker put up his hand. "For fuck's sake, you look like you're gonna make a testimonial speech. Just take the damn money and shut up about it."

"Fuck you, both." Python raised his beer bottle. "And thanks."

Cobra patted his cut for his smokes. "Our guy at Metro

say anything about finding Demon's body?"

"Nah, but I'm thinking he's barbecue by now." Python threw them a shitty grin.

"You got a weird fuckin' sense of humor." Joker nabbed one of Cobra's cigarettes and held it up. "Daisy thinks I quit this shit so keep your mouths shut." Then he stuck it between his lips and lit up.

Python laughed out loud pointing at Joker. "The guy trashes a bar with a baseball bat, then lights it on fire, and he's worried about his ol' lady catching him out."

"Damn straight." Joker dragged deep on the smoke. "That fiery wildcat is way scarier than anything the cops can throw at me."

"Plus, she'll cut you off and you'll be making friends with your right hand," Cobra said.

Python motioned between the two men. "You're both pussy-whipped."

"You're not far behind us, brother," Cobra said.

Python's brain locked in on Virginia, and he couldn't help the smile covering his face. Cobra and Joker both laughed, but he didn't give a shit.

Rattler's voice came through the door. "Hey, boss."

"C'mon in," Cobra yelled.

Rattler filled the doorway, then he ambled into the room. "Madeline texted me. Just a few stitches. They're gonna release her later."

"Good," Cobra said. "She kept it together."

Python dug his hand into the duffel bag. "Give her this." He tossed three bundles of hundreds at Rattler.

"You sure?" Rattler gazed at the thirty thousand dollars.

"I got what I need." Python patted the backpack. "If it wasn't for her, we wouldn't have known it was there."

"She won't believe it," Rattler said.

"Putting you in charge," Cobra pointed at Rattler. "Make sure it goes to her kids."

"Should be easy duty." Python smirked. "I've seen the way you've looked at her when we go up there. And how you made sure she was all covered up before you took her to the hospital."

"Couldn't have her walking in there buck-ass naked." Rattler grinned.

Joker pointed to Python. "He's got the same stupid look on his face as you when you talk about Virginia."

The brothers razzed each other, drank more beers, and congratulated themselves on a job well done. All in all, a good fuckin' day, and it was only nine in the morning. He'd texted Virginia earlier, but she hadn't gotten back to him. She was probably awake by now, so he'd surprise her with a little morning action, then tell her the good news about the money, and plan their future. He'd even gotten a text from the vet informing him he could pick up Kobi later today. Yup, good fuckin' day all around.

CHAPTER TWENTY-ONE

A half hour later, Python dragged his body up the stairs to his apartment, tired, but relieved all the bad shit was behind him. It was a nice feeling to want to share your life with someone, and he knew Virginia would be happy to hear the good news about Kobi, and most definitely about the money. Her offer last night was typical Virginia, but of course he wouldn't take it. Now, it didn't matter. Sometimes things did have a way of working out.

He unlocked the door, entered his apartment, and bent to pick up an envelope on the floor as if it'd been shoved under the door. He ripped it open and found two pieces of paper. A check made out to cash for fifty-thousand dollars and a note.

This is to assure you stay away from my daughter.
Chet Curtis
He read the letterhead on the check.
Chet Curtis, CEO, Owner
Century Media, Inc.
Los Angeles, CA
A cold sweat chilled his spine. He called out for Virginia, and when she didn't answer, he stomped into the bedroom

and stared at the empty room. The bed was made and every-thing of hers was gone, like she'd never been there. Python stormed back into the living room, then the kitchen, already knowing she wasn't there. He dug his phone out of his jeans pocket and called her number. When it went immediately to voicemail, he texted her, but he already knew it wouldn't be returned.

He stilled for a few long minutes, the weight of the back-pack filled with money reminded him that without Virginia it didn't matter if he paid off Harry. When he slumped into the kitchen chair he saw a lined piece of yellow paper like Virginia used for taking notes. He slowly reached out and drew it closer, not sure if he wanted to know what it said.

I know you don't understand why I did this, but I did it for both of us. I could never live with myself if something happened to you knowing I could've helped. Giving you up, giving us up, is worth saving your life.

Please don't try to contact me because my father is very vindic-tive, with powerful people at his disposal. He can make it bad for you and your club.

I will love you always.

Virginia

He didn't know how long he sat at the table rereading the note and then just staring at her scrolling handwriting. So like her to handwrite a note. His beautiful Virginia who went back to a life she hated to save him.

———

Three days later, Python walked into the Gold Mine and sat at the end of the bar. Rattler popped the cap off a Corona and set it in front of him. "You look like you could use this."

Python tipped the bottle to his lips and drank deep. "Had my first GA meeting. I basically found out I'm a selfish piece

of shit with an addictive personality. Big surprise." Python
swigged from his beer again. "Believe it or not, there're
fuckers even more screwed up than me. And although this
sounds shitty, it made me feel better."

"Proud of you, brother. Ain't easy to do the right thing."

"When did you get your psychology degree." Python
laughed.

"Standing behind this bar you hear all kinds of shit. Some
of it I wish I could *unhear*."

Cobra slapped him on the back and sat down next to him.
"Any word?"

Cobra's not so discreet way of asking about Virginia, and
Python didn't blame the man for being worried. The day
Virginia had left, Python trashed his living room, then sat
amid the broken glass and got shitfaced on Jack. The second
day, he swept up the broken glass, nursed his hangover, and
took Kobi back to the vet for his post-op checkup. Good
news, his beautiful German shepherd's wound was healing
nicely; bad news, Python's wound was wide open and bleeding
profusely. By the third day, he got his ass in gear, went on a
five-mile run, then attended his first Gambler's Anonymous
meeting.

"Nah, she ain't answering so I stopped calling and texting,
but that don't mean I'm giving up." Python took another hit
off his beer. "Crazy right? One week ago I had Virginia, but I
didn't have the money I owed Harry. Now I got double that,
but no Virginia."

"Sometimes life is just one fuckup after another."

"I'm meeting with Harry later to settle up. He's been
pretty quiet since we took the Shangri-La down, but I want
him off my back. I'm thirty-five fuckin' years old. 'Bout damn
time I got my life in order."

"Hey, shut up and listen to this." Rattler hit the volume on
the TV remote over the bar.

An anonymous source from our sister station in California has released information regarding charges against notorious Las Vegas bookmaker, Harry Smith, also known as Harry Houdini, for extortion, human trafficking, and prostitution. Our sources say an indictment should be reached later today. They are also tying him to the mysterious fire of the Shangri-La earlier this week. The mayor of Las Vegas is outraged and taking a stand against this latest barrage of violence, although many tie his concern to the upcoming election.

"Interesting coincidence," Cobra deadpanned.

"I thought you didn't believe in coincidences," Python countered.

"I don't, but you said her father was some media hotshot, and now all of a sudden Harry's off the streets," Cobra said.

"You think she did that?"

"Yeah, I do."

Virginia not only went back to a life she hated but ended up using her story to save him. She'd told Python she was doing investigative work, but he never imagined she'd gotten that deep.

"She gave up everything she wanted for me."

"I think it's about time we do some investigating of our own." Cobra leaned in. "Starting with where Mr. Chet Curtis goes and what's important to him."

"I can tell you it's not his daughter." Python pulled a face. "From what Virginia had told me, her old man is a heartless fuck who only cares about business."

"That could work." Cobra got that look on his face that said he was formulating a plan. The man had a mind like a steel trap. "I'll put in a call to our friend down in Laughlin."

"Thanks." Python clapped him on the back.

"You got me straight with Sheena, stood by me after Danny. I own you, man."

———

Two days later, Python turned off Sepulveda Boulevard and wound his way to the Bel-Air Country Club. He'd purposely taken his black and gold Fatboy for its growly throttle and overall rumble. It fit his mood and it got attention.

After turning onto a private road, he drove another half mile down a tree-lined drive. He stopped at the end of the road to read the signs, then pointed his bike in the direction of the clubhouse. He circled around the back of the main building and parked in a side lot. This time of the afternoon there wasn't too much activity. He suspected most of the golfers were done, and the caddies were cleaning the carts and counting their tips.

True to his word, Cobra came through with some amazing intel from a computer genius they used in Laughlin. Information Python planned on using to set Virginia free.

Python received a fair amount of side-eyed glances until a guy with a patch on his shirt that said *Bobby - Golf Pro* stepped into his path.

"Can I help you, sir?"

"I'm looking for Chet Curtis." Python gave him the signature smirk and waited as Bobby examined his tats and cut, the worn jeans and dusty boots, quickly assessing that Python outweighed him by about sixty pounds.

"What is this about?"

"It's about none of your fuckin' business." Python widened his smirk and stepped into Bobby's space. "So, either you go in and get him or I will."

Bobby's eyes darted to some of the caddies standing by the pro shop.

"I don't think you wanna involve them. And I really don't think you want me to go in there, right?"

"Oh, n-no, sir," the guy stuttered.

"Great. Tell him Python wants to see him."

"Just wait here." Bobby rushed to the back entrance of the clubhouse.

Python sent a threatening glare toward the caddies, and they went back to wiping down the carts and putting away the golf bags.

A few minutes later, Chet Curtis walked his way, eyes narrowed, fists balled at his sides. Python guessed him to be about fifty, toned and tanned from days on the golf course and a Peloton in his home gym. The kind of douche who was used to getting what he wanted, one way or the other. Until now.

Along with the information their Laughlin connection provided, Python scanned his bio on Wiki. Yeah, he was that fuckin' important, and the combined info gave him everything he needed to make this deal work.

"What's this about?" Chet squared his shoulders, but Python still had five inches on him. "You got your money. Plus, I let Virginia anonymously leak the story that led to the other criminal's arrest."

"That was sweet, but I have a feeling you did that more for the illustrious mayor than me, especially since he's only interested in getting votes for the next election."

"Then why are you wasting my time?" Chet rolled on the balls of his feet, then slammed his fists on his hips in a show of power.

"I want more."

"You want more money?"

"Nah, I want Virginia."

"Impossible." Chet's lips thinned, and his brows furrowed. Probably scared the hell outta them in the boardroom, but it didn't quite match staring down the barrel of a .45.

Python cracked his neck. "That's really not working for me. If I had known, I never would've let her go through with this deal." He slipped the folded check out of his cut. "Take

it. I didn't want it then, and I don't want it now." Python held
it out to him. "Then we can say we're even."

"You and I will never be even." His tone dripped with
sarcastic superiority. "And you will never be around my
daughter again."

Python hoped he'd resist. Now for the fun part.

"I understand you've got an important meeting coming up
this week with CBS." Python grinned when Chet's eyes
widened, then narrowed. "I've been keeping up with Forbes,
CNBC, and Bloomberg Business, and they all say this is a
pretty big deal."

"And what would that have to do with Virginia?"

"You give me or her any trouble about getting back
together, and I might have to let some pictures leak."

"What kind of pictures?"

Python gave him the *what kind of pictures do you think* look.

"You wouldn't dare."

No, he wouldn't do that to Virginia. Truth, he didn't even
have any pictures, but this dirtbag didn't know that. Chet
already thought Python was scum, so why not play the role
and give him exactly what he wanted.

"I'm thinking those big shots at CBS might not wanna do
business with a guy whose only daughter hangs with an
outlaw biker. I got some great shots of us at the Serpents'
clubhouse, on my bike, and of course a lot of other pictures
with more exposure." Python cocked his head. "Just sayin'."
Sometimes it scared him just how sleazy he could be.

Chet sucked in a deep breath, and Python relied on Chet's
obsession with his reputation.

"Fine, but I have some conditions. First of all, if she goes
back to you, she relinquishes her trust fund and any money
from my estate. I'll contact my lawyer when we're done with
this conversation, so be aware—there will be no money
coming her way."

"I don't give a shit about your money. I didn't even know who she was when we first got together and I don't care about it now."

"And her mother and I certainly don't want you coming for holidays or family gatherings, so going forward, she is to never have anything to do with me or her mother again."

"You're a real fuckin' prince, Chet." Python spent a lot of his earlier years wishing for a family, feeling sorry for himself, but now he was sorry for Virginia.

Chet was a first-class asshole, willing to cast his only daughter out because she didn't live up to their rules. Python felt lucky for the first time in his life because he had a real family, the Serpents.

"Do we understand each other?" Python heard the voice he must've used at all those big deal meetings. Controlled, in command, and cold as piss.

"Loud and clear." Python stepped into Chet's space. "And when you get old and are looking for somebody to take care of your sorry ass, don't go calling for Virginia. Do *we* understand each other?"

Chet glared at him and Python held out the check, then ripped it up and let the pieces float to the stone pavers.

Chet huffed out an entitled breath, turned on his heel, and walked into the clubhouse without a second glance. Python had seen all kinds of people in his thirty-five years, but that was one cold-hearted bastard.

EPILOGUE

Python dragged his ass out to Beverly Hills two days ago and fought with Virginia's father. Then he called and texted Virginia before he straddled his bike in the country club's parking lot. Only problem, she didn't respond to his calls or his texts.

Now he sat at his table in the back of Ecstasy with two empty shot glasses in front of him. The number two seemed to be his curse.

He tried to convince himself he was over Virginia, his brothers tried to convince him he didn't need her, but in the end he was fucked because he wasn't over her and he did need her—badly.

"I'm looking for a guy named Python." The soft, smooth voice surrounded him, drowning out Metallica and the bachelor party clustered around the stage. "I understand he runs this place."

"Yeah, he does." Python slowly lifted his head, afraid it might not be her.

"I'm a reporter doing a story about gentlemen's clubs in Vegas," Virginia continued.

"Sounds interesting."

"Yes, they say this guy, Python, fixes faulty locks and sends outrageous gifts."

"Sounds like a real pushover when it comes to women."

"So I've heard, but he's also sweet, generous, and beautiful."

Python smiled at the three words she used to describe him one of the first times they were together.

———

"Move over, you big baby." Python pushed at Kobi, who had snuggled his furry body between him and Virginia on the bed.

Virginia tried to rearrange the protective plastic cone Kobi still had to wear around his neck to keep him away from his wound. "Be nice. I feel sorry for him. This thing must be so uncomfortable."

Python smiled, watching her cuddle the animal that was almost as big as her. "Do I have something to worry about here?" He joked.

She waved her hand between them. "Not after what we just did."

He leaned in and cupped the back of her neck, then captured her lips with his, and when he tasted himself on her tongue, he sighed.

Their banter in the club lasted for about ten minutes before he had dragged her up the back staircase to his apartment. Five minutes after that, they'd stripped naked and fallen into bed. The first time was a blur of emotions, and fuck if his eyes hadn't teared up. Luckily, he wiped them away before Virginia noticed. He sure didn't want her thinking she got stuck with some pussy who cries after sex. The second time was off-the-charts hot, and oh yeah, he had her moaning and screaming out his name. Best thing ever, seeing his woman splayed out under him, knowing he'd brought her to that place.

Now, she lay sprawled across his chest with Kobi snuggled in on her other side.

"I got one question." Something bothered him for the last two days. "I'm sure your father told you what went down between him and me, so why didn't you return my phone calls and texts?"

"I couldn't." She hesitated, and Python mentally made plans to hurt her father if he'd done anything to Virginia. "After I left you that morning," she continued, "I stopped along the shoulder of I-15 and crushed my phone under my shoe, then threw it into the desert. Very cathartic, while cutting off all ties with Vegas." She mashed her lips together. "When my father filled me in on your visit, I had no way to reach you. I had a new phone but didn't have your number in it, so I came in person."

"So you drove four hours not knowing how this would go down." He raked his fingers through her hair.

"I hoped it would go the way it did, but of course my father calling you a degenerate hoodlum who was only interested in money and would probably beat me was upsetting." She scooted up on her knees, tucking her legs under. "Even tried to bribe me with a new BMW, but I packed up my things, took my Toyota, and left." She cocked an eyebrow. "Since you let me ride in your jeep and on the back of your bike, I thought it was the least I could do."

"You're too much, babe."

Virginia leaned in and kissed Python's neck. "I didn't think I'd ever see you again."

"I had your father right where I wanted him. I know a little about negotiations too."

"Yes, I understand there are some pictures you used as leverage?" She waggled her eyebrows.

"You're old man was more gullible than I expected, but there are no pictures."

"I know, even though I was, as you said, 'fucked-dumb,' I think I'd know if you were taking pictures."

"I used his worrying about his rep and the fact he thought I'd do something shitty to my advantage."

"That's my father, always seeing the worst in people. One of the reasons I used my mother's maiden name, but now I don't want to use that name either."

Python shifted on the bed discreetly, wiping his sweaty palms on the sheet.

"I know I got a lot to work on, but I'm going to Gambler's Anonymous meetings, and I'm even starting to see why I do crazy shit. I'm not gonna say it's going to be easy, but I'm tired of blowing my life apart and for you—"

"Not for me," she interrupted. "You have to do this for you."

"I am, but you believing in me, too, makes it that much better." He drew in a deep breath. "Plus, I came into some money, and I got my eye on a nice piece of property just outside of Vegas, and now that I won't be pissing it away anymore, I think I can swing it." He'd spit the words out so fast he was breathless. He figured if he didn't give her a chance to talk, he could delay the disappointment if she turned him down.

He gulped in one more breath. "I've never had anything real in my life, and just those few days without you was too much. I need you in my life, and I want you in my life."

"Python, I—"

"I'm not done. There's something else. I was also thinking you could start writing that book you were talking about."

"My book." The two words came out flat, and it saddened him to think that maybe she'd given up on her dream.

"It's what you talked about and I think you should do it. Give it a shot."

She nodded her head but didn't respond.

"Cobra's got a cabin up at Mt. Charleston. It's a beautiful spot. Quiet, surrounded by pine trees, secluded, and out of the way."

"That's nice."

"We could go up there for our, well, you know, or if you'd rather go somewhere else—"

She stared at him so intently that her brown eyes darkened. Sure, he'd laid out all the ways he'd been thinking about their future over the last few days, but he still hadn't said the words. He'd fantasized that after his big lead up, she'd get the hint or maybe even jump into his arms and say the words herself, but no, she just stared at him.

Here he was, a six-foot-five sergeant-at-arms for one of the toughest MCs in Nevada, and the only club in Vegas. He'd spent his life fighting for what he wanted, staring down wired-up cons and strung-out junkies, yet Virginia, all five-foot-nothing of her, had him spinning out of control.

Python swallowed hard. "So, since you don't wanna use your father's name or your mother's maiden name anymore, how about you take my name?"

She cocked her head, and her eyes grew wider, but fuck him, she stayed quiet.

Even Kobi sat up on the bed, probably sensing his terror.

———

Virginia's head spun. Being able to write her book, Python laying out their future, and was that a proposal? The sincerity of his words tugged at her, and she hadn't missed his attempt to hide his tears earlier. Seeing her tatted, tough guy break totally blew her away.

She wanted to find the right words, and she also wanted to clarify his words, especially since he hadn't actually asked her to marry him. Bikers took ol' ladies, but it sure sounded like he was talking about forever.

Python balled up the edge of the blanket in his tight fists. "And of course, I'm done with all those other women. I only want you in my bed, and from now on—"

"Will you please shut up."

His back stiffened and he opened his mouth but then snapped it shut.

"You're right, I want to change my name. I also want you in my life. I've never wanted anything more, but I don't know what exactly you're asking me."

Python's jaw tightened, then he sucked in a huge breath. "I'm asking you to marry me." He spewed out in one elongated, breathless sentence.

She had to bite her cheek to keep from grinning at the sheer terror in his eyes, and the absolute fear in his voice.

"I would be honored to marry you."

———

Python blew out a long-held breath that made his head light from the lack of oxygen.

"Holy-fuckin'-hallelujah." Python gathered up Virginia and held on tight. Having her in his arms made the crazy in his life right. He needed this woman more than the blood that ran hot in his veins. With her at his side, he could conquer his demons and help her build up the confidence that her parents tore down. The confidence she needed to write and publish her book. And although he knew nothing about writing a book, or even writing a sentence, he would be there for her. Together they were unstoppable.

Kobi got up on all fours, lifted his head toward the ceiling, and barked twice—like he was giving his okay too.

A rumbling growl swelled in the back of Python's throat as he twisted her under him. "I sure hope you didn't plan on sleeping tonight 'cause I'm in the mood to celebrate."

Virginia nipped at the metal bar through his nipple and he hissed in a breath.

"Play nice, and you just might get what you want." He waggled his tongue piercing.

"I already have what I want."

THE END

BEYOND RETRIBUTION/BONUS CHAPTER

Boa was having a first-class, grade A, shitty day.

After getting a phone call at five in the morning from the alarm company telling him the security system at Ecstasy flaked out again, he dragged his ass down there, met with Metro, and shut off the head-banging, shrieking alarm. Before heading back home, Boa did a walk-through of the empty club—nothing more depressing than a strip joint in the early morning hours.

Stupid shit kept cropping up the last two weeks in and around the Serpents-owned strip club. Nothing too serious, but just enough to be a pain in the ass. Since Boa didn't believe in coincidences, he'd be bringing it up at the next church meeting.

Later on that day, he rode out to Joker's shop, J&D Custom Bikes in Henderson, to find out that not only couldn't his club's VP get the part he needed, but the manufacturer didn't even make it anymore. Boa would have to put off rebuilding his Harley softail, maybe indefinitely. Bummer.

On his way back to Vegas, while cruising along Boulder

Highway, some smart ass in a Lamborghini decided to tail Boa, then zipped past him so close he almost laid down his bike. The jerk-off paced him, but as soon as Boa slipped his hand into his cut, his eyes widened seconds before he sped off. Boa gave his Kimber a loving pat. Nothing said "Get the fuck away from me" like a 1911.

Other than that, Boa was having a fan-fuckin-tastic day.

All these screw-ups messed with his brain and had him angling his bike into the McDonald's on Sahara on this 95-degree fall day in Las Vegas. With any luck, the blonde with the bangin' body would be working, but of course, because he was having a shit day, he found two guys with bad skin and a woman in her sixties behind the counter instead. Yup, it was a fuckin' lousy day when Boa couldn't order a hot and juicy while ogling a hot and spicy.

He could almost taste that Big Mac, large fries, and chocolate milkshake sliding down his throat as he waited in line. Yeah, his personal trainer would say he was "eating his feelings," and once upon a time in the bad old days when he was the fat kid everybody made fun of, that was true. Now at six foot six, weighing in at two-forty, and pierced and tatted from head-to-toe, nobody made fun of Boa. Except Rattler. The Serpents' road captain razzed everybody. Sarcasm was in his DNA like peanut butter and jelly. They just went together.

He'd just nabbed the warm bag of his greasy, two-thousand calorie lunch when a blood-curdling scream echoed through the restaurant. He spun around in time to see a woman drenched in what looked like a supersized soft drink. She frantically tried to wrangle three kids out of the booth also dripping in the thirty ounces of sugar and syrup. He couldn't help the smile tilting his lips because the older kid was putting up a fuss. Boa didn't have any kids of his own, but he loved their energy and spirit, and this kid had it in spades.

He was about to head out to his bike and unwrap his junk food when the woman straightened, and her profile made him look closer. Shit, it was Madeline. Madeline, the stripper from the Shangri-La with the knockout body. Madeline, who helped the Serpents take down a notorious MC president. That Madeline.

His booted feet sent him in her direction, and a few seconds later, he was standing in a puddle of Coke.

"I told y'all not to be horsing around and causing a fuss," Madeline scolded in a heavy southern drawl. He'd only had a few words with her in the past but never detected any accent.

The boy, who looked to be nine or ten, paid her no mind and continued to swirl the spilled soda over the Formica tabletop with a smirky smile while two other younger boys complained their fries and hamburgers were drenched and soggy.

"Shit, shit, shit," Madeline squawked each word louder than the last.

"Hey," Boa's deep voice cut through the chaos. Madeline flinched, and now he had four pairs of big brown eyes staring up at him.

"Boa? Geez, you scared the shit outta me. I figured it was the freakin' manager telling us to leave." She shot a look to the boys. "*Again*."

The middle boy averted his eyes while the younger one stared at Boa looming over the table, but the oldest one, defiant and challenging, held Boa's glare.

"I'll bet you begged your mama to come here today, right?"

The two younger ones nodded their heads, but the older one continued to scowl at Boa.

"And now 'cause you all were acting out, it's ruined." Boa waved his hand over the uneatable food. "That ain't right, and you should be apologizing to your mom."

Madeline remained still and quiet as the younger boys each mumbled, "Sorry."

Boa shot his mean mug to the older one, who finally spit out an apology too. Yeah, this kid was a handful, but there was something admirable about him that tugged at Boa, something the biker hadn't learned until much later in life.

"Now go up to the front and nicely ask the girl for some rags to clean this up, and we'll see what we can do about getting some new food."

The two little ones scurried out of the booth, whereas the older one continued to hold Boa's gaze for a few extra seconds, as if he didn't trust this good luck. Smart kid.

Madeline narrowed her eyes and cocked her head like she was just as confused as her oldest son. The little he knew about her told him she couldn't afford to waste food. According to the talk around the Gold Mine, these three kids all had different daddies, one of them up in Ely State Pen. Her last job had her stripping at the Shangri-La until the Serpents torched it in a turf war. Supposedly, Cobra gave her some money for her part in setting up the sleazy owner, but feeding and housing three kids on her own had to be tough.

An uneasy silence settled between them. Boa sensed her skepticism mixed in with a hint of pride, probably where the older kid got his spunk.

Madeline had been a platinum blonde the last time he'd seen her. Today, her hair color was dark red with purple streaks—and her makeup?—a bit dramatic for McDonald's at two in the afternoon or any time in a fast-food restaurant for that matter. The spill from the soft drink molded her thin t-shirt, showing off her amazing tits, and even though he'd seen her topless at the Shangri-La, this was turning him on even more. Flat sandals, denim shorts, and a drenched t-shirt, Madeline still looked like a porn star. Boa didn't mean it in a negative way, but with all that big hair, her curves and height, she oozed sexy.

"Thanks, but you don't have to do that." The southern accent disappeared.

"I want to." And for some reason, he did. With all her glitzy makeup and tough attitude, she seemed desperate and … kinda shy?

"Come over here and get this shit cleaned up like Boa said," she yelled at the boys as they approached the table, rags in hand. "Then plant your skinny asses in those seats."

Well, maybe not shy, but something.

"I'll be right back." The crowd thinned out, and Boa was able to order more food quickly. He gathered up the bags, headed back to Madeline, and dropped them on the now clean tabletop.

"Thanks," the little ones mumbled while older one still wondered the reason for this reprieve.

"Just remember to be good to your mama and do what she says."

Madeline reached up and circled her slender fingers around his forearm. "Thanks, again."

Boa's face split into a grin—the first one today. He left McDonald's with his now cold food and didn't even care, which was fuckin' crazy 'cause the only thing Boa liked better than food was screwing. Since neither one was in the near future, this easy, stupid sensation confused him.

———

Later that night, Cobra called a special church meeting to assess and discuss the wonky shit going on at Ecstasy. All the brothers filed in, dropping their phones in the cardboard box on the table by the door.

They settled into their usual seats around the scarred oak table etched in the middle with a coiled serpent. Cobra lit up a smoke and turned his icy blue eyes on Boa. "Fill us in on what happened this morning."

Typical Cobra—no dancing around shit but just right to the point.

"Something or somebody tripped the alarm again for the third fuckin' time this week."

"Along with our mouse infestation, which had every half-naked dancer squealing and standing on chairs the other night." Python rubbed his stubbled chin. "It took me twenty minutes to settle them down. Believe me, it was like some X-rated *Tom and Jerry* cartoon. I felt sorry for the mice."

"Then the graffiti scrolled on the outside wall," Joker said. "Took the prospects three days to clean that shit up, and I had to listen to them bitch the whole time."

"Before that, it was roaches in the kitchen on the very day the health department decided to pay a visit," Rattler added. "I know none of us believe in coincidences, and since we've never so much as had a fly in that kitchen, I'd say someone's fuckin' with us."

"Desert Rats?" Python offered.

"Nah, after we took down the Shangri-La, most of them split up and hit it to Cali," Cobra said.

"Then it's an outside force. Somebody with a grudge … Somebody looking to mess with our shit." Cobra rested his eyes on every officer. "Any ideas? Rumblings from other Nevada clubs? We got a sweet deal with Ecstasy, but maybe we also got some envious fuckers trying to move in."

"Anything's possible," Python agreed. "But our rep's too tight. No other club would want that kinda blowback."

They all nodded in silence.

"Then it's coming from another source." Cobra turned to Boa. "Nothing on the cameras?"

"Nah, whoever they are, they're smart," Boa said. "They position themselves so all I got are the backs of some guys in black hoodies. I couldn't even get a profile, not enough to do a facial recognition."

"Bottom line is, we need to find out who's behind this shit and put a stop to it."

"I'm on it." Boa leaned into the table. "I'm setting up heat sensors so I know the minute somebody's in the lot or anywhere around the building after closing."

Rattler tipped his head. "Torching the Shangri-La put a lot of bartenders, bouncers, and strippers out of work. You think, maybe it's tied to one of them?"

"Nah, I hired some of the bouncers and bartenders at Ecstasy." Python said. "Most of the strippers scattered, which is fine with me. A lot of them were into shoving shit up their nose, a headache we don't need."

Cobra glanced at Rattler. "You saw Madeline afterwards. What was her attitude?"

Madeline's name perked up Boa.

"Her attitude was grateful. The nice pile of cash you threw her way for helping us out smoothed over torching that dump of a strip joint."

Boa forgot Rattler's involvement with Madeline. When they ambushed Demon, the former president of the Desert Rats and owner of the Shangri-La, Madeline stepped up. She even got grazed by a stray bullet. Rattler took her to the hospital, and the club kicked in some money with the stipulation she use it for her kids.

"Plus, she hated Demon and all the shit he made the girls do."

"What kinda shit?" Boa's neck tightened.

"Fuckin' for money, whether they wanted it or not."

Rattler's usual blunt observation hung over Boa. Word was, Madeline had money troubles, maybe even a problem with blow. It didn't mean she was selling herself, but still.

"Did she get another job?" Cobra rested his eyes on Rattler.

"I don't know, but this seems like more than some petty revenge," Rattler added.

"You still seeing her?" Cobra asked.

"Off and on." Rattler shrugged his shoulder, and Boa knew what that meant. Rattler had a stream of hot- and cold-running women. His bedroom at the Gold Mine was like a revolving door.

"Make it more *on*, and feel her out. See if she's heard anything."

Rattler huffed and shifted in his seat.

"You got a problem with that?" Cobra challenged.

"She lives in this shitty trailer out by Sam's Town. Fuckin' AC don't work right. It's like being stuck in a tin can."

"Shouldn't be too much of a hardship." Cobra added, "She's got a body like a goddamn porn star. Plus, I hear she's pretty hot in the sack."

"What was her stripper name?" Python looked toward the ceiling for guidance, then snapped his fingers. "Oh yeah ... 'Kitti Kat.' She used to wear a cheetah thong with the black tassels on her—"

"We get it." Cobra rolled his eyes at Python, then turned to Rattler. "So, suck it up for the club. Drag your ass out there and see if Madeline knows anything."

Rattler mumbled under his breath.

"Work your charms." Cobra slid him the side-eye. "If she's blowing on your dice, she can't be too picky."

The other brothers joined in with comments of their own, mostly about how Rattler would fuck anything with two legs and a pussy, but Boa still didn't like the undercurrent regarding Madeline's reputation.

"She's got kids, ya know." Boa didn't understand why he said that or why his voice came off sounding like a bitch, but it pissed him off the way they were talking about her.

"The only thing she's missing is the baby daddies. One of them is up in Ely." Rattler laughed. "I guess they don't celebrate Father's Day at her place."

"Can't be easy raising them on her own." Boa's fingers balled into a fist. He pictured her drenched in Coke, trying to wrangle her unruly kids.

"Might help if she didn't hook up with druggies who do disappearing acts and can't keep their asses outta jail." Rattler grinned around his comment.

Boa leaned in, his back tense. "Says the outlaw biker."

"Since when are you a knight in shining armor?" Rattler loved egging him on. "What are you gonna do, ride in on your Harley and sweep her off her feet?"

"Fuck you." Heat surrounded Boa's neck along with an urge to crush Rattler's perfect jaw.

Cobra got in both their faces. "What the hell is goin' on with you two?"

"Nothing," Boa grumbled.

"I didn't even think you knew her." Rattler slouched back in his chair, dismissing Boa's pissy attitude. Typical Rattler. The prick didn't take anything serious.

"Just don't think you should be talking about her like that," Boa mumbled.

"If we're done with this intriguing analysis, could one of you pay her a visit and see if she's heard anything?" Cobra slammed down the gavel.

Boa shot Rattler another look, and the asshole laughed, then grinned at him. Rattler could take anyone down with a smirk. It always amazed Boa how he still had all his teeth intact. Probably because guys knew he didn't give a shit, so why bother.

To read more of Beyond Retribution hit the link or the QR code.

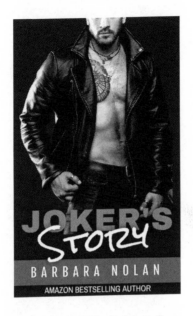

FREE PREQUEL: **Joker's Story**

There was still so much that needed to be uncovered about Joker's past, that I felt compelled to write his backstory.

Don't miss out on the crazy way Joker and Daisy met
Beyond Redemption

and how their love is tested in
Redemption

ALSO BY BARBARA NOLAN

Serpents MC Las Vegas

Beyond Redemption/Joker

Redeemed/The Ultimate Scam

Beyond Remorse/Cobra

Redemption/Joker and Daisy

Past Regrets/Python

Beyond Regret/Python

Beyond Retribution/Boa

Serpent Boxset Vol 1

Paradise Series

Beyond Paradise

Dangerous Paradise

Forbidden Paradise

BEYOND REDEMPTION

Read an Excerpt: https://amzn.to/3jBsxZH

The risk of death is about to meet the reward of desire...

On the sizzling streets of South Beach, Joker needs to make a deal with the cartel to free himself and his son from his outlaw biker club. A chance meeting with a gorgeous mystery woman who hates all things biker quickly ruins his plans.

Daisy's savvy skills and killer looks make her Miami's premier con woman, but she wants to leave the game behind. When her plan to get out goes awry, she's surprised to find a biker of all people coming to her aid.

With his vicious club president and her murderous boss to handle, Joker and Daisy concoct the biggest con yet. Pitting two larger-than-life powers against each other is dangerous enough, but setting them up while navigating their uncontrollable desire proves downright deadly. Soon this pair is out-of-control and teetering on the razor-thin edge dividing what they want from what they need.

REDEEMED/THE ULTIMATE SCAM

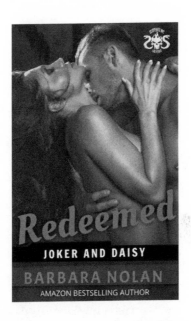

JOKER AND DAISY

BARBARA NOLAN

AMAZON BESTSELLING AUTHOR

Sometimes you have to do wrong for the right reasons . . .

Joker tries to put his past behind him, but when his son is caught in the crossfire of an old grudge, Daisy comes to his rescue.

With the help of the Serpents MC, Daisy uses her conning skills to lure their enemy to Vegas for a final showdown—but will reliving her past tempt her in a way she never expected?

An outlaw biker set on revenge, a conwoman seeking redemption, and a ruthless psycho bent on retaliation. What could go wrong?

Joker and Daisy wager it all in the City of Sin for vindication, and absolution, but can they finally be Redeemed?

BEYOND REMORSE

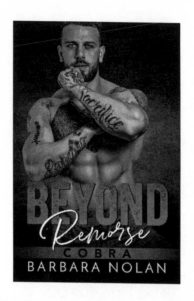

Read Excerpt: https://amzn.to/35JFxrg

They're two rebels on a crash course with passion and disaster...

Cobra, President of the Serpents MC Las Vegas, can't resist getting tangled up with Sheena, even if peeling back the many layers of this gorgeous card mechanic threatens his equilibrium.

Dealing high-stakes poker games is how Sheena pays the bills, and turning over a new leaf isn't so easy when the rent comes due and dinner is a bowl of cereal. Las Vegas is full of temptations, like returning to a life of crime. Or an irresistible bad boy biker with crystal blue eyes.

When a vicious mob boss threatens the future of the MC and lures Sheena into his web, Cobra must take a stand. Will he be forced to sacrifice everything he feels for Sheena in order to fight for his club?

REDEMPTION/JOKER AND DAISY

JOKER AND DAISY

BARBARA NOLAN

AMAZON BESTSELLING AUTHOR

They had everything they always wanted. Until they didn't...

Redemption was never an option for Joker until Daisy strutted into his life, but the love of a good woman won't absolve him of his past. With the soul of an outlaw and the sense of a biker, he can't shake his desire to ride, even if it means jeopardizing his marriage.

Reformed from her life of cons and crime, Daisy can't forget what the biker life cost her. So Joker's decision to join the Serpents MC as she prepares to give birth to their first child leaves her questioning his love for her and his devotion to their growing family.

Only hours after Joker accepts his VP patch, his life is turned upside down. Daisy and their unborn baby are now in peril, and everything he believes to be true is a lie. Turning to the Serpents for help is the only option he has left, but as Joker tries to save his wife and unborn child, it's hard to know who to trust. Is the club the reason his life has imploded, or are his new brothers his true shot at Redemption?

PAST REGRETS/PYTHON

When they were young, life tore them apart. Now, fate throws them together again, but will their reckless passion threaten to separate them forever...

Abandoned by the people who were supposed to care for them, Python and Zelda meet in an Arizona group home. Finding strength in each other they forge an incredible bond while coping with life as troubled teens—then fate interferes.

Eight years later, destiny thrusts them together again.

Fresh out of prison, Python never expects to see Zelda riding with the vicious president of the Night Devils. He patches-in to unearth her secrets, and their passion reignites. Secret rendezvous and stolen moments only make them yearn for more, but if they are found out the consequences will be fatal.

They tempt fate once too often, and when the MC president spirals out of control, Python must make an impossible decision: admit his love for Zelda, and put both their lives in jeopardy, or deny his feelings, and live forever with PAST REGRETS.

BEYOND REGRET/Python

Read Excerpt: https://amzn.to/3fm7ysw

Her ambitions are larger-than-life, and so is the biker she's falling for...

Women, work, and dodging his bookie keep Python on his toes, but the Serpents MC Sergeant-at-Arms doesn't truly understand bedlam until a case of mistaken identity makes a petite, blonde reporter the third woman in his bedroom during his birthday celebration.

KLAS news reporter Virginia Swanson is desperate to build a life of her own away from her influential family, and making a name for herself in broadcast television is part of her grand plan. Interviewing Python about Ecstasy, the Serpents' strip club, should be the story that fast-tracks her career. Staying focused, however, proves difficult as the thought of the six-foot-five biker's tattooed muscles seem to invade her every thought.

A showdown with a rival club and a vindictive bookie bent on collecting no matter the cost force Python to push Virginia away, but when the chaos lays Python's life on the line, it seems only Virginia's prominent background can save him. As she prepares to sacrifice her new life to return to the old one she detested, can

Python conquer his demons to deliver them both to a place Beyond Regret?

BEYOND RETRIBUTION/Boa

He wants to save her. She wants revenge. Can their love survive?

Boa, the cyber genius for the Serpents MC, takes his job seriously. Madeline, the sultry stripper has a rap sheet longer than Boa

Boa, the cyber genius for the Serpents MC, vows to break down Madeline's walls and her secrets. Madeline, the sultry stripper has a rap sheet longer than Boa's. But when her children are threatened, she reaches out to the only man she can trust. Boa. Can he save her, or will her need for retribution put them all in danger?

PARADISE SERIES/Mobbed Up In Manhattan

BEYOND PARADISE

BEYOND
Paradise
BARBARA NOLAN

Jonny Vallone, the dark, brooding owner of Manhattan nightclub, Beyond Paradise, doesn't need any more complications in his life. Then savvy con artist, Cheryl Benson, barges into his office and spits out a confession that would make most men run for cover.

Cheryl's fast-paced, out-of-control life is closing in, and bad boy, Jonny with his powerful connections might be her only hope against a ruthless crime boss. Her knight in black Brioni has a body made for sin with enough baggage to fill a 747, but when a near-fatal attack throws the two together, they implode in a night of steamy, sheet-gripping passion.

Their wild ride whisks them from the high-powered glitz of Manhattan to the sultry beaches of Miami in a desperate attempt to break free of their shady pasts while trying to tame their explosive passion and the dangerous deceptions swirling around them.

DANGEROUS PARADISE

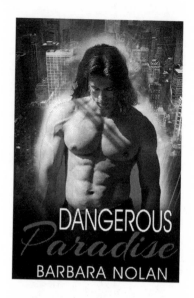

What do a Long Island heiress and a Harley-riding nightclub owner have in common? Absolutely nothing.

After an innocent dinner party goes straight to hell, Paige can't forget Eddie's gentle touch, or his deep rasp when he whispered in her ear. Eddie knows he's way out of his league with Paige, but damn he can't get her out of his head.

Can Paige take a walk on the wild side without getting hurt?

Can Eddie gamble everything he's worked for to keep Paige in his life?

FORBIDDEN PARADISE

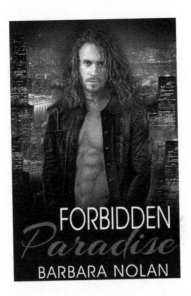

FORBIDDEN
Paradise
BARBARA NOLAN

Dylan Benson, car thief extraordinaire, knows he has to make some solid changes in his life, but then Lena Vallone, and her desperate, ebony eyes turn his whole world sideways.

Lena is eager to escape the controlling ways of her wealthy older brother but taking his Maserati and going to a dive bar in Brooklyn isn't the best decision. Especially when she interrupts the theft of the custom car by an intriguing carjacker with haunting, silver eyes and an air of innocence—Like someone dropped him into this life of crime by mistake.

The two never expect to see each other again, but when her powerful brother seeks retribution, she steps up in Dylan's defense and pleads his case. Dylan promises to reform, so to please Lena, her brother gives Dylan a job with one stipulation—Stay away from Lena.

Dylan is determined to turn his life around, but he can't ignore the simmering passion between him and Lena, or the threats from his thug friends unhappy with his new career choice. Maybe living the straight life isn't as easy as Dylan thought.

As pressure mounts, the chemistry between them sizzles. Keeping their relationship a secret is hard, but keeping Lena safe from his underworld ties might be deadly.

ABOUT THE AUTHOR

Barbara loves her emotional, passionate alpha males and the women who tame them. Her writing is sexy, spicy and seductive, and her goal is to have fun while taking the reader away from their world and into hers.

She is proud of this second act in her life and loves meeting and getting to know her readers, fans, and all the wonderful people in the writing community.

Her passion for reading and words make this a journey of love. She considers reading a luxury and writing a necessity.

KEEP IN TOUCH

Website: http://www.barbaranolanauthor.com

twitter.com/bforlenza5

instagram.com/bnolan26

Made in the USA
Columbia, SC
01 November 2021